THE
GRANT LEGACY

John A. McKinsey

Martin Pearl Publishing
http://www.MartinPearl.com

Published by
Martin Pearl Publishing
P.O. Box 1441 Dixon, CA 95620
www.MartinPearl.com

This is a work of fiction founded upon several alternate theories of history that involve persons alive during the early years of the United States of America. All modern-day events and all other persons are products of the author's imagination and any resemblance or similarity to actual persons, living or dead, is entirely coincidental.

ISBN: 978-1-936528-15-8
Library of Congress Control Number: 2014917267

PRINTED IN THE UNITED STATES OF AMERICA

10 9 8 7 6 5 4 3 2 1

THE
GRANT LEGACY

PROLOGUE

Gettysburg, Pennsylvania, June 30th, 1863

Anna rushed through the already-hot morning air trying to suppress her fears about the forces colliding on their otherwise quiet town. Rumors and cries of alarm had started circulating the day before. The Confederate Army, led by General Robert E. Lee, was supposed to be approaching from the north. Advance units were being reported on the little ridges to the north of town. That made little sense to Anna. *How could the Union Army have let the rebels get so far past them that they could approach from the north?* In the meanwhile, even more frustratingly, some Union Calvary soldiers had ridden through town and Union forces appeared to be setting up on the hills to the south of town rather than defending the town itself.

They're abandoning us to an invading force, Anna fumed as the bottom of her dress swirled near the ground while she ran through the alley behind her home. *How could they do that?*

The town was in a fluster. Some folks were packing up belongings and headed in any direction they thought was not occupied by any army. Or they were headed towards the reported path of the Union forces with an assumption they would be treated fairly and allowed to pass. But most people were afraid of the entire situation and were simply fleeing or collecting food and water to hide in their homes. There were thus people rushing everywhere. Horses galloped. Wagons creaked, squeaked, and generally rushed about, fully loaded.

Anna personally hoped that the excitement would turn out to be "much ado about nothing," one of her favorite phrases. But she was glad her children were out of town for the month with her brother's family at her parents' farm, a three days' ride to the east. Her husband Earl had, of course, volunteered. That had been something she had dreaded until it happened. But then she had accepted her fate and refused to show fear in front of her children. She had seen him off with a unit of Pennsylvania volunteers that she understood to be south of the national capital. Until now she had feared for him but had not felt overwhelmed by gloom. Now she understood that this war was going to be much worse and much less predictable than the bragged-about version espoused by too many northern politicians.

Anna's home was a quiet small brick affair a few blocks west of the town square. She intended to hole up inside and pray to God for fair treatment by whatever people came. But she had one task she knew she had to do first. She pushed open the back door and raced to the small study off to one side of their kitchen.

Dear God, I pray you will see this into good hands that will treat it with the care it deserves, Anna prayed to herself. With trembling hands, she pulled open the bottom right drawer of her husband's desk and took out a rolled oiled-leather pouch that was about twelve inches long. It had two thick leather laces that were tied to keep it tightly rolled. Anna paused and thought about how so much importance could be placed on the piece of paper inside.

Of course it is not the paper, but the words on it, she thought. *And the signature too, of course. A signature* is *really what gives almost every document its real importance.*

Coming out of her short reverie, she turned and shoved the pouch into a tulip-shaped blue clay vase that was about twice as long as the pouch. Then she grabbed and crumpled up some other writing paper and shoved it into the neck. She shook the vase and inspected it. Then she gently felt the weight of the vase.

No one will know you are in there!

Anna then ran into her bedroom and quickly pulled a medium-sized satchel out of the closet. She yanked some clothes off pegs and wrapped them around the vase and shoved the bundle into the bag. Then, hurrying back to the living room, she pulled a few family mementos and some papers from the desk and placed them on top.

She lifted and examined the leather satchel. Satisfied, she strapped the satchel shut, raced out the door and headed back down the alley.

*****

A few minutes later she arrived at the back of another house a few blocks away. Behind it, a young family was just getting into a dual axle buckboard loaded with family possessions. There were two young boys and their parents who looked a few years younger than she and Earl. Just as the lady was stepping up onto the wagon, she saw Anna coming. She immediately stepped back down and rushed towards Anna. Her blue eyes were just visible under a white bonnet that failed to entirely cover her golden hair.

"Oh, Anna!" she exclaimed. "I'm so glad you are coming." She looked toward her husband and his hands holding the reins.

"John, Anna can fit on our wagon, can't she?"

John seemed to look concerned for a moment but then a nervous smile filled his face. "Of course, we can squeeze her in next to the boys."

Their two boys were half hidden among the possessions in the wagon, but their eyes were very visible, wide with a mix of astonishment and fear.

"No, Linda, I am not here for myself," Anna said firmly. "I need for you to take this bag with you. It has Earl's family letters and my family bible along with a few other special items."

Linda reached her arms around Anna and Anna briefly returned the gesture before backing up and holding out the brown satchel.

Linda looked confused and shocked. John actually looked relieved.

"But General Lee is coming! The rebels will be all over this town shortly," Linda began. "You cannot stay here."

Anna looked at Linda with a confident smile she did not really feel.

"Linda, I am not going. I must stay with our home. Earl would expect me to. I am not afraid of General Lee. I hear he is a southern gentleman and will not tolerate many of the things you are afraid of."

"But, but…" Linda mumbled.

"Besides, nothing may come of this but some theft of food. Why would two great armies fight over this little town?"

Linda looked unconvinced, but John spoke up.

"Linda, we have to go, now. Anna's right, her children are not here. Ours are. We owe it to them to leave now."

Anna then reached out and pressed the satchel into Linda's hands. She weakly accepted it.

"Take very good care of this. It's more important than you could understand. Give it to Earl's brother, Caleb, in Harrisburg or bring it back with you when you return."

Linda took a deep breath.

"Okay," she said with a short but deep breath. "Caleb."

"Now go," Anna ordered her friend. She looked up at John with a stern stare.

John spoke loudly.

"We'll see this back to you as soon as this is over," he promised. "Come on, Linda."

Linda took one last look at Anna and then turned. She stepped up onto the wagon, clutching the satchel to her. John took one last look at Anna, looked down at the boys and then turned to his horse.

"Giddyup," he called as he twitched the reins. The wagon creaked forward gingerly.

Anna watched for a minute, noticing that the boys' eyes were fixed on her. She then turned herself around and began rushing back to her house, trying to think of what she needed to find or do to get ready for the coming day.

CHAPTER ONE

Harrisburg, Pennsylvania

By noon, a nice late spring day had unfolded on the eastern side of Pennsylvania. It was very pleasant with blue skies, a comfortable temperature and little wind. The cafe that straddled the sidewalk along Third Street in Harrisburg was teeming with guests of seemingly every type. At one table a college student hunched over a laptop with a textbook open next to it. At another, an elderly couple enjoyed a light lunch. Several families were there.

At one table, a middle-aged man sat with a simple cup of tea in hand and a newspaper unfolded in front of him. He was tall and lanky and the hand holding the teacup seemed too large for the task. Gray hairs sprinkled his brown hair and some wrinkles in his face gave a hint at his age. His slacks, shirt and sweater seemed to perfectly fit the casual atmosphere of the sidewalk cafe. As a result, it was easy to overlook him as being unimportant. Anyone who had looked closer at him, though, would have been captivated by his eyes and what they saw in them. They were an alluring hue of green that seemed full of intensity. Right at that moment they were locked on an article in the paper in a manner that contrasted harshly with the mellow, relaxed atmosphere of the cafe scene. He was closely reading an article about a startling historical discovery in a cave in South Carolina. He sat that way for many minutes, the teacup almost suspended in the air by his hand.

Finally, he pushed the paper down and lifted his gaze to look around the cafe. He examined the various groups around him as if to satisfy himself that no one meant him any harm. Then his attention seemed to drift towards the street where he stared, deep in thought.

Fascinating! he thought. *Amazing! They could be just the ones!*

He stayed that way for several minutes, clearly contemplating something. Suddenly, the chirps of a car alarm being armed a few feet away brought him out of his trance and back to the table, the cafe and the teacup in his hand. He smiled slightly and lifted the mug to his lips. Just before he sipped the tea, he whispered a simple toast: "To the free states."

He then put the tea down, and reached into his pocket to pull out a black cell phone. He looked slowly around one more time and selected a number to call. Bringing the phone up to his ear, he listened to the ringing until someone answered, "Hello?"

With a simple smile on his face and a sheen in his green eyes the man spoke. "Fred, this is Joe. Freedom's time has come, we need to meet."

He waited for the response.

Greenville, South Carolina

Professor James Enloe lay in his hospital bed looking fairly miserable. A history professor in his normal life, he now was splayed on a mattress with various tubes and wires connected to him and various equipment and machinery surrounding him. There was a gentle beeping coming from one machine that seemed to be monitoring his vital signs. A clear bag of liquid hung from a pole and a steady drip fell into the intravenous line that was plugged into James's wrist. Several tubes ran into his midsection, where they disappeared under his hospital clothes.

He looked miserable but there was also humor in his gray eyes. It echoed the smiling faces of the three people gathered around the bed. There was a tall athletic-looking man next to a brunette woman who appeared to be the mother of the teenage girl on the other side of the bed.

The man, Sean Johnson, was leaning with both hands on the handrail near James's feet. His hands had some relatively fresh cuts and he had a bandage on his forearm. His short-sleeved plaid shirt and blue jeans suggested casualness, but there were also some signs of tension in his posture. Sean looked capable of being dangerous when he needed to be. He spoke.

"Well, I'm glad the surgery went well. There has been enough loss in the last few weeks. To lose you would have been too much. After all we've been through, you feel like family to me."

James grunted, "Humpf, well if this is how you treat family, getting them shot and dragging them around in the woods on a rainy night, I'd hate to think how you treat enemies."

He stopped short after saying that and looked at the two females around him. They in turn looked a bit uncomfortable. They had all just witnessed how Sean treated enemies and the reminder was unsettling. James spoke again to get them off of those memories.

"That's just an expression, of course. I've thoroughly enjoyed your company and our adventure. I'm glad we solved the mystery." The professor's hand reached out to hold the teenage girl's hand where it rested on the edge of the bed. "And you, Abigail, I owe you my life. You were brave and it's something I will never forget. Thank you."

Abigail's young eyes looked a little embarrassed but a smile spread across her face.

"You scared me, Professor. I was scared. I'm not sure I really did that much. But, for whatever reason, we're all here."

Abigail's mom, Kim Poole, spoke next. "You were brave, Abby, and I am proud of you. I'm so sorry for getting you into this in the first place." Kim's face looked pained.

"Nonsense, Mom. It was scarier being kidnapped, really, but I'm not complaining in any case." Like only a teenager could, Abigail had a look of undaunted enthusiasm and determination on her face.

Sean spoke up. "When this began, we really had no idea where it would go. But it's over. And, I think, we are now a bit famous. We found a historical treasure that is going to be keeping people busy for a while. My phone has been ringing off the hook." He took one hand off the handrail and pulled his cell phone from his pocket as if to show everyone.

"What I still think I do not completely understand," Kim said, "is how Abraham Enloe fit into all of this. Was it just coincidence?"

"As much as anything that happens is coincidence," Sean replied. "The Union captain decided that the best way to preserve what he had learned was to bury it with the treasure he had stumbled onto. Though Atlanta had fallen, he and his team were still in enemy territory and quite a ways from the main body of Sherman's army marching to Savannah. It was coincidence again when that information got tied to the Abraham Enloe mystery."

"But what they all had in common," James interrupted, showing some energy, "was war and secrets. In war, people take extreme actions that they hide from others. It leads to mysteries like the ones we unraveled. It was amazing, though, that one of those secrets was still very much relevant to people living today."

Sean looked over his shoulder at the hospital room door. "Speaking of which, I think that FBI guy in the hallway is also interested and finds it relevant." He smiled at everyone. "You guys keep entertaining the professor. I'm going to go entertain the FBI."

Sean reached out and clasped the professor's other hand for several long seconds. Then he turned and walked out of the hospital room while James, Kim and Abigail watched him go. James's other hand was still holding Abigail's. He turned to look at her.

"So, young lady, you saved my life." James was shifting into his normal warm personality. "Tell me, how do I ever pay you back for that?"

*****

Out in the hallway, the conversation was more serious. Sean was sitting next to a very FBI-looking man. He was dressed in a dark suit with a white shirt and blue tie. Because he was sitting, his jacket was pushed to the sides, showing a badge clipped to his belt. The butt of a handgun in a shoulder holster peeked out from under his left armpit. Across the hall, directly next to the entrance to the door of the professor's room, stood a police officer. Underneath his flat gray service hat, his alert eyes were watching the FBI agent interview Sean. He could see frustration on both their faces.

"So, Mr. Johnson," the FBI agent was saying, "you have to understand the issues here. You have admitted to shooting and killing two people, one who was a special agent." The FBI agent grimaced a bit, his short blond hair shifting down on his scalp slightly. He continued. "Admittedly, Special Agent Nazimi appears to have been acting outside his role and function and also appears to have been acting recklessly and criminally. But the other dead man, and the injured man, come from a very prominent political family in Georgia. When anyone is killed, a very thorough investigation must be completed. The accusations you have made, while supported by other witnesses, are going to be very hard to accept by other people."

Sean nodded, smiling slightly. The agent seemed even more frustrated. "And you just don't seem to care."

"Special Agent Redman," Sean responded, "please do not think that I take the loss of either of those lives lightly. But I have no guilt or regrets. They were both killers acting evilly and violently. My actions, which I have described for you and others several times, were taken to protect my life and that of the others in that room."

"You've killed before." The agent did not really ask a question, but was making a statement. Sean's smile went away and a hint of anger came across his face.

"Have you?" Sean paused, looking in the other man's eyes. "I didn't think so. Yes, I have killed before. But I cannot and will not tell you anything about those circumstances because what I was doing was, and still is, classified. But I will tell you this. Not only have I killed a human being before, I have also watched comrades get killed, die. I still have nightmares about that. You do not forget either of those things. But I learned. And I vowed a long time ago I would never lose another comrade, that I would never see another person that was depending on me die. What happened two nights ago was just one of those situations."

Sean paused and seemed to calm himself down a bit. He looked the agent in the eyes.

"I respect the job you're doing and understand it. I respect you. But do not sit here and try to pretend like you really know what it is like to be in a firefight or to have made snap decisions that take lives and risk lives. It sucks. It's stressful."

The agent smiled grimly at Sean. "Understood, Mr. Johnson. Let me ask another question of you."

With that, the agent looked down at his notepad and began another of a long list of questions. Sean sighed and looked across the hall at the police officer guarding James's hospital room. They exchanged blank stares.

The people in that room are now the closest thing I have to family, Sean thought, thinking of James, Kim and Abigail. *But what is going to happen next? Do we just go back to our normal lives again?* He then tried to focus his attention back to the question the FBI agent was asking him.

Murphy, North Carolina

Edna Fortuna settled into the chair behind her desk at the museum. Around her, the historical artifacts and holdings filled nearly every available space. Located at the extreme western end of North Carolina, Murphy was a small town perched in the soft southern end of the Appalachian Mountains. Indian country, where Cherokee County drew its name, Murphy's history was mostly a story of settlement and conflict with the Cherokees. The Civil War had touched the area some, of course, but Murphy was so rural and remote, it was of little consequence to the battles and struggles of white men. It had also never been a significant slave holding area, mainly because its hilly lands were ill-suited to the plantation industry that had fed on slavery. Today, Murphy was a modest community surrounded by beautiful woods and sporting opportunities.

Edna was the Executive Director of the Cherokee County History Museum. It was located in an old pre-1900 building and filled the basement, main floor and second floor. It was late spring and what little tourism the area enjoyed was starting to pick up for the summer. That meant there was a chance for a few families or individuals to come up the stairs into the museum and pay the entry fee. *That would be good. Every penny counts,* Edna thought. *But times are tough, including for us.*

As she began sorting her inbox and mail, the phone rang. She answered it. "Cherokee County Historical Museum."

"Hi, Edna, have you seen the news?"

Edna recognized the voice of one of the governing board members and active volunteers, Cynthia West.

"Hi, Cynthia," she began. "No, not really. It's all quiet here. I don't even have the radio on. What's happening?"

"Oh my gosh, it's Abraham Enloe. Someone over in South Carolina has stumbled into some kind of a treasure, you know the G. O. L. D. kind of treasure. I guess there was a shooting and an FBI agent was killed."

Cynthia was starting to talk fast, like she did when she got excited. Edna put the brakes on.

"Hold on. What does any of that have to do with Abraham Enloe?"

"Supposedly they were looking for him or for something by him." Cynthia paused. "Actually, I'm not really sure. I think some descendent of Enloe was involved. But Abraham Enloe and the rumors of him being the real father of Abraham Lincoln are in the news and are somehow related. You need to go online and read about this!"

Edna chuckled, but her curiosity was aroused. "Okay, okay, Cynthia, I will find out what is going on, just as soon as I finish my morning projects."

"Okay, I just wanted you to know."

Edna and Cynthia said their goodbyes. Edna cradled the phone and thought for a minute.

"Abraham Enloe lives again," she said aloud, chuckling. "Who'd have thought?"

She then turned back to her morning tasks, which kept her busy until near noon. Just as her stomach growled to tell her she needed to eat, she recalled her conversation with Cynthia and decided to go online and see what the story was before she ate.

Turning to the computer on one side of her desk, she quickly started up her browser and did a quick search for "Abraham Enloe," "South Carolina" and "Treasure." She had thought that would be a good start, and that she would need to tailor her search from there. But instead she was surprised at the flood of hits mostly leading off with headlines such as "Treasure Discovered! Two dead!" She had clearly found the event, but nothing was apparent to her about how the treasure related to Abraham Enloe.

Edna clicked on one promising-looking article from a major news service. She began reading. They had not been searching for the treasure apparently, but for Abraham Enloe. Well, not exactly Abraham Enloe, but something about him. Edna smiled to herself. *We know where Abraham himself is. That is not a mystery.*

She finished the first story, completely amazed. Lunch now forgotten, Edna pulled out a notebook and began reading the next story. She sensed that whatever this event had been, it spelled opportunity for Murphy and her museum.

CHAPTER TWO

Greenville Airport

The lobby of the airport was small. The airport was small. Still, it had a plane that would connect to another plane that would get Kim and Abby home to Kansas City. To Sean's relief, no one had really noticed who they were, even though stories about them, some including photos, had covered every single newspaper he had seen today. Also to Sean's relief, no television crews had found them. They were not being allowed into the hospital either, so they managed to have some peaceful and quiet moments there.

When it was time to go, a couple of hospital staff had arranged to sneak them out of the hospital in an ambulance that had pulled into a general delivery dock behind the hospital. They all had grinned as they ducked down but then peeked back at the news media people camped on the lawn in front of the hospital. Sean had counted at least four big vans with big letters on them and antennae raised above. *What a crazy world,* he thought. *They're like robots reacting as they are programmed.*

They had camped out in the hospital last night, and taken turns using a shower to clean up. What few belongings they had with them were there, but they all felt like they had been on a two-month trip with two days of supplies. *Not far from the truth either,* Sean thought.

Sean had booked Kim and her daughter on their flights from the hospital, after they agreed that Kim needed to get Abby home to school, and also see what had become of her business back in Kansas City. She had left it hurriedly several weeks earlier. Kim was also nervous about her ex-husband, who was acting furious with her for endangering their child.

Of course, it was actually his neglect that let her get kidnapped in the first place! But in his calls, mostly with Abby, he had been loudly blaming Kim for what had happened. He was yelling so loudly at one point that Abby had simply handed the phone to her. She waited for him to stop and then interjected, yelling back at him.

I cannot believe I ever married him, she thought. *He's just an arrogant, rude lawyer.*

Kim's mind was also on her new relationship with Sean, whatever it was. *How can you fall in love in the middle of a crazy adventure? Is that love? Or just convenience?* But Kim could not deny the attraction she felt towards Sean. And she actually knew almost nothing about him. *Some journalist he has turned out to be*, she thought, cracking a smile.

Sean saw the smile and smiled back as they sat next to each other in the uncomfortable seats in the gate area.

"What are you smiling at?" Sean asked.

"Nothing, you goof, I was just realizing that I have yet to see you do anything that really looks like journalism." Kim paused. "Do we even know who we are?"

Sean chuckled, but then answered more seriously. "I think we learn more about people when we see them under stress than we do when they are under control."

"You never look like you're under stress though."

"Looks don't matter. I was as stressed as you. Besides, we will have some time to get to know each other better after things calm down and our lives get back on track."

"Hah," Kim protested. "You probably don't remember, but you live in Seattle and I live in Kansas City. Are we going to sit around talking on the phone?"

Sean thought for a moment and then said carefully and slowly, "Well, once I get my actual career as a journalist back on track, I was kind of, well, hoping, you wouldn't mind me spending some time in Kansas

City...." Sean let his voice trail off, seeming nervous.

Kim waited about ten seconds and then said with a peaceful smile blooming on her face, "Yes, I think I would like that. Abby would too."

They looked at each other for a moment before Abby's voice interrupted.

"Uh, guys, I am like, right here," she said sarcastically. "Can you not talk about me like I'm somewhere else?"

Sean and Kim looked over to Abby, where she sat staring at them, and then looked back at each other and laughed.

"Sure, Honey," Kim said. "At least I know you were actually listening to me."

"Whatever," Abby said, pretending to be hurt. "But just in case you want my opinion, Sean, I wouldn't mind you hanging around either."

Sean sensed the seriousness of Abby's words and nodded solemnly.

"Okay, well, for at least a few more days, I am sticking around here, I guess," Sean said. "I owe it to the professor to see him get home or at least out of the hospital."

Kim nodded in agreement. "I wish I could stay, but I really can't."

Sean took Kim's hand.

"No worries, I understand and agree. I can get my life back together from anywhere, really. In fact, what I need to do is sit down and write some articles for my editor. That will get me in good graces. But writing about something that I was in the middle of is a lot harder than I ever understood."

Kim patted Sean's hand. "That's okay, Honey, I know you can handle it."

Greenville Hospital

James tried to reposition himself in his hospital bed. He felt significantly better than he did the day before. But besides the pain in his stomach area, he was now starting to notice that every body surface he rested weight on started feeling achy after about thirty minutes. Moving to one side (but slowly!), lifting one leg (gently!) or shifting higher up the bed (carefully!) all brought some relief.

It's a sad statement about medicine, the professor thought grumpily. *Our ability to find problems and fix them is incredible but we have not fig-*

ured out how to improve the comfort of a hospital bed!

James looked around his now-empty hospital room. Just a few hours ago it had been full of the noise of his newfound companions. He had not realized how much he had come to enjoy being around them until he had to face the quietness of being alone in his room. They had not left him alone since he woke up from his surgery. When he was being interviewed by the police officer, Sean had reluctantly agreed to leave the room.

Now, with the group off to see Kim and Abby to their airplane, he finally had to come face to face with what had happened. And that brought him back to thoughts of his sister Mary. Just as emotions were starting to overwhelm him, the ringing of his bedside phone startled him away from that ledge he was trying to avoid.

He looked at the phone with a puzzled expression for a moment. It rang again and he suddenly realized what was startling him. It had not rung once since he got here. That made him look at the phone for another moment until the third ring burst through and triggered his reaction to answer it. Gently rolling to one side, he reached over to the little wheeled table next to the bed and picked it up.

"Hello!" James answered, determined to sound confident and strong to who he assumed was Sean or Kim or Abby.

"Professor Enloe?" a strange voice asked. James instantly assumed some reporter had finally managed to get through.

"Perhaps, but perhaps not," James replied, trying to sound friendly but only mildly interested in the caller. In truth he felt a little rush from what he assumed would finally be a chance to talk to the outside world about what had happened. He had not resented all the protective efforts his friends had taken, but he was now eager to have someone to talk to and a reporter could be all the better.

"To whom do I have the pleasure of speaking?" he continued.

"Ah, Professor, so good to get through to you. It was not easy, you know." The voice sounded to James more like a calm man making a hotel reservation than it did a reporter.

"Maybe so, Sir, but you did avoid answering my question," James said, feeling a letdown in his excitement level.

"Well that was partly intentional, Professor, but not in any bad way. I had to lie and say I was your long-lost brother just to get your number. I am not a reporter nor am I anyone from the government or a company trying to exploit you." Now the voice was a bit off to James, as if it were purposely shifting into some other tone.

"Then why are you calling?" James asked, letting some irritation sound in his voice.

"You can call me Joe, Professor," the voice responded, yet again not answering James's question.

"Okay, Joe," James replied. "Why are you calling?" He repeated his question with more firmness, hoping to make it clear that he wanted an answer, not an evasion.

"I am sorry, Professor. I am calling to see if you and your group would like to turn your great talents to an even better mystery. I must say your accomplishments are amazing, if not miraculous. Tell me, are the stories really true that you accomplished everything in just a few weeks?"

James felt a bit more appreciated. "Well yes, though to tell you the truth, things moved so quickly it seemed almost like a few days."

James paused and then repeated his earlier question even though he had gotten one answer. "Who are you really?"

"For now, let's just use Joe. But let me tell you that my benefactor may be willing to pay a substantial fee for services like the historical investigation you just completed. But for the moment, confidentiality prevents me from telling you more about who I am."

"Humph," James said, expressing some skepticism as he best knew how. "If you won't tell me more, and you won't tell me who you are, why should I think you are anything but a crackpot?"

Joe responded promptly, exuding a confident tone. "Because I know people, Professor, and I know that you can sense when something is real and I am very confident you will not let a great opportunity pass."

There was a pause while James considered the statement. Joe continued.

"Besides, Professor, I am actually mostly done with this call. But let me tell you this. I will call again. I actually want to talk to Mr. Johnson. After all, I assume that for a little while you can't go anywhere. If your team will accept my preliminary offer, I will immediately fly Mr. Johnson to meet me and then tell him much more in person. But I will call again, probably tomorrow. Please discuss this call with your friend and await my call."

"Hold on," James began. "It does not work that way…"

"It will have to for the moment, Professor," Joe interrupted. "Just for the moment. Rest comfortably, please."

The phone went dead. James pulled the handset away from his ear and looked quizzically at it. At first he pondered the call and what to make of it. He realized he had started and ended the call looking at the phone in the same puzzled way. He also realized that "Joe," despite his mysterious air, had actually hit the nail on the head.

"Rest comfortably," James said aloud with a chuckle. "That is exactly what I need to figure out how to do."

With that, he placed the handset back in the cradle and went back to trying to find a new comfortable position.

Washington D.C.

The Free States of America were of course not yet free nor even in existence, Steven thought. *Yet,* he added with an emphasis, if only to himself.

Steven Ableman was sitting at a table with three other men. It was a windowless interior room in his office building and Steven was confident that no one would intrude or spy on them. Being that they were meeting in the nation's capital, they had exercised many precautions for this rare face-to-face meeting of the "principals," as they called themselves.

The senator was there, looking as polished as he always did under his tightly cut blonde hair. The general was there as well. *But he never looks like a general, except when he's in uniform,* Steven thought. *And he is certainly not in uniform today.*

And of course "Joe," as he insisted he be called at all times, was there. It was a request that Steven thought bordered on paranoia, but perhaps Joe knew better than any of them what they were getting themselves into.

Joe broke the silence.

"I believe it is time to take action, Gentlemen. Fred has agreed with me and will provide the next stage of funds if we all agree to act."

As Joe spoke, Steven reflected on how much he hated the name "Fred." It stood for their benefactor, their financier. It was someone that no one but Joe could identify. Or at least he presumed that no one present in the room could identify Fred. It was certainly possible, he mused, that the senator or the general were in deeper than they let on. Steven had even wondered if either the senator or the general was in fact "Fred." But he had eliminated that possibility by realizing that neither was as rich as their benefactor. Major amounts of money had been provided already. Ted Hines was a financially comfortable senator from Pennsylvania. They had known each other for a long time. General Frank Huerta had been a military man his entire life. He seemed to need the money he got from his current positions in the Army Reserve and the Pennsylvania National Guard. *No, they could not be Fred.* Steven knew that. But that left the possibility that Joe was Fred. Except Fred had been on a call with Joe and Steven once. So unless Joe had hired an actor, he was not Fred either.

But we really do not know much about who Joe is either, Steven thought. Steven listened as General Huerta spoke next.

"If I understand your position, Senator, you believe the time is ripe politically?"

Senator Hines cleared his throat. "Yes, the nation is both divided and distracted. The average citizen has such a low level of respect for government, let alone any trust, that we probably face the most receptive climate we have ever had."

The senator looked slowly at each of them in turn before continuing.

"I vote yes. But I do so with both trepidation and excitement. We are not past the point of no return yet, but we will be setting things in motion that expand the awareness of our effort. As we have discussed, the moral right that we feel we have in our heart to take this action, and the legal right we feel we have, will not hold the day. We will be physically challenged and we have to win that challenge."

Everyone turned to look at the general. His brown eyes twinkled as he rubbed two fingers together, as if making a final measure of the air around him.

"If you say, Senator, that the political time is ideal, then I can say yes as well. Our military and strategic plans are sound and as ready as they can be without taking the next step." General Huerta paused for effect. "If our benefactor is ready to fund us, we can begin to expand. We will then have about one to two months before everything will collapse back upon itself if we do not act. So this is a very important moment. I think there is no turning back if we take it to the next step. At a minimum I will be exposed. You all probably will be exposed as well."

All four of them absorbed the general's ominous message, before Joe spoke again.

"General, you are always so dismal." Joe smiled and lifted his arms with his palms facing forward like a minister in the middle of a sermon. His green eyes connected with each man in turn and then he spoke, still smiling. "I believe in our cause, I believe in our plan, and I believe in our ability. I trust all of you, just as you trust me."

Joe turned to Steven. "Steven, what do you say?"

Steven spoke immediately. "I too believe in our plan and our team. I say yes as well. But I am also nervous. I too think this is really the point of no return for all of us."

He tried to sound as confident as he could, but he was really very scared. His reason for being part of this was very different from the others', and they knew that as well. He wanted revenge. But now that the day was at hand to move forward, an ominous feeling was tightening his stomach.

"You think you have found the man that can find our document?" he continued.

Steven was their historical and political foundation as well as responsible for crafting most of their propaganda. "You all know I have said we do not have to have it, but I believe it will help us significantly when we go public. When we appeal to Americans."

"I do," Joe answered. "But, it's a team, really, of sleuths. The ones that made that find in South Carolina. We will see how they do."

Joe stood up. "Unless anyone else has something to say I think we have been in the same place long enough. Time to disperse." He looked around and saw agreement.

"To the free states," he stated firmly.

"To the free states," the others responded in unison.

Joe then stood, turned and exited through the door into the hallway.

Steven glanced at his watch. "Three minutes, then you, Senator." Steven hated this part more than anything. But they had agreed on strict procedures when they met. No phones or devices with them. Never leave or arrive together. He sighed and began making small talk with the general.

CHAPTER THREE

Greenville Hospital

"So, Professor, how are we doing today?" Sean was leaning in the doorway of James's hospital room with his arms crossed.

James looked up from a book he was reading, slightly startled. He had the bed propped up, but his head had been so slumped down toward the book on his lap, Sean thought he might have caught the professor napping. He looked mildly irritated as he snapped back.

"That's what every nurse says when they come on shift. I don't need you sounding so condescending as well." He paused, looking hard at Sean for a moment.

"I ache, I'm tired, but I think I hurt less than I did yesterday. And that's with less drugs."

Sean smiled as he entered the room. He walked over to a large whiteboard next to the professor's bed and looked at the all the notes written on it and at the documents attached to it with magnets. James watched him with a grouchy look on his face.

"Don't try to make any sense out of all that. They tell me it says I am doing well. My organs are working, and my body is healing. And no signs of infection."

"That's good," Sean muttered, as he examined the board.

"Did the girls get off okay yesterday?" the professor asked, his voice softening somewhat.

Sean gave up on the whiteboard and turned to sit in a chair next to the bed. "Yep. It went very smooth. Nobody bothered us at any point and they made it on the plane. Kim called last night when they landed to tell me they were home."

Sean looked towards the window.

"Professor, I miss her, you know. Already. And they just left. Hell, we just met . . ." he trailed off feeling a bit foolish.

"I miss them too, but I am stuck here," the professor responded gruffly. "You did not need to stay here and watch over me, you know. You could have gone with them."

"Gone with them?" Sean asked rhetorically. "No, I could not leave you here free to harass the hospital staff. Besides, somebody has to keep the media circus at bay."

James's eyes twitched at the mention of "media."

"Hey, I got a weird call yesterday after you left," he began. "I thought it was a reporter at first. It might have been. But it was weird. Fellow called himself Joe. Said he actually wanted to talk to you. Said he was impressed by what we accomplished and wanted to give us another job."

Sean looked quizzically at James for a moment. "That's it? What did you say?"

"I never got to say much. He is supposed to call back."

"It might just be the FBI trying to dig some more information out of us. I still think they don't believe our story," Sean offered. "Or you're right, it's some nutty reporter trying to get into us."

Sean paused and looked frustrated. "Speaking of which, I am supposed to be a reporter. I need to get writing."

James was about to reply when the ringing of a cell phone interrupted him. Sean reached into his jacket pocket and pulled out a new-looking phone. He glanced at it quizzically, then nodded at James and took the call.

"Hello."

"Hi, is this Sean Johnson?" an older-sounding high-pitched female voice asked.

"Yep, this is him." Sean was already thinking of hanging up and was wondering how a reporter had gotten his new cell.

"Kim said you would be on this line," the voice continued. Sean's curiosity rose.

Not a reporter. Sounds like a nice elderly lady.

"Before you hang up, I'm not a reporter. My name is Edna and I run a museum in North Carolina. But I'm not asking for anything either. At least not anything you found."

She paused and Sean sat there a bit dumbfounded. "Is this okay, can I continue?" Edna asked.

Sean popped out of his trance and replied, "Yes, sure, please do."

"So, as I said, I run a museum in a small town in the very western end of North Carolina, a town called Murphy. Probably never heard of it." Edna paused to give Sean a chance to respond. He took the cue.

"You're right, never heard of it. Why exactly are you calling me, Edna, if you don't want something from me? And how did you happen to find Kim?"

"Sorry." Edna sounded apologetic, but her accent was so strong it was hard for Sean to be certain. "I tracked Kim down. I'm a historian, you know, it's what I do. Called her in Kansas City. Nice gal. Anyways, she liked me enough to give me this number."

Sean smiled at himself but also felt himself losing his patience. Still, he tried to put his "reporter" hat on. "You're right, she is quite a gal. So tell me, Edna, why are you calling?"

"Well, I've dug pretty good into your adventure, you see, and think I understand what you were doing trying to chase down Abraham Enloe. But I am also surprised that your sleuthing never led to Murphy."

Sean was a bit surprised to hear the name Abraham Enloe. He also noticed how she pronounced it, like "Abram." Sean looked over at James, who seemed to be enjoying the one side of the conversation he could hear.

"Well, you're right, I never found my way to Murphy, but I'm not sure why I should have. You certainly have me curious. Or confused. Or both."

Edna cackled. "Well, I guess that makes sense. You see, Abram Enloe lives here. Or he did, anyways, and never left."

"Um." Sean was now certain that he was confused.

"Abram Enloe is buried here. Murphy is the final resting place of that amazing man. The whole town of Murphy would like you to come here and see his final resting place. Since I am the town historian, so to speak, it is essentially my job to invite you, young man."

"Oh." Sean could feel the gears in his brain starting to whirl and click. "I think I'm interested in that. You know I am actually a reporter?"

"I do, which is really kinda why I'm calling you. To be honest, I'm hoping you will do a story on Murphy and the end of Abram's life."

Sean thought for a moment and made a decision. "Edna, your timing is actually pretty good. I've been feeling like I needed one more angle to start writing the story and Murphy might be it. So I do want to come out."

"Great, so what else can I do? We can't pay or anything, but I am certain I can get you a free room in one of our nice bed and breakfasts here."

"Let me get back to you later today," Sean replied. "Can I call you at this number?"

"Yes, yes, please do."

"Okay, thanks, Edna." They said goodbye and hung up. Sean put his attention back on the professor, who still looked sharply attentive.

"Whew, that lady was pretty high powered," Sean said, laughing. He explained the conversation to James.

"Well, now I'm even more jealous," James said. "Murphy is not actually that far from Knoxville. I cannot believe that a town so close claims to have Abraham Enloe's grave."

James paused and took on a lecture-like tone. "But you know they could all be nuts. But they could also be right. There is so much oral history that has simply not made it into books yet."

"Yes, I know, Professor." Sean emphasized James's title in a friendly mocking kind of way. "But it works for me that they think they know something. It's about time that I get back to being a reporter."

"Well, then go there," James ordered. "It's a ways, though. But what about this Joe character?"

Sean thought for a moment. "If he calls back, take his call. If you still think he is serious and for real, then give him my new cell number."

"Okay, I will then. And maybe I'll be let out of this prison soon and can start helping. We were a good team, you know."

Sean smiled and stood. He placed his hand on the professor's shoulder. "We were a great team. This sounds good. But don't expect the kind of excitement we just had. This stuff is as uneventful as, well, teaching history."

James looked up at the remark but could see Sean was smiling and joking. "Get out of here and do something useful," he growled.

Kansas City

Kim felt relieved to be back in her shop, Garden World. It was located in an upscale shopping area known as Country Club Plaza and featured garden and kitchen goods. It had felt like she had been gone for months, but as she settled in she realized that inventory had not changed that much and that really it had been a few weeks. Her able-bodied assistant manager, Bridget, had clearly done a great job in Kim's absence.

Bridget was, in fact, standing in front of Kim's desk smiling, her arms crossed. She looked down on Kim through her horn-rimmed glasses and Kim was again reminded how much Bridget felt like a mom to her.

"See, I told you things would be fine. I can't say I'm not looking forward to a few days off, but I actually enjoyed running the show."

Kim smiled back at her. "I know. I really just felt, and feel, so guilty leaving you here with the responsibility. But I can tell you that I will express my appreciation in many ways in the days to come. The business looks like it did better in my absence."

"Not hardly," Bridget said, clearly enjoying the compliment. Then the beep of someone entering the store sounded and Bridget turned to leave. "Gotta go and let you sit here and do your owner-manager thing now," she called as she headed to the front.

Kim smiled and watched her walk out. She spotted the customer on the security monitor perched on one side of the office. She could see Bridget approaching him.

Definitely a guy, she thought. *And young.*

As she watched she began to get a sense that something was amiss. It might have been in Bridget's posture. Or it might have been that the man just looked out of place. He was not really dressed like, or acting like, a customer. Kim felt tension flow over her body and felt reminded of her recent experience. Then she saw Bridget look up at the camera and stare kind of quizzically at it.

She is telling me she is not sure what to do. But if she had felt threatened she would have a different look.

Sighing, Kim got up and headed out to the floor. As she came around the corner from the back hallway, both Bridget and the young man looked over at her. The man had a nice smile on his face.

Too nice, Kim thought.

"Ms. Poole? Kimberly Poole?" he asked.

It was a simple question but it made Kim realize that among the unanswered questions now floating around in her life was whether she was going to change her name to what she had learned was her real last name: Thomas.

But she nodded, and the man suddenly moved. He reached into his jacket. Kim felt a sudden urge to scream and run come over her. She expected a gun to emerge, but saw it was, instead, paper—white paper.

"For you, Ms. Poole," the man said, thrusting it into her hand with that same fake smile. "Have a nice day." He nodded, turned and left.

Kim felt nauseous. She had gone from feeling relaxed to be back in her store to thinking it was all happening again, to feeling relief it was only a paper, to being overcome with dread over what she knew she held in her hands. All in a matter of moments.

Bridget, ever the watchful one, reached out and grabbed her arm to stabilize her.

"Are you okay?" she asked, knowing that Kim was not.

"Yes..." Kim started to answer but fell silent. She thought for a moment and then an angry look came over her face. "I know what this is without even having to read it," she said spitefully. "And if he thinks this is his big chance to get Abby all to himself, he has another thing coming!"

Kim whirled and stormed back to her office as Bridget began to understand what had just happened.

CHAPTER FOUR

North Carolina, Highway 40, Westbound

To Sean, being back out on the road as a reporter, without the threat of killers on his tail, felt like being born again. It did not hurt that the rolling hills and small mountains of eastern North Carolina were so beautiful. He had his rental car on cruise control and steered the car gently as he mentally worked his way through an outline of a set of stories on Abraham Enloe, Abraham Lincoln, and all things in between.

Nothing like a highway to let you get your head around things, he thought.

Upon leaving the hospital in Greenville, Sean had gone straight back to his hotel, packed up, checked out and then hit the road. He was not sure what Murphy had to offer him, but sensed that just going after a story would allow him to get back into reporter mode and have a chance of keeping his job. He was expecting a call from his editor, Paul, in Seattle at any time. In his mind, he was trying to formulate his plan for a set of stories.

The ringing of his cell phone interrupted his thoughts and he looked down, expecting it to be Paul. Instead, he could see it was James calling from his hospital phone. Sean glanced around to make sure he did not see any police ready to ticket him for driving and talking on his cell at the same time. Satisfied he was safe, he accepted the call, putting it on speaker so he could at least pretend to focus on driving.

"Professor," he called out. "Can you hear me okay?"

"Yes, yes," James grumbled. "Why shouldn't I?"

"Just checking. Are you okay?" Sean winced as soon as he asked it, knowing the response it would trigger.

"Yes, quit asking me that! Now listen, our friend Joe called back and I gave him your number. He was just as mysterious but he seemed even more determined to hire us. He should be calling you shortly."

"Okay," Sean said. "I'll be ready. I'm halfway to Murphy now, I think. Passing Waynesville." Sean remembered being in this very area not that long ago.

"Good, well then don't let me keep you. But call me back after you talk to him." James paused and sounded almost wistful. "I'm pretty eager to do something, you know. Not sure I want to just go back and be a history teacher. Of course I have some great writing to do of my own."

Sean could tell James would ramble on if he did not cut him off. "Got it, Professor. I will watch for his call and call you back. I promise."

They hung up and Sean went back to driving and working his way through his own writing. But his thinking period lasted only a few minutes before his phone rang again. This time is was an unknown caller.

"Of course, Mr. Joe, you would be blocking your number," Sean said aloud as he took the call. This time he decided to pull off the highway to free up his hands and his attention.

"Hello," Sean began as his car came to a halt on the shoulder of an off-ramp.

"Hello, Mr. Johnson," a kind-sounding voice replied.

"I assume this would be our mysterious Joe calling?" Sean asked. Sean looked around briefly, satisfied he was stopped in a safe, good-to-talk location. He could hear the cars rolling by on I-40 below him, but the environment in his car was relatively quiet.

"Correct, Mr. Johnson."

"Okay, well, if all I get to call you is Joe then please just call me Sean."

"Certainly, Sean. Thanks for taking my call. I assume Professor Enloe has told you why I am calling?"

Sean could tell that Joe was used to smooth talking. *Former salesman, I bet. Or he still is.* Sean chuckled.

"He has told me what little you told him. I assume you're going to tell me a lot more about your proposal?"

"Yes, but let me begin by telling you that I am most impressed with your recent accomplishments. I have been seeking a lost piece of history for quite some time. I represent collectors and this particular piece would be worth a lot. In fact, I have a buyer who is eager and willing to pay the right person or persons to find it. But it is a bit urgent, I'm afraid. I think the buyer has a short window to sell it to someone else."

Sean sensed he was getting a less-than-full story; the speech was a bit too "prepared." One concern came to mind.

"Look, Joe," he explained. "I'm a reporter, really, not a historical investigator. But overall, I would not be afraid of taking it on if it has a good story and I can write about it. But that relates to this issue."

Sean paused, to see how Joe reacted.

"Go on, Sean, I'm listening."

"Well, whatever this is, it has to be legal and public. Nothing stolen, nothing that is questionable morally. And I have to be free to write about it."

"That should not be a problem at all, Sean. The buyer will probably remain a mystery, but I assure you that this is entirely above board. If you find this artifact, you will be empowered to buy it. And once you have completed your task, you can write all about it."

Sean thought for a moment while he jotted down a few notes with his free hand.

"Well then, I think I want to know more about how much you're proposing to pay us, what this thing is and probably more about you. I'm not sure I'm going to be willing to work for someone I can't at least verify is a real person."

"Let me tackle those in reverse," Joe said. "If you agree to take this on, I will provide you my full identity. I am being secretive because there is competition out there to find this artifact. My buyer, in fact, might even have another agent like me. The object is an early American painting that disappeared during the Battle of Gettysburg. A key part of your focus will have to be on Gettysburg, the battle and its aftermath. I will tell you more when we meet and you agree to take on the work. I will pay all your reasonable expenses, plus $10,000 to attempt to find it. If you succeed in acquiring it, you will earn a $50,000 commission. You will only have a month in any case."

Sean liked the amount of money he was hearing, but he was still feeling suspicious. "Look, I don't mean to be difficult, but why can't you provide me a name now? Who are you?"

There was a pause and then Joe replied, "My name is Samuel Franklin. I am the owner of an art advisory company called PAF Services. You will find it is headquartered in New York and duly registered in Delaware. I reside in Harrisburg, Pennsylvania, when I am not traveling around the world."

"Samuel Franklin, PAF Services, got it," Sean replied as he jotted the information down.

"I do ask that you and your team refrain from telling anyone right now that you are working for me or my company. We are to be an undisclosed principal, if you know what that means."

"I think I do now," Sean replied. "So assuming you vet out okay, what's next?"

"I would like to meet with you in two days in or near Harrisburg, if that is acceptable. I will pay you an advance on expenses and the $10,000 stipend at that time. Do you have an email I can use to exchange our contact information?"

"I do, Samuel, or Joe, or however you want me to refer to you."

The man laughed. "My nickname has always been Joe. I actually prefer it, Sean."

"Okay then, Joe it is," Sean replied.

Sean gave Joe his email address and they hung up. Sean then immediately called James. The phone barely rang before the professor's voice bellowed out, "Professor Enloe."

He is definitely starting to sound like his old self, Sean thought.

"Hi, Professor. Joe called and we talked."

"And what is the outcome?"

"I think it's a go. I'm going to research the personal information he gave me, but my sense is it will check out." Sean proceeded to explain what he had learned.

"Hmm," James muttered. "I think I will have a student back in Knoxville put together some material for us. He's a nice kid and probably eager for something to take on. His name is Thomas Adams. Is that okay?"

"Sure. I guess we can split this between the two of us and you can pay him what you want," Sean proposed. "Oh, wait. We should give Kim a chance to be involved also. Not sure she will though. But if she does, then three ways?"

"That's fine, Sean," James replied. "I'm mostly just pleased to have something to do."

"Okay then, I'm going to get back on the road and find a place to stop for the night out here in the Appalachians. Any suggestions?"

James gave Sean a few ideas and they said goodbye.

Greenville

After hanging up, James lay back and thought things through for a few minutes. He understood the basic concept: a painting went missing from Gettysburg at the time of the battle of Gettysburg. His general recollection was that the looting or taking of goods by the rebels while they occupied the town for several days was limited to mostly food, guns, and simple things of value. James had a hard time thinking a painting would have been stolen. Moreover, he thought such a fact, if reported, would stand out and still be talked about.

In any case, time to see if young Thomas has some time and interest in researching!

Thomas Adams was a history graduate student who should have just finished his first year towards his Master's in American History. James had used him for research in the fall semester and found him competent and engaging. But one issue was that James had no idea what his phone number was. He did not have any of his normal travel materials with him.

James called the only number he knew by heart, the main number for his department. His fellow professors and staff at the University of Tennessee had sent some nice flowers, but he had not even bothered to call them. Now he knew just getting through all their inquiries might take some time.

When he called, he was proven right. What he wanted was the number for Thomas Adams, but that took talking to four different people, all of whom asked the same questions. Still, the professor survived and soon had Thomas on the line.

"Thomas," James began, "do you have summer plans?"

The young energetic voice responded with a New England accent that reminded James that Thomas hailed from Boston, where he also did his undergraduate work.

"Only some small research work for two other professors," Tom replied. "I'm game for anything you throw at me."

James was elated. "Excellent then. Get a pen and paper and I will walk you through what I need. This is pretty hot, so if you can get right on it, that will be great."

"No problem, Professor. I'm ready. Fire away."

The professor then proceeded to walk Thomas through several specific, immediate tasks. James guessed he had given Thomas a week's worth of work, but in increments he could bite off in about a day each. They ended the call with James feeling like things were moving nicely. He even felt like it might just be time for him to get out of the hospital.

Washington D.C.

The table was not very expensive looking. In fact, it was several tables shoved together. Emmitt Talie reflected on this as more people strolled into the room for his meeting. Here he was, now running task forces for the FBI from within the National Security Branch at headquarters. But he still just rated an internal conference room with old tables and equipment. *Good luck even trying to get that speaker phone to work*, he thought.

As he watched his "team" members settling in, he reflected how much more diverse the FBI had gotten in recent years. *It used to be a bunch of us white men. Now we've got every religion, ethnicity and even gender fully represented.* Not that he minded. Just the opposite. He knew and felt that an important law enforcement agency should be made up of all members of the community it protects, and that doing so made it more effective. But Emmitt was a traditionalist in most other ways. He was old-school enough to appreciate the role of having a dress code. He adhered to that tradition and today was no exception. His dark tailored suit was lightened only by his crisp white dress shirt and blue tie. He still felt fit for a mid-fifties, soon-to-retire FBI agent with more than 25 years of service. But his shortly cropped gray hair and the wrinkles around his eyes showed not just his age, but also the wear and tear of those years. But now he had a true desk job: run task forces investigating security threats. *Except today it's an "old table" job,* he thought, noticing now how the tables did not even seem to fit correctly together, leaving gaps where all sorts of things could fall to the floor.

His team was now assembled and looking at their phones or reading the briefing file. He had seven members, including two field agents. The rest were research and investigation staff.

"Let's get started, Ladies and Gentlemen," he announced. This caused almost every head to look up immediately, giving Emmitt a small sense of satisfaction from the authority he clearly had.

"You are all assigned as members of taskforce Supernova. As you know, the name itself is classified, in addition to the entire investigation. You can't repeat the name of this taskforce, nor share information from this investigation unless it's in the direct conduct of your duty and the disclosure is necessary. Some information, classified as secret, cannot be shared or disclosed. Period. Is all of that understood?"

Heads nodded. Emmitt heard at least one grunted "yep."

"Okay, then. I think we all know each other, so let's skip introductions and get to it." Emmitt paused, looked around the room one more time, and then checked his notes.

"Supernova is the working name we are giving to the investigation of a potential terrorist group that might be operating in D.C. and the larger metro area of Baltimore/Washington. One of our sources of this information is an anonymous informant. Three messages have been left with a field agent here in the building. The field agent looks to have been picked at random. You have transcripts of all three voice messages. Generally, they warn of a high level conspiracy to harm our government. We would have probably put these off as some crackpot except the third message included details regarding the murder of a Maryland state trooper that had not been publicly released. Needless to say, these messages now have our attention."

Emmitt looked around the room. "Questions? Comments?"

Dana Misler, the young researcher, spoke first. Emmitt knew this was one of her first jobs. *So she's eager. That's good.* "I think we should challenge the assumption that the selected agent was found at random. The names of agents are not generally public knowledge. This agent in particular was at a desk job at the time. I think the fact that the three voice messages went to him in particular is worth investigating. Why this agent was selected, or even how he was found, could tell us something about who or what Supernova is."

"Good. Okay, Dana, that's your task then. Interview the agent and find out everything you can about when and how his name and work assignments have been published or made public. Take a good look at his personal daily habits and life right now as well. This could be incidental contact, like someone at a gym for all we know."

Special agent Ryan Lentz went next. He was a very large and burly man in his mid-thirties, but his smile and charm often seemed to produce a very different impression than his size and presence might otherwise have. He smiled even as he spoke. "Obviously, we need to investigate the murder. He was shot while off-duty in his personal car at a shopping mall outside of Baltimore. This certainly suggests that he stumbled into something by chance. I think agent Chapman and I need to look closely at all the reports and forensics and see what we can turn up." Ryan turned and looked to his immediate right, where a very diminutive, dark-haired, Asian woman grimaced. Alice Chapman spoke.

"I agree. But Maryland's finest may not like us stepping into their investigation. We can be gentle, but you know how these things go...." Her voice trailed off as she shrugged.

Emmitt nodded. "Yes, they will resent interference and be suspicious that we're trying to take over the case. They will also want to know why we are looking at his death. We can't tell them why, as that could expose our unknown source."

Ryan nodded and Alice replied, "Understood."

Emmitt continued on with the meeting, already satisfied that he had a good team. He felt, though, that there was something they were not thinking of. Identifying the source, he thought, was critical. But there was something else in this that he sensed he was missing.

Kansas City

For Kim, it felt great to be back in her own kitchen cooking dinner. A light stir-fry of vegetables and beef was almost done. The salad was ready.

Abby had made the table. Everything was perfect. Except for the summons she had been served with. Her ex-husband, now living in Dallas with his new girlfriend, wanted to take sole custody of Abby.

Probably just to avoid child support, she thought angrily. *No, that's not fair. He is an idiot, true, but he really just thinks that Abby is much better off with him.*

The truth of it was that Kim was really scared. Abby had been on an adventure. She had missed school. She had been kidnapped. Kim had, indeed, not cooperated with the police. Abby had been shot at and had helped a professor avoid bleeding to death from his wounds. Kim had run off with a high-flying reporter all across the country dragging Abby along. All of that and more were alleged in the petition that her ex, Jason Wilcox, had filed with the court in Kansas City.

Of course he omitted how she was kidnapped after I had dropped her off for his safekeeping! And how he did not even notice her missing until I found out the kidnappers had her!

Kim felt her anger rising and took a deep breath. She tried to tell herself that things would work out. Her next task was what she was dreading: talking to Abigail about her father's move. Abby was sitting on the sofa, just past the little dining nook they ate in, watching an entertainment news show.

Okay, now's the time.

"Abby, I have something important to talk with you about," Kim called, trying to sound like a normal mom.

Abby looked up and saw that her mom was serving their dinner. She popped up from the sofa.

"Okay, what's up?"

They both sat down at the table. Kim avoided passing the salad and instead came out with it.

"Today I was served with a petition to award your father full custody over you."

She watched Abby's face, which showed surprisingly little shock, and then a little anger.

"Dad? He ignores me when I'm there, Mom! Brenda's nice, I guess, but I do not belong there. And I do not want to be there!"

Kim felt relief over her biggest fear, that after all that had happened,

Abby might actually want to move.

"Well, unfortunately, our recent adventures have given your father an opportunity. The petition he filed is pretty ugly and very hard on me." Kim paused. "I'm meeting with a lawyer tomorrow. Hopefully she tells me that he doesn't have a chance. I do know that the court will listen to you also though."

Abby did not look very upset or concerned. Kim was not sure if that was because Kim was not being scary enough or if her kid was really that brave. *After what I took her through, she might just be the toughest sixteen year-old around.*

"Okay, so I will keep you informed," Kim said. "In the meantime, how was it being back in school today? How many days are left of the school year?"

With that, their conversation drifted to normal family dinner conversation. Nothing about killers, kidnappings, or even history.

CHAPTER FIVE

Murphy

To say Edna was excited was an understatement. She was standing at the entrance level of the two-story museum building trying to keep herself busy. Roland, her general maintenance man, had managed to find an excuse to be there. He was pretending to work on a loose banister leading up to the second floor where most of the displays were located. Edna had tried to shoo him off, but he had firmly resisted. So she had given up. Sean was due anytime, based on his last call. He had apparently spent the night near Cherokee, North Carolina. Today and tonight he would be the guest of Murphy. *Or at least some of Murphy.*

She heard the outer door of the museum entrance swing open, and turned to see if it was her waited-for visitor.

A tall man, dressed in slacks and a sports shirt, was striding through the entranceway. Edna was certain it was him.

"Roland, be useful and get the door for Mr. Johnson," she directed Roland, who was also watching the guest's progress.

Roland gave up his pretend effort to fix the banister and quickly walked over and opened one of the inner double doors. Sean walked in as the door opened. He smiled sheepishly.

"Thanks," he said.

He then turned his attention to Edna. "Hi, are you Edna?" he asked.

"Yes, Sir, and you must be Mr. Johnson."

"I am but please call me Sean."

"Yes, Sir, Sean," Edna replied, realizing she was probably still sounding too formal. "Quite a few of us are really excited that you have come to visit us. Especially so soon after your discovery in South Carolina."

Sean took a moment to look around the museum. He could see glass cases with mannequins dressed in clothes and uniforms of various eras.

"Well, please, I'm really not a celebrity," he replied. "Truthfully, your invitation was very interesting to me and it allows me to get back out being a reporter instead of sitting back there in South Carolina, trying to avoid all the other members of the media."

"Well, we feel like we have a celebrity visiting us," Edna crowed. "How long will you be here?"

"Probably just tonight," Sean admitted. "I have another appointment all the way back in Pennsylvania in two days. So I plan to hit the road back east tomorrow morning."

Sean could see a small look of disappointment flash in Edna's eyes.

"But you have my full attention today and tonight," Sean went on. "I'm very interested in learning more about how Abraham Enloe came to be buried here. And I'm honored that you are so excited to have me. So I will be a very appreciative guest, if only for one day."

Edna's face changed from disappointment to excitement again.

"Yes, well we are excited to have you," she replied, looking at her watch. "It's eleven now and we have lunch for you at noon. But if we get busy we can walk through our Abram Enloe history."

Sean noticed again how Edna pronounced Abraham's name without the middle syllable.

"Great then, I'm ready," Sean replied. He glanced again at the man in coveralls who had opened the door for him.

"And who might you be?" he asked.

Roland extended his hand. "Roland White, Mr. Johnson. I take care of this old museum building. This was actually our courthouse years ago. Did you know that?"

Sean accepted the handshake. Roland's eyes twinkled as they shook hands.

"No, I did not, but I was admiring all the marble and I guess that explains it."

"Yes, Sir. All this marble was cut and brought in here from a quarry not too far away."

"Okay, Roland, thank you," Edna cut in. "Mr. Johnson does not have a lot of time before the luncheon, so I need to walk him through our Enloe history."

Roland grinned at Sean. "You can see how it is here. Ms. Fortuna runs a tight ship. Perhaps we will see each other later."

"An honor meeting you, Roland," Sean replied. He then turned to Edna as Roland turned his attention to the banister on the stairs going up. "Now Edna, I can see it's going to be hard for you. But my name really is just Sean."

"Yes, yes, Sean," Edna replied, clearly struggling with referring to Sean by his first name. "If you come over here I can walk you through our materials on Abram Enloe. Then we can head over to the cemetery."

They walked to the table where Sean saw some books laid out and what looked like photocopies of various documents.

"I took the liberty of making a copy of everything I thought you might be interested in," Edna began. "There is a note on the first page of each document I copied telling the full name of the source."

Sean was impressed by Edna's attention to detail.

"Abram, or Abraham as you know him, came to Murphy in the winter of 1840-41 to visit his daughter, Margaret Mingus, and her family, who had moved here. He was to visit his grandchildren," Edna continued. "It is believed he was caught in a winter storm on the way here, caught pneumonia and died. He was buried about 200 yards from here at the old Methodist church and cemetery. His headstone reads 'Abram' not 'Abraham'."

Sean interrupted. "So how is all of this known?" He sat down at the table she had prepared and thumbed through the documents as she spoke.

Edna laughed lightly. "Well, most of this story is an oral history that was captured in writing in the early 20th Century. One of the documents I copied for you is from a county history book published in 1919 that describes interviews with some of the then-elderly citizens of the town.

"What we know for certain," Edna continued, "is that a woman that was probably his daughter lived here then. Her family shows up on the 1840 census. We also know we have a man buried here by the name Abram Enloe. We also have a death record for him. There are supposedly some concurring records for the county where his home was that shows his will being probated in 1841."

"Okay, I'm convinced," Sean said, stopping her. "Let's go look at his grave."

*****

A few minutes later they had walked about two blocks, all up hill, to a small white church near the top of Murphy. Sean learned it was the Harshaw Chapel, a former Methodist church that was now more of a historical landmark. A small, old cemetery was spread around behind it and to one side. Edna led Sean across the tightly mowed grass to a relatively simple rectangular headstone that read:

ABRAM ENLOE
BORN 1770
DIED 1841

Sean stood in front of the grave for a minute pondering the magnitude of what he was seeing. Edna stood patiently behind him. Finally he spoke. "Amazing. So this could be the real father of Abraham Lincoln."

"Yes, yes. That is what some believe," Edna replied behind him, "But, one way or another, I am confident that this is the same Abraham Enloe of Rutherford County that is alleged to have been Lincoln's father."

"This headstone looks newer than other ones from that era. And it's a pretty big stone compared to most here," Sean noted.

"Yes," Edna replied. "Very observant, Mr. Johnson. Oh sorry, Sean. Anyways, yes. And it is likely that Abram's daughter's family was quite poor. So this stone was probably put here much later, perhaps even about the time of the publication of that county history book. Back in 1840, it would have been more likely that Abram would have had a simple stone, flush with the ground. Like these."

Edna pointed around her at numerous stones that were sunken an inch or so below the level of the grass.

Sean looked about the area. "Well, let's get a few photos and then you can get me to this luncheon."

Edna smiled. "Certainly."

Kansas City

"Kim, you need to understand that the facts he pleads are not good."

Kim was sitting in a comfortable chair in a plush lawyer's office not too far from her shop. Her new lawyer, Katherine Edsen, looked to be in her mid-fifties. She was wearing a dark suit and her brown hair hung down just low enough to reach the collar of her blouse. Kim had expected to hear this advice.

"I understand that," Kim replied. "How do we fight back?"

"Well, we can challenge his story with your own. He makes a case for you to be endangering Abigail in a reckless and negligent way. How is his story not correct?"

Kim frowned. "Mostly, his story is accurate. He does omit a few facts though. A couple of months ago, I came across a letter left to me by my father who passed away several years ago. It was a shocking letter that revealed that our family name was not Poole, but Thomas. It had something to do with Abraham Lincoln, the Civil War and a man named Abraham Enloe."

Kim paused and looked at her lawyer to see if she was paying attention. She was, so Kim continued.

"As I began researching these things online, I connected to a genealogist in Arizona and a reporter in Seattle. It turned out there was still a cover-up going on for some things that happened back in the Civil War. In fact, the genealogist was murdered."

Kim stopped again and observed Katherine's eyes light up.

"I wound up teamed up with that reporter and a history professor from Knoxville, Tennessee. We found three hidden caches of documents, the third of which is the one that has been in the papers. As you know, two more people died that night of the final discovery.

"I was worried about the well-being of my daughter, so I took her to my ex-husband in Dallas. She was kidnapped from there and the reporter and I rescued her in a parking lot in Georgia. It was my ex-husband who was derelict, not me. From then on I kept her with me. It turned out we even had a corrupt FBI agent involved."

Kim stopped speaking and looked plainly at her lawyer who sat quietly for a moment, clearly trying to decide what to say next. Finally she spoke.

"Well, okay. We do have some issues but your facts are certainly better than the way he paints them in his pleading. There is a hearing tomorrow where your ex-husband's lawyer is going to press the court to immediately award custody of your daughter to his client. And he may prevail, candidly."

Kim stiffened. Before she could speak, her lawyer continued.

"Please listen. The court is going to be amazed that you chose to rescue your daughter on your own, did not report your success to the authorities and then proceeded to race across the country with her, ultimately greatly risking her life in an encounter with criminals. These are both bad and good facts."

Kim was ready to scream but she forced herself to remain calm. "They would take Abby away from me? Would they send her to Texas…?" Kim let her second question dwindle as she visualized such circumstances.

"That is a complicating factor, yes. Your ex lives in Texas. But if the court thinks that your daughter is not safe with you, then they might give him custody, yes. It would be a temporary decision at worst and he would have to promise to come back for a final decision."

Kim was flabbergasted. "There is nothing you can do?"

"No, there is something I can do. I will argue this as best I can. We may prevail. But, again to be candid with you, the odds are not in our favor."

"Do I need to bring Abby?" Kim asked, trying to think her way through her options.

"You can. She is old enough that the court will be interested in what she wants. But it may not be willing to allow us to orally argue as much in front of her. And if he has a full schedule, this judge often does not want to take the time to allow argument in his chambers. So, it might be better if you leave her behind. This will turn more on what happened than what your daughter wants."

"Okay, I understand, Kim replied." What else do you need from me?"

Knoxville

Thomas was sitting in a chair in the school's library, deeply absorbed in a book that described the story of the Battle of Gettysburg. He had never gone to Gettysburg and really only read very high-level summaries of the famous battle. He, like many Americans, understood how the battle was often thought of as the turning point of the Civil War, the point where the Confederacy's star began to wane. It was certainly the "high-water mark" for the South's push into the Northern States. And as a historian, admittedly a new and young historian, he had read about a few of the famous people involved in that battle. The famous Confederate, General Robert E. Lee, had led the battle for the South.

But now, for the first time, it was his task to learn everything he could about the battle and how it affected the town. The Confederacy actually held the town itself during the battle. The Union forces had set up on a curve of hills that provided a superior defensive position. The rebels had not taken the town really, but rather the Union forces simply never attempted to defend it, so there had been no real battle over Gettysburg itself. Instead, the fight had occurred on terrain at its southern boundaries. The battle in 1863 had ironically happened on a very hot and humid Fourth of July.

There were several stacks of books on the table around Thomas. He had known there would be lots of books on Gettysburg, but he was surprised by how many were sitting on the shelf in the main library of the University of Tennessee. So he decided to spend a few hours reading the most comprehensive story of the battle he could find among all the books he had pulled. And now he was deeply into it.

As the story reached the end of the second full day of battle, Thomas stood up and stretched his lanky arms. Tom decided to take a walk around the perimeter of the table to collect his thoughts. The spring quarter was over and most of the students had left for the summer. Certainly, there were not many using the library. He was the only person using one of thirty-odd tables in the reading area adjacent to the history section.

The day was nearing its end and he was due to report to Professor Enloe on the overall impact of the battle on the town and what resources were available that went into specifics of the town's citizens at the time. He realized he had allowed himself too much time digging into the full battle history. He now needed to determine what information was available, whether in book form or some other medium, on the town residents and how they dealt with the battle. That was going to require that he turn his attention to the Internet and some historical databases and search engines.

Thomas had reached the far corner of the table area and spied a drinking fountain. He turned towards it.

Murphy

It had been a long day for Sean. The luncheon had been interesting, with about a dozen town residents, including the mayor, asking him many questions about his earlier Enloe quest. The mayor had bluntly asked him if he was going to write about Murphy itself. Sean had hinted that he probably would and had explained that he thought the final resting place of Abraham Enloe seemed to provide a great tangible point of reference for the story.

After the luncheon, he had been shown his room at a small bed and breakfast a few blocks from the town square and about six blocks from the museum. It turned out the library was almost right behind the museum.

After Sean spent some time talking with the two sisters who owned and operated the bed and breakfast, he walked back to the museum and library. He spent about three hours at both and another hour walking around the town to flesh out his feel for the place. Then he had called James to check in.

Now, finally, after a quick dinner at a small restaurant in town he was ready to sleep. But he really wanted to call Kim. Now that she was probably home for the night, he thought it was a good time. He pulled her number up on his cell and clicked on it.

"Hi, Sean," Kim answered. "Hold on just a second."

Sean could hear a door open and shut and then Kim came back on the phone. "Okay, I'm back." To Sean, she sounded a bit on edge.

"I've missed you," Sean began. He then proceeded to tell her about the new mystery and also about why he was in Murphy. But he had barely gotten into introducing the topic of the missing painting when Kim interrupted him.

"Sean, I need to talk to you." She now sounded almost angry.

"Okay," Sean replied. "I'm sorry, I should have asked about how you're doing."

"'Not good," Kim replied curtly. She then told Sean about the legal battle she had found herself in the middle of.

"He wants to take Abby away, Sean!" she finished, almost yelling. Sean now understood that Kim had gone into another room, or perhaps even outside, so that Abby would not hear the conversation.

"Wow. This is my fault. I dragged you into this."

"No, while I do want to blame you," Kim began and Sean could sense she was smiling, "this is my fault, not yours."

Sean thought for a moment. "Do you think you have a good lawyer?"

"Yes, but I think I am screwed."

"Well, let me offer this. First, what matters is that we did take good care of her, when it comes down to it. She was not hurt. Second, I think Abby has grown and become stronger from her experience. So we actually helped her. Finally, I don't see the court keeping her away from you forever, even if it awards full custody to him at first. So I think you need to be calm and not overreact."

"Not overreact!" Kim exploded. "That's easy for you to say, she's not your daughter!"

"Sorry, that was bad choice of words. You know I care very deeply for Abby as well."

"I know," Kim replied, calming down some. "Listen, I have to get dinner done. I will call tomorrow and tell you how it went."

"Okay," Sean said, sensing her distant tone. He felt frustrated, though probably not as much as she did. "Talk to you tomorrow."

After they hung up, Sean sat at the small table in his room looking out at the now-lit-up town of Murphy, trying to see something positive.

CHAPTER SIX

Roads Towards Pennsylvania

Sean's car was now pointed in the other direction. He was driving east again. He had made it out of the winding canyons immediately east of Murphy and now was in the flatter land of North Carolina that lay south and below the Smoky and Blue Ridge mountains that separated the state from Tennessee and Virginia.

He felt that the Murphy trip had been worth it. He had managed to complete the outline of an initial feature story telling about Abraham Enloe and the story of his earlier quest. But he had gone to sleep thinking about Kim and Abby and his relationship with them. He had concluded that he needed to give Kim some space. If they were meant to be, then they would find themselves together soon enough.

Now, today, he was trying to shift his focus to the new job that he and James had taken. Things about it still seemed a bit odd. He had done some Internet searching two nights ago and again last night in Murphy and was satisfied that "Joe" and his company were legitimate. But now, as he began a very long day of driving to get to Harrisburg, his mind was coming back to the oddness of a sudden urgent need to find a painting that had been lost for about a hundred and fifty years. Oddness aside, though, if they got paid like Joe had promised, then it would not matter.

And it might also make a good story.

So long as this is clean and legal.

Sean thought about how looted art was supposedly all over the world and how it was being bought and sold on the black market daily. *If the art went missing during a Civil War battle, then was there not some person out there that it was stolen from? Probably, but that's not what's really bothering you.* What was odd was how Joe suddenly wanted Sean and his team, that he was willing to pay so much, but that he was not willing to tell him exactly what he was looking for until they met in person.

Sean decided to check in on James and sound things out with him. He had managed to configure his phone's wireless signal to work with the rental car's system. He hoped he could now call using the car's microphone and speakers. He punched up James's number and shortly the professor's voice boomed over the speakers.

"Good morning. Professor Enloe."

"You're getting better sounding all the time, Professor," Sean replied. "They must be ready to kick you out by now."

"Good morning, Sean. Yes. There is a chance I might even be released today. If not, then maybe tomorrow. My staples will come out in a few hours. And I'm walking around pretty well."

"Excellent. Keep me posted. I am headed to Harrisburg for the meeting with our Joe fellow and will be driving all day. If you are there for another day or so I may be able to get down there and pick you up. Otherwise, you're probably on your own."

"No worries, Sean. I am quite capable of taking care of myself."

Sean knew that James essentially had no family anymore, though, so he felt that the professor's words, while sounding good, were probably hollow.

"No, no, I got you into this. Besides, we are now partners of sorts."

"Yes, that's right," James replied. "What about Kim?"

Sean then gave a brief summary to James of her situation and "their" situation.

"Well, I have no doubt she will make out fine and the two of you will be running around together soon enough," James assured Sean. "In the meanwhile, it sounds like it will be the two of us on this new matter."

"Yes," Sean replied. "I have to tell you, I still think there are some weird things about this." Sean proceeded to walk James through his thoughts on Joe and the painting.

"I agree, Sean, that we should be careful. But as you say, even if Joe is a nutcase, if we get paid, and do not break any laws, we'll be fine."

"Yes, you're right. So what do you think we will need to do to find a painting that has been missing for 150 years?"

"I'm not sure. Right now we should focus on the Gettysburg connection, whatever it is. I have put Thomas to work getting a good compilation of what is known about the town and its residents at that time. He reported in last night. Today he is fleshing out the armies and that side of the documentation. I think by the end of tomorrow we will be ready for whatever you learn tomorrow. So if Joe proves true to his word, we will be off and running."

"Okay, so if Joe comes through, what information do I need to get from him?"

"Everything he knows. Everything about the painting and everything about its Gettysburg connection," James explained. "Have you ever been to Gettysburg?"

"No," Sean admitted. "In fact, I am embarrassed to say I know little about it."

"Well, you will know a lot more about it before we're through then."

"Admittedly," Sean replied. "Okay, listen. Keep me posted on your health. Call if you need me or need to tell me anything. I'm going to keep driving and make some more calls."

"Okay, Sean, take care," James replied.

They hung up and Sean returned his attention to the road ahead of him. The valley had been getting wider and the hills flatter and he knew he would turn north into Virginia soon.

Time to touch base with Joe.

Sean pulled up Joe's number and soon it was ringing on his speakers.

"Hello, Sean," Joe answered.

"Hello, Joe. I'm headed to Harrisburg now and will be available to meet tomorrow as proposed."

"Excellent! How about lunch? I can text you the address for a nice Italian place we have here."

"That sounds good. You and your company have checked out fine."

Sean decided to prod Joe some. "Of course you knew that would be the case. But if this is super urgent, anything more you can tell me now might help us get started more effectively."

"No worries, Sean. I know this seems a bit weird to you, but the world of art is full of oddities. I really want to meet you and affirm my expectations. Plus, then I can pay you your advance and that should make you very motivated."

"You're right on that," Sean replied. "But I have some research already starting."

"No worries, Sean, it will work out fine."

"Okay, see you tomorrow."

"Tomorrow," Joe replied.

Harrisburg, Pennsylvania

Joe put his cell phone down. He was sitting in his home office, where he had been working on some of his formal business affairs when Sean called. One of his hardest challenges for the last several years had been maintaining separation between his public life and his private life. The Free States of America had been most of that private life. He knew that soon, one way or another, he would no longer have to work at keeping his private life both private and largely secret.

The biggest secret, of course, was that he was not really any of the people that he was thought to be. He was not really Joe. He was not really Samuel Franklin. In truth, he was no longer sure "who" he really was. Instead, he mostly just thought of his purpose and it was now at hand. He intended to see it through. "Joe" was the closest person to that purpose and he reflected that he might really be becoming Joe. If so, then, he was probably going insane. But that did not scare him. Because all he cared about now was his purpose.

His primary existence for a long, long time had been as Samuel Franklin. Samuel Franklin owned the house that he was sitting in. It was a nice house. It had been his home for a long time. The room he was in, his study and office, was on the second floor and looked out on a highway that led out of Harrisburg.

Up until now, he never did anything related to his private life in his house, let alone his study. He would not have had Joe's cell phone on and on his person while sitting in his study. Only Samuel had lived or existed in his private house.

He had maintained his life as Joe by going to other places. And he had been very careful. Of course, he had been trained carefully when he was very young. He could only barely remember the person he was before he had become Samuel. His persona as Joe was not as ancient, so that was one whose origins he knew and understood.

Now things were being set in motion that could not be undone. Some of his partners at his last meeting had sensed that. There really was no turning back. That was going to be true for others. Some wittingly and some ignorantly. Sean and his team fell into the ignorant category. But, Joe suspected, Sean could prove to be most valuable to the purpose. In several ways.

Time to update Fred. And no reason any longer to go somewhere. I could probably even use my landline at this point. But Fred would not like that.

Joe lifted his phone and entered a number he knew by heart. Fred did not answer. He was not supposed to. But five minutes later, on the minute, Fred called Joe back.

"Greetings," Joe began.

"Greetings to you," Fred replied. "I assume you are calling for a particular reason?" Fred had a deep melodic voice that certainly could have been on radio.

"Yes, I most certainly am. We have begun the expansion and the move towards our final step. Our team is ready for and expecting the funds to be transferred and available by early next week." Joe spoke plainly and simply. Fred had always preferred that.

"Very well. I will transfer funds. Do our expectations on support remain the same?"

"Actually, in Washington and within the guard, we think we will do better than our baseline."

"What about our political position. Do we have the documents we want?"

"We have all but one and I am deploying someone that might even find us the last one."

"The declaration?"

"Yes," Joe confirmed. "You are asking many questions. You said that you would not do that. For security purposes."

"I know. But we are now at a point where none of that matters. You know that, don't you, Joe?"

Joe was surprised at this admission by Fred. *So you too are on a path of no return?*

"Yes. I was just thinking about that very fact."

"We have talked long enough. I will do my part," Fred stated and then paused. "Good bye, Joe."

"Good bye, Fred."

The line went dead and Joe turned his cell phone off, took the battery out and then put it on his desk. He stared at it for a moment and reflected that his conversation with Fred had been very unusual. Fred clearly understood things the same way Joe did. Joe wished he knew more about who Fred really was.

Highway 83, Virginia

Sean had crossed into Virginia earlier and was feeling pretty good about the time he was making. It was midday and the rolling countryside he was driving through seemed so fertile and productive. *Even the bushes seem as big as trees*, he thought. He was being more cautious about his speed though, given the reputation Virginia's state troopers had for ticketing out-of-state speeders. He was listening to a country music station on the car radio when the song playing was interrupted by the ringing sound of a call on his phone. Sean hit the button on his steering wheel to answer it without even bothering to see who was calling.

"Hello, Sean here," he called out.

"Mr. Johnson, Agent Redman here."

Sean recognized the voice and the name as being the FBI agent tasked with investigating Sean's involvement and role in the shootout in South Carolina. *I thought I was done with him by now?*

"Hi, Agent Redman, how can I help you?"

"I'm just following up on a few things and wondered if you could answer a few more questions for me?"

"Sure," Sean replied. *Just what I wanted to do on this nice afternoon.*

"Is this a good time?"

"Yep, I'm on the road driving, so fire away."

"Oh, are you still in South Carolina?" Sean detected a change in the tone of the FBI agent's voice.

"No, no. I was in North Carolina. Now I'm in Virginia, but headed to Pennsylvania."

"Oh, I see." There was a long pause and Sean could tell Redman was trying to decide how to best say something.

"I probably should have said this, but we would prefer if you kept us informed of your whereabouts and travel plans."

The comment irritated Sean. If the agent had said this to him earlier, Sean would have questioned why that was necessary. But now Sean felt he was better off just ignoring the comment. But he could not help be a little witty back to the agent. "Well now you know. I'm going to Pennsylvania."

"Thank you," Agent Redman replied, followed by another pause. "Where exactly are you going in Pennsylvania and what is the purpose of your trip?"

Sean felt he was losing his sense of self-control.

"Look, Agent Redman, you and the FBI are not my mother. I am not running away from anything. My colleague, Professor Enloe, is still sitting in the hospital in Greenville. I am a reporter and a journalist. I'm working on a story. I'm generally headed to Harrisburg, but I'm not sure where I'll stay tonight nor where I'll go after Harrisburg. Is that enough for you?"

"I guess so," Redman replied. "But please do keep me informed."

"You said you had questions for me," Sean prompted, hoping to get the call over with before he grew so tired of the junior agent that he hung up on him. *Then they might really want to track me down,* Sean thought, chuckling to himself.

"Yes I do. So, first off, can you confirm that you had no prior relationship with or awareness of the lives of the other people involved in the shooting?"

Sean paused and thought for a moment. "Only the FBI agent. He had come looking for me before. I suspect now that he was acting personally. But I have told you that."

"But nothing else?"

"Yes," Sean said, continuing to work at keeping his tone polite and civil.

The agent continued with more questions, some of which Sean thought he had asked before. Other questions, Sean noted, seemed like misstatements of what the agent should have already known. Sean could not decide if this was on purpose of if the agent was following some interrogation manual.

Finally, Sean had enough. "Look, Agent Redman, I'm willing to answer your questions directly. I sense you are circling around topics. I do have other things to do today."

"I understand, Mr. Johnson," the agent replied. "Perhaps we can take this up tomorrow or the day after? Where will you be then?"

"I can be wherever you need me to be if it'll bring this to an end."

"Could you come to D.C.? If so, I can probably set up a meeting with our team there that is handling the investigation."

"I certainly could, perhaps the day after next," Sean replied.

"Okay, let me see if that is a go. I may not get back to you until tomorrow."

"Fine," Sean said. "Goodbye, Agent Redman."

It was now early afternoon and Sean had one task to do that he had put off: he was to call James's assistant Thomas to get an overview of the battle of Gettysburg. While trying to pay attention to the road, he manually entered Thomas's number from the note pad on his lap. Once in, he pressed the call button and set the phone down on the passenger seat. The country music was again replaced by a ringing sound. Then Thomas's voice came on. "Hello?"

"Hi, Thomas, Sean Johnson here. I think Professor Enloe told you I would be calling you."

"Oh, hi. Yes he did."

"Great. Well, if you have time, I would love to get the story on the battle of Gettysburg. A condensed version, anyway."

Thomas replied that he could and proceeded to walk Sean through the basics of the battle. Some of those things Sean had known. Some things were new to him.

"So when the battle was over, the rebels just left?" he asked.

"Yes, after the failure of Picket's Charge, they concluded they were beaten and withdrew."

"They left the town intact?"

"Yes, no real burning or anything. The town was just one of their positions in a large semicircle that surrounded the ridges that the Union forces were defending. They quietly withdrew that night, leaving the town mostly intact."

"So what kind of data do we have on the town and its people?" Sean asked. "And its art, I guess."

"I have put together a list of sources of information. I even have some of the files electronically, already downloaded. Overall, there is a lot of writing about the battle and a decent amount about the town. But, like many things, the mundane matters, like who lived where, did what, et cetera, are harder to pin down. Now, if you ask about a particular house or person, results can be much better."

Sean liked the eagerness and clarity that James's assistant seemed to possess.

"Thanks, Thomas. I will learn more tomorrow, hopefully, and then perhaps we can get more specific. Are there any stories of missing paintings?"

"I haven't found any," Thomas replied. "But there could be records. I have a few books that I'm now reading. They tell the story of the town and its aftermath."

"Okay, well don't let me keep you then," Sean advised. "Talk to you soon."

Washington D.C.

The desk phone lit up and rang, signaling Emmitt to turn from his computer and see who was calling him. It was Agent Lentz. He took the call.

"Talie," he said.

"Ryan here, Sir. I wanted to give you a report on what we've learned so far."

"Go ahead, Agent Lentz." Emmitt loved to be formal. Ryan and he had known each other for quite a while, but Emmitt felt formality and professionalism in agent relationships were of the foremost importance.

"Yes, Sir, Agent Lentz reporting, Sir."

"Don't mock me, Agent Lentz!"

"Never, Sir."

"Just report," Emmitt ordered, trying to sound irritated.

"Yes, Sir. Agent Chapman is meeting with the forensics examiner that studied the site, so she is not available at the moment. We have had good cooperation with the Maryland State Police. They seem appreciative that we are involved and seem to hope that we might help them break this case. But that, Sir, probably tells you where they are at, a dead end. No witnesses and no video recordings found."

Lentz paused and then continued. "Matthew Grismond was found shot dead in a parking area near a highway commercial stop on 1-83. He had been shot once at close range. The lack of witnesses to the shooting suggests a silencer. A nine-millimeter bullet entered the lieutenant in his right eye and failed to exit. He was lying face down. Several people noticed his body on the pavement and called 9-1-1. It is believed the calls to 9-1-1 were made within ten minutes of the shooting. They found no forensic evidence at the scene nor on his body. His car was about 75 feet from his body. His badge and gun were in the car. It was unlocked and his keys were in his pocket."

Lentz paused again. Emmitt could tell that he had been reading from notes. "So what do you think happened, Lentz?"

"It seems like he stumbled upon something and was approaching someone who chose to shoot him. This could be put off as a random cop-hate crime except for our informant. The informant told us the caliber of bullet and said that it was with a silencer at very close range. Our informant even told us that the shooter picked up the bullet casing. So, I think the lieutenant saw something he was not supposed to see that connects to this supposed conspiracy. Perhaps it was a weapons sale."

"Very good, Lentz."

"But I don't know how much more we can find out here. Alice and I examined his car, his clothing and his possessions. Alice, as I said, is meeting with the forensics examiner now. Once we finish that, we're going to close up here and head back to D.C."

"Understood. Thanks." Emmitt hung up before Agent Lentz could respond. Emmitt was frustrated. The kill was too clean to produce anything. It had to have been a meeting of people who could not be seen together or a sale or transfer of objects that could not be seen being transferred. *But it was going to be a dead end. We will have to focus on identifying the informant.*

He would put Lentz and Chapman on the task of both tailing and investigating the FBI agent who had received the calls. They already had his phone line monitored so that if he got another call they might be able to trace it. Misler was digging into the agent's past. That was still a possible path.

"But what else can you do, Agent Talie?" he asked out loud. No answer came to mind.

Roads Towards Harrisburg

The day was getting long. Sean had stopped three times for gas or food, but had otherwise maintained a steady pace. It was going to take him less time than his GPS had originally predicted, but it was still going to be a long day. For many hours now, Sean had been alternating between silence and the radio. He had used the silence to think his way through some of the topics percolating around him.

One was his relationship with Kim and Abby. He had not talked to Kim since he said goodbye to her in Murphy the night before. He decided it was late enough that she should be home and dialed her number.

"Hi, Sean," Abby answered. "Do you want Mom, or are you willing to talk with me some?"

Sean laughed. "I think I can say that I will always be willing to talk to you. How is school?"

Abby replied, explaining that she was taking several incompletes and that she had been given summer assignments to complete to convert her grades to passing.

"So, it should work out fine. Except English, which never works out fine. But now that I have a writer around I'm going to expect some quality editing."

"Just send it to me," Sean promised. "But you have to do the work."

"I know," Abby sighed. "Here's Mom. She is going to tell you that I'm still here, at least for now."

Sean could hear a short verbal exchange between mother and daughter and then Kim came on the line.

"That girl," Kim said. "I told her I would tell you about it."

"So what happened?" Sean asked.

"The judge was not too harsh, but definitely seemed to be supportive of Jason. But he asked a lot of questions about Jason being down in Texas. He put off a decision today. That will happen next week. We have another hearing in a week."

"Well, hang in there," Sean replied, not knowing what else to say.

"In the meantime, I called James and he is ready to leave. So Abby and I are going to come back, pick him up and drive him home to Knoxville."

"What?" Sean asked, surprised. "How can you do that?"

"Abby is on her own with assignments and is not taking exams next week anyway. I have to be back for the hearing next week, but candidly, I kind of miss James. I also think that Abby will get a lot out of seeing him home."

"But, but...." Sean tried to come up with a reason to object. But he could not.

"Besides, the professor told me about this painting job. I might enjoy helping with that too, you know."

Ah, there it is, Sean thought, feeling pleased.

"I meant to tell you last night, but you were pretty out of it," Sean explained.

"I know, that summons threw me for a little while. But I thought about all that I went through in the last month and realized Jason's pathetic attempt was an easy one to deal with. Besides, I really did enjoy that." Kim paused and then continued. "I mean the sleuthing part, history, you know. Not the graves, really, and definitely not the shooting."

"No worries, I don't think we're going to have anything like that happen to us again in our lives."

"Us?" Kim asked. "What do you mean by that word, Sean Johnson?"

"You know exactly what I meant. Or at least I think you did."

They bantered for a while longer until Sean said he needed to pull off for gas.

"Okay, well I'll call you tomorrow to let you know how things went," Sean said. "Keep me informed of your schedule. Are you going to drive James back?"

"Yes, he's not supposed to fly for a few weeks."

"Okay then. Perhaps I'll come back that way also, depending on how things go in Harrisburg."

"That would be nice, Sean," Kim replied warmly. "Goodnight."

"Goodnight."

Sean heard the click of the line dropping and then the country music came back on the radio.

It sure would be, he thought wistfully.

CHAPTER SEVEN

Harrisburg

Sean scanned the restaurant, looking for a man sitting by himself. He spotted just the person, sitting in a booth across the room.

Straight brown hair, tall, black sport coat. That must be him.

Sean had arrived in Harrisburg in the mid-morning after staying the night at a highway motel about thirty minutes south of the city. He had walked around the downtown area of the city enjoying the architecture and history that had been blended with modern hustle and bustle. The restaurant Joe had told him to come to was a classy one that put on a nice display. Lunch was doing well with only a few tables available. Joe, or the person Sean had pegged as Joe, had one of a set of booths set into a wall along the far side of the dining room. Light peered into the windows along two walls of the old building. The stone and high ceilings amplied the noise arising from the patrons and wait staff.

A good place for a private conversation, Sean thought, his suspicions of Joe suddenly rekindled. *Why the secrecy?*

As Sean navigated his way around tables to reach the booth, the man looked up and spotted Sean coming. He slipped out of the booth and stood just as Sean reached him.

"Sean Johnson, you look just like the picture they're using in the newspapers," Joe said and then extended his hand. "I'm Joe."

Joe said his name simply and tersely and Sean sensed that he really did think of himself as Joe and not as Samuel. He was slender and about as tall as Sean. He looked to be in his sixties.

"Very good to meet you," Sean replied, extending his hand. They shook firmly with Joe's green eyes meeting Sean's for a moment. Then they sat down.

"No issues getting here?" Joe asked.

"No, I got a lot of things done while driving yesterday. I explored Harrisburg this morning a little also," he explained. "Nice town. Are you a native?"

"No, but this is my adopted hometown for sure," Joe replied. "Before we go any further, let me give you the items I brought."

He lifted a thick, page-sized envelope from the booth seat and placed it on the table next to Sean. It seemed heavy and was at least an inch thick. "As promised, advance payment for your efforts. I included a nice sum for reasonable expenses. There is also some information in there that I will explain to you." Joe seemed confident and comfortable.

Sean looked at the envelope and then reached out as if to pick it up. But, instead, he pushed it with one finger back towards Joe a few inches. Sean had clearly done this to slow Joe down for a moment and it seemed to have just that effect. Joe's face subtly switched from a pleased look to one of slight amusement.

"Okay, I assume you have some questions for me first," he said to Sean.

"Yes. You checked out, no issues there. But my long drive gave me a chance to think through the things about this that seem strange. Don't get me wrong, you're paying a substantial sum and my team wants it." Sean nodded to the envelope. "But I want to understand both the secrecy and the urgency here. Why the sudden rush to find a painting that has been missing for a hundred or more years?"

"Nearly one-hundred-and-fifty years, Sean," Joe corrected. "But point well taken. I think I told you that there is a buyer who will pay a substantial sum for the painting, but only if he can get it soon. I never ask my clients why they want something. But I can guess. I think the buyer has promised it to someone else. Or has promised someone else he could get a painting by this artist. Or something like that. Is that enough?"

"On the urgency point, yes," Sean answered. "Why the secrecy? Are there competing teams looking for this painting?"

"No. Or at least not yet." Joe was smiling smugly again.

Sean was immediately struck with the thought that Joe was relieved. As if he were prepared for a different question. *But what else is there to ask?*

Joe continued. "You see, if the word does get out that a team is searching for it, and even more so if the word gets out that it might be found, then there will be all sorts of competition for it. I am a fair man, but I need to get this from the owner's hands as quickly as I can before the owner finds out what he might actually get for it. If he senses there is a bidding war, I would probably still win, but it would take too long."

Sean studied Joe. Finally, he gave in. "Okay, then you have a deal. Or at least so long as what we're doing is legal. What is this painting I'm supposed to find and what makes you think I can find it?" He reached his hand out and pulled the envelope towards him.

"It's a painting by an artist named George Munger. One of his paintings hangs in the White House. It depicts the burnt-out wreck of the White House in August of 1814, after the British burned it when they occupied Washington during the War of 1812. Another of his paintings depicts the Capitol building in a similar state. They are watercolors. There is supposed to be another one that he mentions in a letter. It's supposed to show the Capitol, the White House, as well as a good portion of the city."

"What happened to the painting?" Sean asked.

"Overall, I'm not sure. It is believed to exist, based on the letter by Munger. An 1835 will suggests a Munger painting of Washington City was inherited by a merchant. That merchant's daughter wound up living in Gettysburg. The trail would not lead to Gettysburg if it were not for a story told by her son. The son, when he was an adult in the late 1800's, wrote a letter to an art dealer explaining that his mom had lost a painting while living in Gettysburg during the battle and that she had always hoped to find it. He supposedly described this missing Munger painting."

Joe could see that Sean was about to say something and anticipated his question. "I used 'supposedly' because we do not have that letter. Instead we have a letter by an art merchant in New York describing a painting he is looking for. His letter says it was at the request of a man who wrote him. So the merchant's letter tells us the story of what is probably the painting we want."

Joe paused to give Sean a chance to absorb what he had said. Then he continued.

"So we have a letter saying it existed, and then a will and a letter telling us where it might have gone, to Gettysburg," Joe summarized. "But it may have been destroyed or taken from Gettysburg during the battle. We do not know. All of this and more are in your envelope."

"So you want me to pull off a miracle and find this painting?" Sean asked. "Within a month?"

"Even less than a month if possible. 'As quickly as you can' is my request. I am saying you can stop after a month. I might stop you sooner. You keep that payment in any case."

Sean sighed. "Okay, we will give it our best shot. I do think we have proven ourselves to be a pretty good team. Either that or we got lucky."

"I think you accomplished an amazing feat. Which is why I want you to try this one. I think you are very capable. If you find it, or even if you make headway, keep me informed. If we are getting closer to it, either I or a buyer will be ready to purchase it."

"What is this painting worth?"

Joe laughed. "Worth? Who knows? But I can tell you right now there are plenty of people who would pay millions for it."

"Millions. Amazing," Sean replied shaking his head side-to side. "I guess that's why you can spend so much money trying to find it."

"That's right, Sean. But, to be honest with you, for me, it's a thrill to find missing objects. You understand that."

"Yes, yes I do," Sean mused. He looked around the restaurant as if lost in thought and then seemed to bring himself back to the moment. "Shall we eat?" he asked, grabbing a menu from the table.

"By all means," Joe replied. "The fish here is excellent, by the way."

Eastern Pennsylvania

The building was part of a large light-industrial, heavy-commercial complex located off a highway that runs through the rolling hills and meadows that make up the part of eastern Pennsylvania about 30 miles west of Harrisburg. There were seven massive buildings, some divided into sections and some a single place of business. Most businesses located there were installers of sorts. One unit was a distribution warehouse for a national supplier of appliance repair parts.

Frank Huerta had leased this building using a company they had created solely for the purpose of acquiring such resources. This particular complex was conveniently amid or close to several of their targets, so it was essentially their home base. It was also nice that they had their own building, separated by parking lots from the other ones.

Less chance of any neighbors ever seeing something going on here that seems strange, General Frank Huerta thought.

General Huerta was dressed in civilian clothes: slacks and a collared, short-sleeved shirt. The shirt was white and he looked like any other ordinary business manager. He was sitting in the meeting room of their facility at a large table with two other men. The room was part of a set of offices built into one side of the building. The meeting room was on top of offices and had two small windows that looked out on the mostly empty floor of the building.

Huerta was Hispanic in appearance with darker skin and brown eyes. The two men he was meeting with had fairer skin; one had blonde hair and blue eyes and the other brown hair and eyes. All three of them had tight, short haircuts. In front of them were cell phones sitting on top of the boxes they had been sold in. They all had manila folders and organizers spread around them. "Are we good to go, Gentlemen?" Huerta asked, looking at the other two.

Ken, the blonde, spoke first. "Yes. I have said for a while to count me in. I'm good."

"Me too," Alex, the other man, chimed in. Alex and Ken both looked to be a decade or more younger than General Huerta. "I think it's funny that Ken and I never knew you had recruited the two of us."

"Sorry, it had to be that way, you understand," Frank said. "Maintaining secrecy and deniability was the best way to limit risks."

The two nodded.

"I recruited both of you because I saw the same frustration in you that I had. The same philosophy. You will see in your list the others that I have recruited. My intent is to have them all report to one of you. Your first step is to reach out to your new unit of men and establish that they are still committed. If they are, you bring them into our efforts. If they are not, you quietly and quickly thank them."

Frank paused and took a breath. "Just as when I reached out to you, the moment you contact them is a big moment of risk. Someone that says no might report you and your contact to them. The only person they know of to be involved is me. I am assuming that out of the 80 or so people there, you will have at least a ten percent failure rate. I think it is inevitable that one of them will repeat this to someone else and that eventually authorities might hear about it."

Frank looked as serious as he ever did. "But there is nothing to fear about that. If we never do anything then their comments or even accusations will not lead anywhere. And if we do take action, it will probably be before they say anything and, in any case, it will not matter anymore that they have talked."

His last sentence ended on an ominous note. Ken looked at Alex, and then back at Frank, nodding. "We understand. We're committed to this cause."

"Good," the general said. "You have two weeks, maximum, to complete the forming of your team. Some advance work should begin being done next week. A few of the men who live or are stationed around here, who are ready and willing to start right away on preparatory tasks, should be called into service right away. If everything goes as planned, we will be mobilized and operating within a month's time.

"Treat this like all the missions you have been trained and prepared for in your military careers. Follow our communication protocols. Observe your surroundings. Be alert. Pretend you are in enemy country." Frank looked thoughtful for a moment. "Actually, that really might be true depending on where you are. Some people will think we are heroes, others that we are criminals. Probably even terrorists. But we believe in what we are about to do. Always remember the key to our success is to convert as many people to our cause as possible. So we must not be thugs or terrorists. We must be heroes."

Road Out of Harrisburg

As Sean drove south on the highway out of Harrisburg he considered detouring over to Gettysburg that afternoon, but he decided it would not be useful. He really had no idea where to go or what to do. *I do not know enough about any of this. Time to call the professor.*

The professor answered his phone on the fourth ring, sounding a bit out of breath.

"Hi, Professor, Sean here. You sound like you've been exercising or something."

"I would not quite call it exercise," James replied proudly. "But I'm walking and free from the little drip unit following me around. Even going to the bathroom on the toilet."

"That's great," Sean replied, laughing. "Kim tells me that they are going to run back and take you home."

"Yes, she told me that too. I told her I did not need that, but she insisted."

"That's Kim. Listen, I had the meeting with Joe. We've been provided the $10,000 fee and also $10,000 for expenses. So we're in business."

"Good," James replied, still sounding out of breath. Tell me all about it."

"It's a Munger painting of D.C. after the British burned it in the War of 1812."

"The one in the White House?" James sounded confused.

"No, a missing painting that is from that series. It's a small watercolor I guess." Sean continued to explain what he had learned. He had only skimmed the documents in the envelope. There had been some history on George Munger and his work and copies of letters, a will, and even some kind of a research paper on the lost piece. When Sean finished there was a pause before James responded.

"Okay, so I guess we start with Gettysburg and this family history. But how do we have any idea where it might have gone?"

"I think the answer lies in the story the son told the art dealer. It has some details about a vase. So we are probably looking for a vase. I think we start with Gettysburg. The vase might still be there for all we know."

"True, true," James muttered. Sean had learned that when the professor was muttering he was deep in thought. Sean had learned to let him stay that way because often good ideas sprung forward afterwards. Finally James spoke up.

"The painting could be hanging in plain view too, you know. I don't mean directly, but behind a larger, plain or ordinary painting. That was a common way to hide things from thieves and plunderers. Recall the copy of the Declaration of Independence found that way."

"That's right," Sean replied.

"Well, what are you doing next?" James asked.

"Actually I'm headed down to Washington D.C. Our friends at the FBI seem to be having a hard time accepting our story, as true as it is, of how we wound up in our situation," Sean explained. "I'm meeting with them tomorrow in a last attempt to get them off our backs. They should be ecstatic at what we found. Instead, they seem to want to treat me like a criminal."

"Hmm," James paused. "I would try and not annoy them too much. Besides, most of the D.C. community is excited about our find. The FBI is just not into history like, say, the Smithsonian."

"That's true. And not everything we did was exactly legal. There was a breaking and entering or two. I have avoided telling them how we got a few documents, which is probably why they're frustrated. They can tell I'm holding back some information. But I'm not about to confess to any crimes so they can then turn around and prosecute us." Sean paused, thinking. "So, I think that after D.C. I'm going to head back up to Gettysburg. Perhaps we should all meet there? Kim could drive you up there."

"I was thinking the same thing. In the meanwhile, why don't you call Thomas? He can go over some more history of Gettysburg with you and tell you what he has found."

"That's a great idea, Professor. I'll do that next."

They said goodbye and hung up. Sean promptly called up Thomas's cell phone.

"Hello, Mr. Johnson," Thomas's young voice said.

"Hello yourself, Thomas. But please, just call me Sean."

"Right, sorry, I think you asked me to do that once already. So how can I help you?"

"I want to tell you what our exact task is and also learn some more from you about your research to date."

"Sounds good, let me get hold of a pad of paper."

Sean could hear some rustling and other noises. "Okay," Thomas said. "Fire away."

Sean explained his meeting and the decision to zero in on Gettysburg first. Thomas interjected a few times and asked good questions. It was obvious to Sean that Thomas was very engaged and focused on the task.

"Okay, now that I have walked you through it, any questions?" Sean asked.

"Um, no, not yet. Can I comment though?"

"Sure."

"Well, this painting could have gone anywhere, you know. It's probably not that large. But if anyone knew they had it I would think that they would have it on display. So others would know about it." Thomas paused, trying to think of how to express his thought. "I guess what I'm saying is that it seems more likely that, if this painting still exists, it is probably hidden in something. In other words, whoever has it doesn't know they have it. So we're really not looking for the painting, we're looking for the object or place that it's hiding in."

He finished and waited for a few moments for Sean to reply. Sean, though, was thinking through what Thomas had just said. *He really is a sharp kid. Brilliant idea.*

"Does that make sense?" Thomas sounded hesitant, probably from Sean's silence.

"Yes, yes, it does. It's brilliant even," Sean replied. "Sorry, you had me thinking. So then the vase the painting was in is supposedly one option. We would be looking for a vase tall enough to hide the painting. One that would typically be in a home in the 1860s."

"Yes, exactly. That is my point," Thomas replied, sounding excited. "Can you send me a scan of the letter describing how the painting was hidden?"

"I will do that tonight," Sean replied. "Assuming I can find a scanner."

"Just use your phone, assuming it has a camera. Send me a decent quality photo. I will convert it to a text document and email it back."

"Great," Sean replied. "I'm glad we have you on our team."

"I'm happy to be here as well."

"So now, one more request. Can you walk me through more details about Gettysburg?"

Thomas replied affirmatively and the two continued to talk as Sean drove south towards D.C.

CHAPTER EIGHT

Washington D.C.

"We got another message from the anonymous informant," Agent Chapman reported.

"I see," Emmitt replied. He was working at his desk when Alice called. He had her on speakerphone. He now turned his attention away from his computer and looked at his phone. "What did he have to say?"

"I just listened to it and took notes, but the transcript is not done yet," Alice explained. "So this is not precise."

"Understood, go ahead."

"He continues to not identify himself. There is background noise so I assume he is calling from some public phone somewhere, which would be the same as the other calls."

They had in fact identified the point of origin of each of his previous calls and had gone to those locations. The calls had been from phones in hotel lobby areas or payphones and all had involved using calling cards purchased for cash at small shops in public places.

"He also appears to have again used a voice distortion device," Alice said.

"Go on."

"He had three pieces of information. First, he said that, quote, 'action is imminent.' Second, he said that this might be his, quote, 'last warning.' Third, he told us that some historical research was being conducted and that the group was particularly interested in getting results from that. This third one was pretty odd. He used the phrase 'historical research' and said that the group wants a particular document. 'Particular document' is a quote."

"That is odd," Emmitt replied. "A dead trooper, some action against the country and a historical document. This case just gets odder and odder."

"Yes, Sir, it does."

"And why tell us he may never call again? And why call it a warning?" Emmitt thought out loud. "It's almost as if he is trying to scare us. But if he was so concerned, why not just tell us exactly who and what? Why string us along? Is he playing with us?"

"Perhaps it's some nutcase who happened to get non-public details of the trooper's murder and is using that to manipulate us?" Alice asked.

"Do you believe that?"

"No, I don't," Alice admitted. "He comes across as being sincere. And if he was trying to stir us up, he could offer more specific information on what the group is planning to do. But we would be remiss if we did not consider that he could be misleading us for some other reason."

"Consider also his use of a voice modulator and the care in which he avoids tracing calls back to him," Emmitt added. "That is the work of a professional. Like a spy. Someone trained. No, I think he is for real but I think also that he has some form of a hidden agenda that we are not privy to."

"So what's next?" Alice asked. "We're still running down the leads on the agent he has been calling. Ryan is looking more closely at who has had access to the records of the trooper's murder."

"Get the transcript and trace on the call and chase down the calling location. Maybe we will get lucky on cameras on the approach routes. Or even a fingerprint. Get a psych analysis on the latest call as well. And send it for voice analysis even if we expect the same result."

"Will do."

"Send me the transcript when you get it," Emmitt instructed. "I will think about what else we might do."

"Okay, anything else?"

"No, that's it for now."

She clicked off and Emmitt swiveled in his chair to look out on 9th Street from his fifth-floor office. Outside, cars, cabs and people were everywhere. Emmitt thought about their Supernova investigation. *Are we chasing our own tail?* What should he make of this latest twist? Why was this informant calling and giving just clues? Emmitt thought again of the profile they had on the informant. He personally did not put much stake in profiles, but this profile had indicated the informant could be some form of a serial killer-style psychopath getting a thrill from risking his own capture. But, weirdly, here he would be risking the capture of a group if he was being honest in what he was reporting. The profile had said that he might have killed the trooper himself and was now using his inside information as a means of gaining attention. *So what do I make of his clue about research on a historical document? Do I have to chase down every history grad student doing research out there?* Suddenly, though, Emmitt did have one idea.

*****

A few floors below Emmitt's office, agents Paul Redman and Lance Dawson were questioning Sean on his role in Agent Nazimi's death. Sean suspected that Dawson had some form of an "internal affairs" position and was involved because of the situation of an FBI agent being killed while apparently being involved in a crime. Dawson was older than Redman. Redman, Sean suspected, was probably a junior field agent.

Sean had come into the headquarters building that morning, been met in the lobby and walked back to a meeting room. There were no mirrors that could serve as one-way glass like so many cop movies seemed to have. Instead it was a plain meeting room that could be found in almost all offices in America. They were seated at a rectangular table in uncomfortable chairs with Redman across from Sean and Dawson to his left. Sean knew enough about interrogation to know that their positions were no accident. It allowed Sean to see only one of them, most likely the more junior Redman. That in turn allowed Dawson to observe Sean's body language and facial features. Sean had turned his chair a little bit to make it possible to see both agents. But then Dawson had simply slid his chair farther to Sean's left.

Sean was now also forced to turn his head to look at Redman. Overall, he was feeling annoyed and tired of the FBI's investigation.

It was their agent who turned criminal, an agent in charge of an office, no less. Why harass me? But Sean knew the answer. An agent was dead and he was avoiding some topics. But he did not see a way to satisfy them.

Sean tried to focus his attention on the questioning. Redman had just asked Sean for the second time how he came into the letter that had pointed at the South Carolina location.

"Look, Agent Redman, you can ask that question all you want. My answer will remain that I am not obligated to tell you how I got that letter. Does how I got the letter relate to why your agent was running around trying to kill innocent people?" Sean tried to speak clearly and calmly but it was getting harder.

He turned to look at Agent Dawson. The agent, who looked to be in his mid-to-late thirties, smiled back at Sean. He had the same dark suit, white shirt, and plain tie look as Redman.

"Agent Dawson," Sean asked, "do you think I'm lying when I say that Agent Nazimi had no legitimate reason to be shooting at me? Or even to be there that night? Do you think I'm lying when I tell you he was there out of simple greed?"

Agent Dawson smiled for another moment and then answered, "No, I don't think you're lying, but you're also not telling us everything. Maybe you have your reasons. But if those reasons relate to the crimes involved then we have a need to know them." Dawson glanced over at Redman and then continued, but without the smile. "Look, if we don't get what we want we're going to keep investigating. We will haul your colleagues in here and grill them just as we are you. You are a tough guy and maybe we're wasting our time with you. But how long will your nice little girlfriend hold up? Or your kind professor? You want to play tough, we can play tough."

Before Sean could respond, Redman jumped in.

"Now hold on, Lance, I don't think that's necessary. Mr. Johnson and his team have done the country a great service." Redman turned to look at Sean. "Just give us some more information, enough so we can complete our report and investigation."

Sean suddenly realized he was getting the oldest interrogation trick in the book and laughed. "Good cop bad cop? Is that all you have? Look, I'm not going to tell you anything else. Threats from Mister Tough Guy here aren't going to change my position."

Sean took a breath and stood up. "I think I'm done with this for today. But understand something. I'm cooperating with you. I'm not sure I or my colleagues will cooperate if you turn heavy-handed. And one thing Redman said is correct. We apparently are heroes. And the FBI looks bad in what happened. The FBI doesn't need the two of you making it look even worse."

Redman's eyes were slightly wide. But Dawson just stood up and smiled. *Like a chameleon*, thought Sean.

"Sorry, Mr. Johnson," Agent Dawson began, "we have a job to do. And I think we understand each other."

Dawson reached out and shook Sean's hand. "I do admire your service record and even what you have accomplished. Let me walk you out."

Sean looked at Dawson for a moment, then reached over and shook Redman's hand. "Okay," he replied. "Lead the way."

As they walked down the hallway towards the entrance to the building, Dawson spoke. "You did not hear this from me. We are under a lot of pressure to find fault with you and your team. I am just doing my job. I am not sure we are done yet either. But I do think you are a good guy."

Sean looked over at the agent. "I understand."

"So don't be surprised if we call again."

"Okay, I won't," Sean replied.

They had reached the end of the hallway. As they rounded the corner, the main entrance room came into view. Agent Dawson pointed toward a path on the righthand side that avoided the metal detectors and security Sean had navigated to enter the building.

"Just head that way," Dawson said.

"Roger," Sean replied, heading for the exit without a look back.

Good cop, bad cop? Then bad cop turns good cop? Sean thought. *I think I've had enough of the FBI for the day.* He exited the building through a set of sliding glass doors and took a breath of good old Washington D.C. air. The horns and car noises felt weirdly reassuring.

*****

Ted Hines looked over at Steven Ableman. He had first met Ableman at a fundraiser more than two decades earlier where the lobbyist had impressed Hines with his political rhetoric. The senator had recognized the political genius of Ableman and had tried to recruit him into his campaign but the lobbyist had demurred. They had become friends anyway and, over the years, had developed and shared a private political philosophy that had grown more and more unacceptable in normal political circles. When Joe entered the picture, they were ripe for conversion, and had both joined up with full knowledge of the path they were going down.

For the senator, the cause was moral and noble. For Ableman, it seemed more about a personal vendetta that he held against a corrupt political system than it did a moral effort. Steven wanted to see the United States government falter. Ted wanted to see the many states achieve greatness. But, in any case, their desired outcome was the same: free states, the way the Union had been meant to be.

They were meeting in a hotel room that Steven had booked for this very purpose. The senator supposed that such secrecy was probably not needed much longer. Things would be out very soon and either their political careers would be over or they would just be getting started. But for now they continued their secret ways.

Hotel rooms were usually the safest way to meet. Steven would book it and call to let the senator know where it was. The senator could slip into the hotel, get lost in the crowd and then find his way to the room. Then they could meet with no record that they had been meeting at all. And they could talk, think and plan as much as needed.

Steven was sitting in a chair by the small window the room had. It was a large downtown hotel with views of the White House, but mostly through small windows. The senator was sitting in the desk chair with a document laid out in front of him on the desk.

"I have about thirty minutes before I have to go, Steven," the senator announced as he read the document Steven had prepared. That was another element of their secrecy. They did not email anything and the senator took very few printed documents or electronic files with him. When he did, he was meticulous about how he handled them. Over the last several years the two of them had developed the political and legal argument for their cause. Today the senator would be giving his final blessing on their material. He would also now begin working on the speech he would be giving shortly.

"There is not much to really look at," Steven replied. "I accepted almost all of your changes and ideas from our last meeting. Take a look at the talking points on the last page. Some of them are new." Steven sounded smug and confident about his work. But he had always sounded that way. The senator was confident but he never let himself feel or act smug. To him, being smug was to be arrogant and that led to overconfidence. Assume the best, but prepare for the worst. That had always been his motto.

"I think we have said things as well as we can say them," the senator announced a few minutes later. "I like that last bullet you added. It echoes the line in the Gettysburg Address, 'government of the people, by the people,' It's tremendously ironic, but perhaps appropriate, that Lincoln's famous speech can provide some vision and moral certainty to our own cause."

Steven smiled. "I thought you would like that."

"I guess the only unresolved question is whether we will get a chance to use our North Carolina argument," the senator said, lifting his eyes from the document. "Any word from Joe on that?"

"No, but I'm not certain we will really find it. Joe says it's worth trying, but I think truthfully he has been trying to find that declaration for several years now. I don't think we need it. The Declaration of Independence itself stands for the rights we claim to have."

"It didn't help the South though," the senator said, mostly to needle Steven.

"The morality of the South's attempt to exit the Union was tainted by their practice of slavery," Steven retorted. "And the end of their effort was not settled by morality or legality. It was settled by force."

Steven saw the senator smiling at him. "Oh, you're baiting me," he said, smiling back.

"I most certainly am, my friend. I love watching you get heated up over these issues. It warms my soul."

The senator pushed back from the desk. "Does this hotel have a mini-bar, Steven?"

"I think it does," Steven replied, getting up from his chair. "Who's paying?"

"You, of course. The room is in your name."

Steven opened a cabinet door and then opened a small refrigerator door.

"Ah, here we are. Two bourbons coming up. No ice, I'm afraid, but the bourbon is chilled at least."

"That's fine," the senator replied. "I'm going to begin preparing my speech now. We will either be hanging from the gallows or be heroes in a short while. Best to drink to our success before things get hot."

"I agree. Here you are." Steven poured the contents of two of the small bottles into glasses and handed one to the senator.

"To the free states," Senator Hines toasted.

"To the free states," Steven replied.

******

"My idea is to reach out to the major historians around D.C. Professors, I suppose," Emmitt said. "We should be asking them about research related to governmental history and if there are any researchers that seem extreme in their views or beliefs."

Agent Chapman and Emmitt were meeting in his office near the end of the day. To Emmitt, the idea was simple. There could not be that many documents or even historical topics that could relate to governmental conspiracy. So why not ask the professional researchers?

Alice did not seem so convinced. "Okay," she said doubtfully.

"What? What's wrong with my idea?"

Alice sighed. "It's just the idea of interviewing history professors. I hated history in school. Now if I could arrest them for putting students to sleep, that might be a better topic."

"Well, I think it gives us a chance to identify the researcher or the topic. Maybe our informant is a nutcase history professor himself. Then you would get to arrest him." Emmitt smiled. "In any case, that is my task for you. Use Misler to develop the list."

"How soon?" Alice asked.

"You mean, can you wait until Monday or do I need you to work on this over the weekend?"

"Well, yes, kind of."

"At least get your list done over the weekend so you can start calling them Monday morning," Emmitt advised. "If this is a real threat and we fail to act urgently and then it explodes in our face, we will look pretty incompetent."

"Yes, Sir. I can handle that." Alice stood up and started to leave the office, but then stopped and turned around. "I should tell you that I listened to all the messages several times in a row today. I think that whatever else our informant might be, I don't think he is making things up. Something in this is real. I think, anyway."

"That is why I wanted you on this team, Agent Chapman," Emmitt responded. "You think. Don't stop doing that."

"Yes, Sir." Alice turned back to the door and left Emmitt's office, quietly closing the door behind her.

Emmitt stared at the transcript of the latest call and tried to see something that had not yet made itself apparent. He glanced at the piles of documents on his desk and decided to go back and look at the files from the beginning. *There's something in there waiting to be found,* he thought.

CHAPTER NINE

Washington D.C.

Sean had returned to his hotel. He had managed to get a late checkout to allow him to get some work done from a non-moving surface for a change. He reflected on his latest FBI interview, concluding he was going to need to talk to the professor and Kim about the FBI's aggressiveness. *I need to protect them as well.* Generally, the professor had not done anything that could be construed as a crime. But Kim had been with Sean on two adventures that certainly could be considered crimes. So he knew he needed to prepare her for any interrogation.

Then his thoughts returned to their new quest. He had the various documents Joe had given him spread out on the desk. He kept coming back to the art dealer's letter. *That's the one that gives us our main clues.* It was dated October 15th, 1886. The copy was not high quality or else the original had been in pretty bad shape. *I wonder how Joe managed to find this?*

Sean thought about his conversation with Thomas, the professor's research assistant. *Thomas is right*, he thought, *our best chance is to track down the vase. But that seems like a long shot in and of itself. The vase might have been destroyed or thrown away a long time ago. The vase was probably not even distinguishable from any other vase of that era. But it might also be sitting on a shelf in Gettysburg right now.*

Sean also tried to think about the circumstances that led to the painting being put in a vase. *Why does someone do that? Doesn't that risk damaging the painting, rolling it up like that? It is a watercolor on paper, so it might have been soft enough. But even if we find the vase, why would we think the painting is still in it?*

Sean felt frustrated. The task Joe had given them seemed like looking for the proverbial needle in a haystack. Why pay someone so much so suddenly and urgently only to find this painting? *Crazy rich people, I guess.* Joe did not seem crazy at all, though. So it must be his client that was nuts. Sean did not mind the chance to pull off a miracle. But he still had this lingering feeling that they were being "played." But to what end?

Sean put the letter down and picked up his cell phone. He pulled up Thomas's number and called.

"Hi, Sean," Thomas answered. "Give me a moment."

Sean heard the sound of a door opening and closing. Then Thomas came back on.

"Sorry, I was in a quiet reading room looking at some old books on 19th century art," Thomas explained. "I'm fine now."

"Thanks," Sean replied. "I don't want to distract you too much. I just wanted to follow up from our conversation yesterday."

"So how can I help?" Thomas asked.

"I'm assuming you got the photos I sent you of the letters?"

"Yes, I did. I printed them and read them as best I could. They were not the best quality," Thomas replied.

"Well, I'm calling to follow up on one idea that we discussed, the vase."

"Yes. That's why I'm reading up on 19th century art. I'm assuming this was a relatively inexpensive vase. And tall enough to hide a rolled up painting that was probably one to one-and-a-half feet tall. The height is actually helping to narrow what to look for."

"Great," Sean replied.

"What I'm trying to do is put together some kind of a searcher's guide with representative pictures and guidelines on how to spot a vase of the right age. Then I can do some online searching."

"We may converge on Gettysburg this weekend. We could always task someone with going to every shop in the entire town. So such a guide would be great."

"I'm not sure how to get it to you. Could you print a color document tonight or tomorrow?" Thomas asked.

"I'll find a way," Sean assured him. "Just email it. What else have you got?"

"I have a pretty good database of names of families in Gettysburg at the time of the battle. I'm hoping to pin down the home of the Wright family for you. But I'm not so sure that line is really that worthy of pursuing."

"Yeah," Sean replied. "I know where you're going. The house was probably remodeled, the vase or really any clues are not likely to be related to the physical location where they lived then."

"Yes, that is generally my perspective."

"But," Sean said, "we are obligated to leave no stone unturned."

"If Anna Wright lost the painting then why pursue her at all?" Thomas asked.

"Because the letter is not clear if and how she truly lost it. We don't know that it left town in a vase or that it did not come back. I also don't really understand why she put the painting in a vase. I could understand something obviously valuable, but even then you would think that a vase would attract attention."

"True," Thomas agreed.

Greenville

"Back in South Carolina!" Kim exclaimed.

Abby, who was walking along next to her, replied, "I think it's gotten muggier in the few short days we were gone."

Kim and Abby were walking from the gate where they had exited their plane. They each had a rolling carry-on bag.

"It's nice to arrive here under much calmer circumstances," Kim said. "But once we get the professor, I think we'll be heading out shortly."

Kim glanced over at Abby, who seemed happy to be rolling her suitcase alongside her mom.

"Are you sure you're fine with coming back here? You have all of your make-up work? No school issues?"

"Mom!" Abby exclaimed. "Yes, for the fifth time. And I know why you're asking these questions. School is fine. I'll be caught up by the middle of the summer. So nothing bad will happen that'll risk you losing custody. That's the last thing I want."

Abby had drawn out her utterance of "last" as if to emphasize how much she wanted to stay with her mom.

"Okay, well I'm nervous about what's going to happen back home with that. But I'll fight to keep you as much as I can. You're almost sixteen and I think I've done a good job raising you for the last decade. It would be crazy for the judge to suddenly change all of that."

"I can't believe the judge could be so stupid."

"It's not a matter of stupidity. Or at least I don't think it is. The system seems poorly designed for judges to make informed decisions. He's hearing all of this biased information from your father's lawyer and all mine can really say is that I have done a great job safely and responsibly raising you. His story is a lot more interesting than mine."

As they talked, Kim and Abby exited the secure side of the airport gate area. Kim spotted the sign for rental cars. "That way," she said, pointing at a doorway to the right.

Just then her phone rang. She pulled it out of the holster on her hip and glanced at it.

"Sean," she said happily as she put the phone to her ear. "We just landed in Greenville. Where are you?"

"In D.C.," Sean replied. He proceeded to tell her about the FBI interview. Kim glanced over at Abby as they continued to walk to the rental car lot. Abby was looking up at her mom.

"So the bottom line is that you may hear from them. Don't talk about our less-than-savory activities."

"Got it," Kim confirmed, not sounding like she was that scared or bothered at all. "We're picking up James in a little bit and then heading north to meet you in Gettysburg," Kim explained. "We won't get there until late tomorrow, though. And we're going to get Friday night traffic."

"Okay, I'll be booking some rooms for us. I'll just find a room for myself tonight, but I better line up our rooms for Gettysburg right now since it may be busy at the park."

"That sounds good," Kim replied. "Let's talk later tonight when we're all done driving places."

"Okay, sounds good."

They hung up and Kim looked over at Abby.

"Maybe you can do a report on Gettysburg," she said to her daughter.

"Hey," Abby protested, "I already have plenty of work to do."

Seattle, Washington

Paul Clovis was perched on a high stool in front of his light desk, examining some graphics that he had put down on the illuminated surface. It was mid-afternoon in Seattle and he was getting ready to head home early. From the window in his office he could see the beginning of a beautiful June evening.

He was interrupted from his evaluation by the ringing of the desk phone behind him. He spun around and looked at the screen on the phone. "Sean," he said. "It's about time I heard from you."

He then shifted over to his desk chair and hit the speakerphone button. "Sean," he bellowed. "Tell me you're emailing your story to me."

"Hi, Paul, nice to talk to you too," Sean replied, trying to sound offended.

"No, no, none of that guilt stuff from you," Paul said, still speaking very loudly and firmly. "You run off and have the story of the year, nearly getting killed, and then forget about your good old friend and editor. Of course you're probably so rich and famous now, you don't really care about us mere peasants who have to work for a living."

"Okay, okay, I deserve all of your attacks," Sean replied when Paul seemed to stop for air. "But let me know when you're done so we can talk business."

"Business? You want to talk business?" Paul continued, unabated. "How about you getting me a story so I can stay employed? I keep telling everyone here how close I am to you, how you will not let me down."

Before Paul could keep going on, Sean jumped in. "Article tomorrow. I've been working on it. It's a single story on the find itself. I'm including details of what was in there, how it got there. My plan is to send a second story on how we found it."

"Keep going," Paul said, sounding mollified.

"A big challenge for me on the second article is not writing about things we did that might get us in trouble. The FBI is breathing down my neck."

"Tell me about it," Paul laughed. "You know an Agent Redman?"

"Is he calling you?" Sean asked, feeling some increased irritation.

"Of course. He called me the other day asking about you. He was trying to verify that you really were a journalist on a story. He asked me if I had sent you to South Carolina."

"What did you tell him?"

"That you were the sorriest journalist that I had ever worked with, but that yes, you were a journalist and, yes, I had advised you on the Enloe story what seemed like years ago," Paul half-joked. "Of course I told him that since you never called me or told me what was going on, I assumed you had converted to some extreme religious faith and that I'd never hear from you again."

"Thanks, Paul."

"Anytime. So are you really going to get me a story tomorrow?"

"Yes. And listen, I'm not rich or really famous yet, but I have been sought out for a new task. My team, really."

"Your team? You have a team now?" Paul sounded incredulous.

"Stop that. Someone is paying us to find something. Paying us whether we find it or not."

"What, more treasure?"

"I can't tell you until we're done."

"Come on, Sean, tell me something believable."

"No, no. I'm serious. Have to stay silent until we're done, success or not. Then I can write the story."

"Hmm," Paul said. "Can you tell me anything?"

"It involves Gettysburg."

"That's it?" Paul asked. "Okay, stop. Don't call me again until after you've sent your first story. Then we can talk about your second one. I'm not going to look beyond that horizon."

"Okay," Sean replied. "I'll talk to you early next week."

"Sounds good," Paul replied. "And Sean?"

"Yes?"

"Try to be careful, okay. I really don't want you getting shot at again."

"Of course," Sean replied.

Paul hung up the phone and looked out his window. "That guy!" he said.

Washington D.C.

Sean hung up the phone in his hotel room and looked at the clock by the bed. He then looked at his computer. Sighing, he decided he had a good hour before the hotel would probably get angry with him for staying any longer. *Or just bill me.*

Sean tried to go back to the story he was editing on his computer, but Joe and the Munger painting crept back into his thoughts. Thomas had the same reservations that Sean had, that the missing painting was more likely to be anywhere other than Gettysburg. But they still needed to go to Gettysburg. Sean sensed that the more he could get his head around who Anna Wright had been, what it had been like when the Northern and Southern armies collided in that little town, and what would have compelled her to hide such a painting, the better chance he had at some form of an epiphany.

Plus, the professor hasn't really gotten involved yet. He was sharp and effective at unearthing things, so if there was some clue waiting to be discovered, James would be the one to find it. With those thoughts, Sean returned to focusing on finishing his story.

CHAPTER TEN

Knoxville

It was early Saturday morning and Thomas was feeling pretty tired. He had napped twice during the night, just enough to keep his brain functional. Now, he was looking forward to catching up on his sleep. When the library kicked him out Friday night, he had headed home with a clump of books and files. He stood up from the small dining table in his apartment and stretched his elbows back.

It's kind of funny. I just did my first all-nighter and it wasn't even for a class, Thomas thought. *Instead I've been up all night working for a professor and his historical team.* "They better pay me good for all of this," he said aloud.

After a short walk around the table, he sat back down and pulled his cell phone over. He called Professor Enloe but got voicemail. Rather than leave a message he hung up and then called Sean. Sean answered on the second ring. Thomas could hear the highway background sounds that told him Sean was driving.

"Good morning, Thomas," Sean called out. "How are you?"

"Tired, but done," Thomas explained. "I've been up most of the night."

"You're excellent, Thomas." Sean clearly sounded like he was trying to make Thomas feel better. "Your timing is excellent also. I'm just getting into Gettysburg now."

"Okay, then I will email them. I think I've managed to put together Anna's family tree, before and after. Also with it I have some documents like wills, a deed or two and the like."

"Good," Sean replied.

"I also have the vase art guide. I've been calling it the shopping guide." Thomas laughed at his own joke but heard nothing from Sean.

"Okay, well anyways, I have that file ready. It's got color photos in it and is worth printing in color. Finally, I have several documents on Gettysburg residents and landowners. I think a lot of that is probably random and extraneous, but you'll see homes I have flagged as possibly being hers. It looks like many homes and buildings from the time of the war survived. Many of them are registered as Civil War buildings. You'll probably see little plaques on them around town."

"Okay. Anything else?"

"No, that's all I have ready for now. I'm going to crash for a while. Later today I'll get back into researching the painting itself."

"Excellent, Thomas, I'm not sure how you're being paid, if it is from us or through the campus. But you're earning every penny of it."

"Thanks. Good luck in Gettysburg."

Highway 40, Virginia

Kim came out of the hotel lobby and headed towards the car. Abby and James were standing next to it. James looked tired. *Probably too much for him so soon after his injuries.* They had driven until pretty late that night, making it north across North Carolina and into Virginia. Kim had talked to Sean before they pulled off the highway but they had only talked briefly because everyone was tired.

"Okay, let's go," Kim called. "Time to hit the road. In the car, Abby."

Abby groaned. "I'm just putting it off as long as possible," she explained.

James looked over at her as he opened the front passenger door. "Don't you start complaining, young lady. You have no idea what I feel like."

As they were settling into the car, Kim's phone rang. She looked at it and saw that it was Sean. She handed the phone to James, who was now sitting next to her in the car.

"It's Sean," Kim said. James took the phone.

"Hi, Sean. Kim's driving. We're just getting on the road to finish the trip up to you and Gettysburg."

"Great!" Sean replied. "How was the driving last night? Tired?"

"No, I feel great," James boasted, rather weakly.

"If I ask Kim, would she agree with you?"

"No, but her opinion does not count," James replied. Kim looked sharply at the professor and James could hear Abby snicker from the back seat.

"Hmm," Sean mused, "I suspect she might not agree with you on that either. Anyway, when do you expect to get into Gettysburg?"

"I think midday if traffic is decent."

"Okay, well I'm almost there. I booked a set of hotel rooms for us at a downtown hotel called the Gettysburg Hotel. It's really downtown apparently, as in right on top of the center square."

"Sounds good," James replied. "Easy name to remember as well."

"Right. Once I get in, I'm going to explore some. Maybe give me a call when you guys arrive so I can make sure I'm at the hotel."

"Will do."

"Oh, and Thomas is emailing us a bunch of documents. Sounded like he worked all night."

"Well, he's young," James replied. "But yes, he's sharp and hard-working. But probably any history graduate student would love to get paid doing the kind of things we are tasking him to do."

"I'm going to find a printer and print copies of the stuff."

"Good. I am still not sure we are going to get much done sitting in Gettysburg, but I guess we have to start there. And it might help us, being there, to sort out the information and facts we have."

"Yep," Sean agreed.

"Okay, see you soon." James heard Sean say goodbye and hung up Kim's phone. "Sean will be there before us and will meet us at the hotel. He should have Thomas's research ready for us as well."

"Great," Kim replied.

"Who's Thomas?" Abby said from the back seat.

Washington D.C.

Agent Chapman strode into Emmitt's office. Dana was already sitting at the round table in the office with Emmitt, so she pulled up another chair.

"Okay, so I think we have something." Alice was grinning. Even though it was a Sunday, she seemed energized. She had called Emmitt and Dana to come in, refusing to say why. She figured they deserved to spend their Sunday in the office with her.

"You better," Emmitt growled, but it was apparent he was pleased.

He was probably planning on being here anyway, Alice thought. *Not young Misler, though; she looks a little less than excited.*

"Oh, I do." She handed an identical-looking file to each of them. As they opened the folders and began looking at the pages inside, Alice explained herself.

"I started with the professor list, and was compiling it when I came across this on the Internet. It's the agent shooting in South Carolina."

"This guy," she pointed at the photo on the first page of the file, "is the ex-Navy SEAL who shot and killed Agent Nazimi and several others at that historical find on the Savannah River."

Emmitt Talie looked up sharply. *He's actually surprised.* Alice felt elated.

"His name is Sean Johnson," Alice continued "He was in this building on Friday being interviewed."

Emmitt had looked back down but his head jerked back up again. *This is so good!*

"All of this is from the reports and notes in our system. Our internal investigation team is evaluating him closely. The basic story is that he acted in self defense and that Agent Nazimi had gone rogue. The facts seem to support that."

Alice paused, letting them turn the page in their files. "But this is awfully coincidental. And look at that note." Alice pointed about halfway down the page of a report filed by the investigating agents. "Instead of being settled down and focused on the historical find they made, he and his team are apparently busy on a new research project. Mr. Johnson apparently spared some time from his work to come down from Harrisburg, Pennsylvania."

Alice had slowed her speech down and emphasized the name of the town, letting it sink in. Emmitt was reading the report closely. Dana was flipping through the other pages of the document. She waited for a few minutes for them to signal that they were ready to go on. Finally, Emmitt looked up. "You are right," he began. "This is way too coincidental. He fits the profile, he matches the informant's information."

Emmitt paused. Just as Alice was about to speak, Emmitt continued. "But it's almost too coincidental. As if the informant is trying to point at him on purpose, as if the informant was trying to make sure we thought of him."

"Right," Alice jumped in. "My thoughts also, but we can't ignore this. Whether it's correct or a red herring, we have to pursue it."

"Right," Emmitt repeated. He leaned back from the table and pulled his right hand up to point his index finger at his temple. Alice had learned a while ago that this was the sign that Emmitt was feeling some clarity. She waited.

"Okay," Emmitt finally continued. "Misler?" Both Alice and Emmitt looked at Dana.

"Yes, Sir?" she replied. She had been continuously reading the file and was clearly more motivated than she had been a few minutes earlier.

"I want you to get everything you can find on him and his team. Let's find out where he is. Same about this professor and this woman, Kim Poole. Our files should already be robust but I want you to go deeper."

"Got it," Dana muttered as she scribbled some notes on the page she was on.

"And everything about the historical research they did, the find they made," Emmitt continued. "And we need to know who is employing them, who was directing them. Perhaps it was…" Emmitt paused, looking back at the file, "the University of Tennessee."

"Yes, Sir," Dana confirmed, still scribbling.

"Agent Chapman?" Emmitt turned his attention to Alice.

"Yes, Sir?"

"First, good work. Now I want you to ruin another agent's weekend. Get this Agent Dawson in here and talk with him. I want to know his thoughts about this guy being involved in our case. Let's not reveal the need-to-know information at this point, though. Give him an abstract, theoretical situation."

"Okay." Alice nodded. She had really expected this task.

"What do you think about this direction?" Emmitt asked.

Alice cleared her throat. "I'm not sure overall. It seems too easy for me. But even if we are simply following a path of bread crumbs set out by our informer, it will tell us something about who our informer is and what his motivation is. I think we can also ask a few of the professors on our list about this recent escapade and what or how that could relate to anything."

Alice felt she had finished rather weakly and had not really added anything. But Agent Talie seemed satisfied.

"Yes, that's a good idea. We need some support on the history subject. Not unless one of us is a history buff," Emmitt said. "We would also benefit from inquiring about this Professor Enloe character with his peers."

"Got it, Sir." Alice paused. "Mr. Johnson is currently in Gettysburg. Don't ask me how I know that, you don't want to know. Ryan is still up north of Baltimore completing his onsite investigation of the murder. We could easily send him up to keep an eye on Mr. Johnson, just to see what he's doing."

Emmitt eyed Alice closely for a moment. "Yes, put Ryan on him for a few days while we dig into his past." Emmitt paused, then said, "Okay, then don't let me hold you up."

Alice and Dana took the cue and promptly headed out of the office. As they walked down the hall, Dana asked, "What if our informant is someone inside our own halls?"

Alice shuddered at that thought. "That's been my fear for a while now. I just hope it's not true."

Gettysburg

Sean had come into Gettysburg and quickly found the hotel. As with many old American towns, the center of town was the four sides of a square located at the crossroads. The driving portion of the square was actually a traffic circle. It was a busy little town with cars waiting their turn to enter the circle and rotate around it to pull off toward their desired directions. *And this is a Sunday*, he thought.

At one corner of the square Sean saw a statue of Lincoln holding papers. After he had checked in and driven his car around to a garage behind the hotel, he decided to take a walk. The statue had attracted him.

In fact, there were Abraham Lincoln markers everywhere. Signs with his name, pictures of him, busts of him.

There were Civil War and Battle of Gettysburg stores everywhere as well. On the square itself Sean could see several bookstores focused on the Civil War.

It looks like this is a good place to come to study the war.

Sean walked over to one of the stores and opened the glass door. There was an old-fashioned sign hanging in the door reading "OPEN." The glass displays on each side were filled mostly with books, though there were some Civil War objects scattered here and there. A bell hung from the inside doorknob that announced his entry and an elderly gentleman behind a counter near the door looked up from his newspaper. "Good afternoon," he said to Sean.

"Hello," Sean replied. "It is nice, but busier than I expected to find a small town on a Sunday afternoon." The man looked to be in his fifties, with wavy brown hair. He was scrutinizing Sean up and down.

"It's like this on Christmas Day, really. I just wish everyone bought things as much as they walked around." The man seemed particularly interested in Sean.

"Business not that great then?" Sean asked.

"Oh, it's not that great, but it's not that bad." He smiled.

Sean held his hand out. "Sean Johnson," he said to the man he now took to be the storeowner.

"Phillip Orion, Mr. Johnson." The man was now closely scrutinizing Sean. Then his eyes lit up. "You're the Sean Johnson in the papers, aren't you?"

Sean smiled. "One and the same, I'm afraid."

"Well, it's an honor to meet you. I must say I did not expect to see you strolling into my store so soon after your find in South Carolina."

"Neither did I, truthfully. This is actually my first time to Gettysburg," Sean admitted.

"Well, welcome Mr. Johnson."

"It's just Sean," Sean replied. He looked around the shop. "It looks like you have some good material on the war?"

Phillip had gotten up from his chair and was now leaning on the counter. He gestured with his hand. "Oh, yes. I'm mostly a book man, but the demands of keeping the lights on have forced me to sell various memorabilia as well. But you will find that almost every book in here is about the Civil War. Books about the armies are over there."

Phillip gestured to the shelves that started right next to his counter. "This side begins with the Battle of Gettysburg and then continues with just about every other battle of the war."

"Great, thanks. Mind if I just look around?"

"Sure, Mr. Johnson, I mean Sean. Just ask if I can help you with anything at all, okay?"

Sean nodded. "I will."

With that Sean began strolling down the "Armies" side of store. He could see that even just one store was going to take some time to look through. And there appeared to be a hundred stores in the town.

It's like the Smithsonian of the Civil War.

*****

An hour and four historical bookstores later, Sean concluded that he was not going to get much done if he kept introducing himself. Two other owners had recognized his name. Sean thought the first shopowner had even recognized him before he had introduced himself. *My damn reporter headshot has been in every paper!* Being surreptitious and discrete in this town is going to be hard to do. He hoped Kim and James would be better able to blend in.

CHAPTER ELEVEN

Gettysburg

Abby looked very bored. She had been following her mom, the professor and Sean at a distance for several minutes now, almost dragging her feet. Kim was not ready to let her run off on her own, though. Not with everything going on back home.

"Abby," she called, "please keep up with us."

Abby looked up, mostly by rolling her eyes. But she quickened her pace a bit and Kim turned her attention back to where they were going. They were on a paved path going slightly uphill between some big boulders and some trees. Sean and James were walking alongside her, both carrying a book and a pamphlet. There were people everywhere. Not just on the path, but sitting on the bigger rocks and leaning against trees. Behind them were also cars, both moving and parked. And buses of course. They all felt a bit like they were at a theme park.

In a sense, that is where we are. It's a cemetery, a battlefield and a theme park all rolled up into one, Kim thought. At first she had felt a little like a voyeur, peering at things that she felt she was not supposed to be looking at. There were monuments everywhere that constantly reminded her that men had died here. It might have been a long time ago, but the monuments made it seem like it was just yesterday.

She also realized that the crowds had helped create that distasteful feeling about being there. To the extent it was a graveyard, it was not supposed to be crawling with more people than a county fair. And the laughing kids running around made that feeling worse. But then gradually Kim got used to all of it and began to just accept that it was normal to be walking all over ground that seemed holy, ground where Americans had fought each other and died. But every now and then she would imagine how horrible the scene must have been during and after the battle and she would almost shudder. James and Sean seemed to be taking it just as seriously. There were a few times when they did not say a word at all, but instead just looked about solemnly.

Kim also needed to get used to the idea that it was a Sunday. She had expected a Sunday to be a quiet day. Instead she was learning that summer days in general, and summer weekends in particular, were this town's busiest days. *Like a fair.*

They had begun early, after breakfast at the hotel. The battlefield was south of town, though right on top of it. So they had piled into her rental car and begun what was turning into a long day. The battlefield was a national historical park, with most parts of it open to the public. There was a large welcome center where they had begun their visit. After parking in what was already a sea of cars at nine in the morning, they went into the visitor center and watched a great movie about the battle.

It was depressing to Kim, though. So much death and destruction. Men shooting and stabbing each other. And then leaving them there to rot as they left town a few days later! Or leaving them there to moan for a day or so while the town tried to deal with what the armies had handed them. Abby had been doing fine at the beginning. There were artifacts and the movie, and even a 360-degree panorama show to absorb. There were also plenty of kids her age around, including all sorts of Boy Scout troops. But after that visitor center experience, their day had turned into one of driving through the battlefield, except there were so many cars, often they would not be moving at all. The scenes had been surreal at first. Large and small monuments had been erected everywhere. The Union side of the lines had more of them and they were often grander. But the Confederate lines were also full of Civil War markers and monuments. All were apparently erected in the years following.

It must have been therapy for them, Kim thought. *A chance to remember fallen friends, colleagues that they had fought and suffered with.*

After a while, just as it was with the sense of distasteful voyeurism, the surreal feeling had worn off. She had gotten used to it. For Abby, boredom had begun kicking in. Kim could not blame her. *Why should a young teenage girl be expected to enjoy a day of slowly driving from one place to another where supposedly responsible, sensible men had killed one another?*

Even Kim was feeling weary of it. James, of course, was like a priest visiting the Vatican. Or an artist visiting the Louvre. He was an American history professor at one of the most famous and important battlefield sites of the Civil War. Sean, on the other hand, had been hard to read for a while. She was not sure if he had been going through the same series of feelings and emotions she had or if his silence was more akin to James's fascination.

In any case, Kim was ready to get back to the task at hand, finding the painting. But at this very moment they were reaching a view down into a boulder-strewn slope that even she now understood was a very solemn place. They were on Little Round Top. In any other place in the United States, this would have been just another little hill. But as they had learned, this little hill was sometimes billed as a place where one unit had perhaps saved the Union by holding off the repeated attempts of the Confederates to take it. Kim was not sure she fully understood how one little hill could have been so critical. The video had tried to explain it. So had James and even Sean. But she was neither a military veteran nor a history professor. *Just Kim, the shopowner from Kansas City. The mother about to lose custody of her child because she keeps running off to weird places like this battlefield!*

She sighed and spoke. "Guys, I know this is a really important place in American history. I know this particular little hill is the saving place of everything American. But it's going to be the place where the women in your life leave you if we don't head back into town soon and focus on our mission."

Abby had caught up with them and looked up at her mom with a mixture of shock and admiration.

Sean chuckled. "Sorry, it's just that, well, it just feels like I owe every soldier who died here the respect of seeing where they struggled and fought. But I get your point and I, too, am feeling a little full of the history and horror of war for the day."

"But this is really an important place," James protested. "There are and were people who would disagree with your characterization of it. And there are those who also argue its importance is overblown." James was starting to sweep his arms in a gesture when Kim cut him off.

"Professor Enloe," she said sharply, "stop. I know where you're going. And I care about this place, I really do. But this is all I can absorb today, not just of battle sites, but also of cars, buses and tourists. And it's getting pretty hot as well."

"If you think this is hot, just imagine what those July days were like for the soldiers all dressed…" James let his voice trail off as he caught the icy look from Kim. "Okay, okay," James laughed. "I get your point. And actually, I'm feeling pretty tired myself." He turned and looked wistfully down the slope. He then turned around and said, "Let's go."

*****

About an hour later, they were all seated in a big booth at a restaurant at another corner of the town square across from their hotel. Like everything else in town, it was busy. The sidewalk in front of the restaurant was crowded with people walking to and fro and there was not an empty table in the place.

In between bites of food, they finalized their plan of attack.

"Okay," James said. "So we will divide up and conquer and meet back at the hotel at four. Sean, you have buildings and examination of the possible homes of Anna Wright. Kim, you have vase-searching north of the square and Abby, you have south. I have historical records in general."

"You mean you're going to have fun talking to all the history buffs around town," Sean clarified.

"I am best suited to learn about and find other historical sources we have not yet identified. The Internet has not yet replaced the value and importance of historical experts and this town is full of them."

"Enough," Sean laughed. "I do generally agree with you. I just wanted to remind you that you will be having the most fun."

"Well, my task is also appealing," Kim said, coming to the professor's rescue.

"I'm fine with anything other than walking around the battlefield," Abby chimed in.

"Okay, okay, I get it. I know when I'm outnumbered," Sean said. "This town is interesting too. So I'll enjoy it."

*****

Sean was walking down a street on the south side of town peering at a list in one hand and a map in the other. He had gotten used to spotting the little plaques on the front of mostly brick buildings that told him which structures had been there at the time of the battle. He was, however, also getting a sense that he was not going to really accomplish anything. The buildings were all remodeled and far from the look and feel of the middle of the 19th century. He had not expected much. But he also knew that just finding the Wright home would help them draw a picture of what might have happened. The idea, though, that this would lead to some serendipitous clue or solution seemed like a silly dream.

"Excuse me. Mr. Johnson?"

Sean looked up, startled, as he realized someone was right behind him. He turned around to find an elderly man wearing slacks and a short-sleeved shirt looking at him inquisitively. The man looked harmless. *Kindly* was the specific sensation Sean had.

"Uh, yes, that's me." Sean smiled, wondering how this man knew him.

"I've been following you for a few minutes." The man held his hand out. "Tom Kinneson."

Sean clumsily shoved the map in his right hand under his left armpit and managed to shake the man's hand. "So, how do you know me?" he asked.

"Oh, I think quite a few people around here recognize you. At least those of us who care about history and hang out in bookstores." The man smiled. "I was in a store you visited this morning. Heard your whole conversation with Phillip."

Sean recognized the shopowner's name and then remembered seeing an elderly man sitting in a chair reading a book. "Ah, yes. You were behind me, looking at a pretty thick book."

"Very observant of you, yes, Mr. Johnson."

"Well, I would like to tell you I'm observant. In fact, I think I am most of the time. But here, you managed to sneak up right behind me and I was ignorant of your presence. Not that you were sneaking, of course."

Tom laughed. "You did look very entranced by your task. What are you doing?"

"Essentially, I'm looking for a former home of a resident of this town at the time of the battle and war," Sean explained. "I am kind of sworn to secrecy, at least to strangers. So don't ask me yet who this resident was."

Tom turned his head slightly sideways and his face took on a quizzical expression. "You are a very interesting man, Mr. Johnson."

"Please, it's Sean."

"Sean," Tom corrected himself.

There was an awkward period of silence until Sean spoke. "So what can I do for you, Mr. Kinneson?"

"Oh sorry, yes. It's Tom, by the way. I live back a block and watched you checking out a couple of the homes on my block." He paused again, looking at Sean curiously. He seemed to make a decision. "So I know this might seem a little odd, but I am hoping to share a story with you."

Sean looked at him for a moment. He glanced at his watch. "Sure, I'm game. But I am due back at my hotel soon."

"Oh yes, well, I understand," Tom replied. "This was a bit of a spur of the moment decision of mine to come out here and talk to you."

"Go on," Sean prompted, beginning to think the man might be a little off.

"So, well, you see, our family has a little mystery we have clung to that I thought might be right up your alley."

"Okay," Sean said slowly.

"I know, I know, you probably hear that all the time," Tom said. "Tell you what. Here's my card." He pulled a small off-white business card from the pocket of his shirt.

"The story comes from my grandfather. It's about a historical document and what might have happened to it. I will tell you more if you want. Over a cup of coffee. Just give me a call. And if you want to share more of your mission here and I can help you, just let me know."

Sean examined the card briefly. Under his name the card read "Kitchen and Restaurant Consulting."

"Retired restaurateur?" he asked.

"You nailed it, Sean. I can see why you have been so successful." Tom extended his hand again. "I won't keep you anymore. But please give me a call. I really think you will like my story."

Sean shook his hand.

"You have me curious now," Sean admitted.

Tom smiled, turned and walked away. Sean watched him for a moment and then turned his attention back to his task. But after staring at his map, he decided he'd had enough.

"And I'm already late," he said aloud to the building in front of him.

Cramming his map and list back into the folder, he began heading back to the hotel thinking about his odd encounter.

*****

Sean and James were sitting in James's hotel room. They had a set of three rooms all looking down on the square through old-fashioned windows. The hotel was a combination of an old hotel and a new addition. They had gotten rooms in the old portion with a view of the town square primarily because that was all that was left. The rooms were not cheap, but given the group was being well paid, Sean had not minded the expense very much.

Kim had called to say that she and Abby were now together going through a long line of antique shops and would be late. Sean had been late as well.

"So, I think we're not going to get very far looking for a home from Civil War days. Even if we find it, what's the value?" Sean asked.

"I feel the same way, really," James said. "This painting could be anywhere. I think we need to focus more on the painting itself. But we are not art experts."

"What's still bothering me is that Joe has to know all of this," Sean replied. "Why pay us so much and be so insistent we take on a no-stone-unturned approach? And so secretly? And urgently?"

"Yes, yes," James said. "That is the question really."

"Let's give your research kid a call and see if he has gotten anywhere on the painting itself."

"That's a good idea," James agreed.

Sean grabbed his cell phone from the top of his papers and dialed Thomas's number. He put the phone on speaker and placed it on the little table between James and himself. After a few rings, Thomas answered.

"Hi, Sean," he said.

"Hi, Thomas, I'm here with James."

"Oh, hi, Professor," Thomas said.

"Good afternoon, Thomas," James replied. Sean noticed a shift in James to a bit more of his professorial tone.

"So, Thomas," Sean said, "the professor and I were discussing our efforts today here in Gettysburg, and we both are growing in our conviction that we're probably not going to find this painting by looking at buildings, looking for vases, et cetera. Not that your material has not been excellent."

"Yes, most helpful," James added.

"Well, I agree with you, but unfortunately it's for a different reason," Thomas replied. "I was just about to try and reach one of you."

"Oh?" James sounded alarmed.

"Yes, well, you see, I don't think you're going to find this painting because I think it doesn't exist. More precisely, if this painting existed, I think it was destroyed in a fire."

Sean and James looked at each other and then back at the phone.

"A fire?" Sean asked.

"Yes. You see I was doing every search I could think of for records on Munger paintings. Earlier today I came across an article about a fire in a home destroying a painting thought to have been a Munger. I dug into that using the location and date period and found court files on a dispute over whether the fire was set intentionally and whether the painting was really valuable. Seems the owner made an insurance claim. The case settled. Anyway, it was in a Boston neighborhood in the 1960's."

"Go on," Sean instructed. "Why do you think it was our painting?"

"The description of the painting matches ours. In fact, one angle the insurance company appears to have taken was to say that no such painting was actually known to exist. But, even more important, this had to be something your client would have known about, don't you think?"

Sean and James sat silently looking at each other.

"Are you there?" Thomas asked.

"Yes. Sorry. This is just a very surprising development."

"Well, if you want, tomorrow I can see if there are any other files available out there that are not online. But I don't completely understand legal systems and the like so a paralegal or law firm might be better equipped to go farther."

Sean looked at James and then spoke. "Thanks. But I think you have earned a bit of rest here. I think I need to have a conversation with our benefactor. Just sit tight. One of us will call tomorrow."

"Okay, will do," Thomas replied.

After Sean hung up the phone, James spoke. "Well, that's just really odd."

"I'm going to call Joe and confront him with this," Sean said. "It's just weird. Why pay us to look for a painting that he had to have known was probably destroyed in a fire?"

"Yes, and it was odd how he just came out of the blue to ask us to find it so suddenly."

Sean looked up. "Oh, yeah. I forgot." He pulled Tom Kinneson's business card from his pocket. "Speaking of out of the blue, this man accosted me today. Well, accosted is not the right word. Very polite and nice. Old restaurant guy. He overheard me in a bookstore this morning and saw me this afternoon and came out of his home and tracked me down."

James looked up from the business card. "And?"

"So he says he wants to tell me a story about a missing document," Sean replied. "He said he thinks it's right up our, or at least my, alley. Said it was a family story."

"Not a painting?" James asked, half-joking.

"No," Sean laughed. "But it was deja vu for me. Not about Joe really, but about Kim's story. A family history thing."

"Well, you should meet with him then."

"Yeah. I was distracted at the moment he found me." Sean's thought came back to their main issue. "Let me call Joe."

He picked up his phone and called Joe's phone number and put it on speaker. After just one ring it went to voicemail.

"Joe, this is Sean and Professor Enloe. We have an important turn of events we want to discuss with you. Please call us as soon as you can." Sean hung up.

"I think I need a shower," he said getting up. "Dinner later?"

"Yes," James replied. "I need a nap, I think."

*****

Kim hung up the phone. "I'm booked."

"I don't like this idea," Sean said.

"I know," Kim said. "I'm probably crazy. But Abby will enjoy the time with you and the professor, and I trust her in your care completely. And I would rather not have her caught up in whatever happens at court on Tuesday. If I lose custody, I can honestly claim it will take me a little while to get her to Dallas, especially if I have to go get her."

"Yes, but you're risking being labeled a kidnapper or whatever the term is for a parent who runs off with a kid they don't have custody of."

"And that would be the case if I was running off with her. But if I don't bring her back with me then I can't run off with her, can I?" Kim asked, sounding irritated.

"True. But the court might say you ran here when you brought her here."

"Look, I'm not going to argue with you, Sean. Are you willing to watch her or not?"

Sean sighed. "Yes, James and I will take very good care of her. You know that."

Kim smiled but her eyes were tearing up. "She already loves you like a dad, Sean. More than her real dad who is trying to get custody of her."

"I know, I already love her that way too." He got up from his chair and leaned over to hold Kim's shoulder. "You too. This has been a whirlwind of events since we met."

"I know," Kim admitted, placing her hand on Sean's. "Now tell me about this painting being burned up. What were we doing looking for it then?"

CHAPTER TWELVE

Highway, South of Harrisburg

The parking lot was almost on top of the freeway and was thus loud, even on a Sunday night. Sean was leaning against the trunk of his car. After dropping Kim off at the Philadelphia airport, he had driven to this location for a meeting Joe had insisted on. He was right across from the entrance to the restaurant and was early and Joe was not yet in the restaurant. He had not felt like sitting inside the building or inside his car.

To Sean it was strange that Joe had insisted on a meeting. *More mystery. Why not talk to me on the phone? Why face-to-face? And why so urgent?*

Sean was also tired. It had been a long day. *And now I'm playing dad as well.* He was not happy about the idea of Kim going back without Abby, but he was loving the chance to get to know Abby and grow the closeness of his relationship to Kim and her family. *Now I'm sitting in a parking lot waiting for a mysterious man to show up so we can talk about why he misled us. Crazy.* The whirlwind that started a couple of months ago when he met Kim simply had not ended. But he knew they were both enjoying it. Or at least somewhat enjoying it. James, on the other hand, was completely enjoying it. He was almost heart-stricken to learn there was probably no painting. Or at least that they were clearly misled.

Finally, and right on time, a white sedan pulled into the parking lot.

Sean espied Joe driving it. He waved to him and Joe nodded, smiling as he drove past and parked. Joe hopped out and Sean met him halfway across the driveway. They shook hands and talked as they walked inside.

"Thanks for meeting me, Sean," Joe began. "I know you have questions and I have more to tell you."

"More?" Sean responded. "I have to tell you, Joe, that I'm not really keen on being misled. You are paying us well, so I know it's rude to complain. But I am. I need you to come clean with us or I think we are done."

"Understood," Joe replied.

They had gone through the outer and inner doors and now let the hostess seat them. She led them to a booth on one side of the restaurant. They sat quietly for a moment until their server came over and then they both just ordered dessert with coffee.

"Okay," Joe said. "First, tell me what you have learned."

Sean explained what they had done so far and finished with the story they had unearthed about the destroyed painting.

"Very good," Joe smiled, pleased. "If you had not found that problem, we would have been done. Instead, in a way, you have passed a test."

"A test?" Sean asked, sounding incredulous.

"Yes. I'll tell you everything now."

"I'm listening."

"What we are really after is a document that may or may not have ever existed. If it did, then it might also be lost. It is called the Mecklenburg Declaration. Ever heard of it?"

Sean shook his head. "No."

"I'm not surprised," Joe replied. "There were, and probably still are, many that don't want that document to be known."

"So what is it?"

"It is or was a declaration of independence by the colony of North Carolina, before what we call the Declaration of Independence was completed."

"Hmm." Sean thought for a moment. "What would be so wrong or bad about such a document that someone would want to destroy it or suppress it?"

"Simple. As tensions began rising between the northern and southern states, a document that suggested one state, a southern state, had declared itself independent on its own was seen as a tool in the argument over states' rights versus the authority of the federal government. That had always been an issue that had made most of the southern states and even some northern states disagree over their reluctance to surrender the autonomy they had won from the British in the Revolutionary War. Completing and ratifying the Constitution required several compromises related to that issue."

Joe paused as their server delivered their slices of pie. After she was gone, Joe continued while he was eating. "So every time the story has come up, there have always been many who say that it never happened."

"Where does the name Mecklenburg come from?" Sean asked.

"It was the name of an area that is now Charlotte, North Carolina. They met there. They adopted one document called the Mecklenburg Resolves. It was published in some newspapers and was a bold statement in and of itself. But whether they also went on to adopt a declaration of independence is not as clear."

"But you think it exists," Sean said.

"No, not necessarily," Joe replied. "But my colleagues do, and it's my job to try and deliver it. The need for secrecy I held you to is real. I will tell you more now and this may also help you understand the urgency. But, first I want to make sure you are willing to continue your task, but now looking for the Mecklenburg Declaration. There is a connection to the painting I had you looking for. Or so to speak there is."

Sean looked at Joe for a moment.

Joe continued. "We will actually pay you more, double what we have offered. I even have another $10,000 for you."

Sean shook his head, but he was smiling. "Have you heard of this thing called a check? All this cash is really a pain."

"Of course, but if I asked you to start right away on something and handed you a check for that much, it would not give you the same level of trust and confidence that you were really being very well compensated. If you want to keep going, I need you to agree to do so."

"Okay," Sean said. "I'm irritated, but less suspicious than I was. But still I think your level of urgency and secrecy seems a little unneeded."

Joe smiled. As he did so, Sean again felt like he had at their last meeting, like he was a fish taking the bait. The feeling was amplified when Joe pulled a small but thick envelope out of his jacket and slid it across the table to Sean. Sean wanted to hesitate or even refuse the money, but Joe was correct that it was a motivator. Reluctantly, he took the money and slid it into his own jacket pocket.

"Good," Joe said. "As promised, here is the real story. I am part of a political movement that advocates for states' rights. We are about to make a major pitch politically that will be very upsetting to our two entrenched political parties and all of their entrenched elected officials. The pitch may be as early as the end of this week. It certainly will occur in the next two weeks. As we are finalizing all of our speeches and documents, there is one outstanding item we have not made a decision on. It is the Mecklenburg Declaration. We really want to hold it up as an example of a state declaring its own independence. Again, I am not sure this document ever existed. I am not even sure it's worth the political weight we are giving it."

Joe sighed. "But my political allies both value and believe in it. In politics one has to compromise to get where one wants to go. I want our political movement to succeed, so I agreed to accept its importance. We are very, very well-funded and our biggest donor is also a believer in this."

Joe smiled. "And now I want you to be. And your team. But let me assure you this is not another nonexistent painting quest. But here is how this ties to the painting. The family you are researching was real. The lady had told her son on her deathbed the story of the document. She said she had possession of the Mecklenburg Declaration and had indeed put it into a vase. She sent it out of town with other valuable possessions and it never came back. Her father had given it to her. It was her most valued possession. She told this to her son near the end of her life. Her son, a banker in Baltimore, had then promptly written a professor at Harvard about the document. His letter turned up in that professor's materials and was found about twenty years ago. A copy of that letter is in your new packet. Everything else you will find in the public domain quickly enough."

Joe looked at Sean, who looked amused. Sean responded. "You want us to search for a document that might never have existed or it might have existed and been destroyed. It's still urgent. You are paying us more, double to be precise." Sean spoke methodically like he was checking items off on a list.

"You're right, though, to some extent. Politics does help explain it better. And you're right, that paying us more is motivating." Sean paused and looked out the window and then looked back. "I think my partner the professor is really going to like this one. It is much more up his alley then a painting. I like this story better too. Not the Mecklenburg story, but the political intrigue side of it. Am I going to be free to write about that?"

Joe nodded. "Yes, as soon as we go public, it's all yours. Frankly, if you do find this document, or even find good firm evidence it existed, that is all we really need. We do not really want the document for ourselves. We want it to be as public as possible. So you would be serving our interests multifold by writing about it."

"Deal, then," Sean said. "I suppose the identity of your members is a secret?"

"For now, yes. I will tell you that one is a very prominent leader in our country, though. He will be taking this public."

"Does your organization have a name?"

Joe thought for a moment. "Yes, I can tell you that now. We are the Free States of America, or Free States for short. Consider us the Free States Party. But don't use that publicly yet either, if you don't mind. I trust you to keep things confidential."

"Understood. Anything else?"

"Not from me," Joe said.

Gettysburg Hotel

"You are right, I love it!" James declared. "A Revolutionary War mystery. But I have heard of this before, and totally dismissed it." He thought for a moment.

"Which in retrospect looks rather foolish of me. I was a denier of the Enloe oral history and look how that turned out. Professors like me should be much more open-minded and less apt to pass judgment on history that looks inconsistent with our teaching."

Sean, James and Abigail were sitting around a coffee table in the lobby. Sean was ready for some sleep but had called them down so they could discuss it. He looked over at Abby.

"So, Abby, how much time do you have to help us? Your mom will kill me if I don't make sure you're doing your makeup schoolwork."

Abby rolled her eyes and shook her head so that her blonde hair twitched funnily.

"Sean, I'll be fine. I need to do a couple of hours a day, and that's on average. I'm supposed to turn in my homework in three weeks. I'll make sure I do it. My mom trusts me."

"Well, unlike your mom, I'm completely inexperienced at doing this parental stuff so until your mom is back, I want you to show me regularly what you have done. Okay?"

"Yes, "Abby replied. Sean suspected that if it were her mom making these demands then Abby would have had a very different attitude.

"So where do we start?" Abby's question caused Sean and James to look at each other and smile. *Just like her mother*, they both thought.

"We start by learning everything we can about the Mecklenburg Declaration," James said simply. "This was a long time ago, so that is more challenging than you might think. Half the material written in that era is hard to understand, where it is even legible. The English of that time was different. Plus, few documents from those colony days survive."

James looked at Sean. "But I do think we can wait until tomorrow."

"I agree," Sean said. "I'm exhausted."

Eastern Pennsylvania

"I trust this man, but he has shown himself to be dangerous. He now knows information that is not public," Joe explained. "So I want you to shadow him and his team. Keep me informed of where they go, who they talk to."

Joe was sitting at a desk in a small office in the warehouse headquarters of the FSA. It was one of three small rooms adjacent to the large meeting room on the elevated platform. Across from him was a middle-aged man with short brown hair and an open-collared, light blue dress shirt. Fred had sent Kelly Foster to Joe a year earlier. Fred had explained that Kelly could be assigned any task, any task at all. Joe understood that meant Kelly would be their "wetback," a phrase the CIA used for private killers who clandestinely handled kidnappings, killings, and other "dirty" jobs. The fact that Fred could provide a wetback to the FSA suggested to Joe that Fred himself was former CIA. In any case, Joe was glad to have someone who could handle the toughest tasks that Joe was certain he would have had a hard time finding "believers" to do. It was one thing to persuade a disgruntled politician or service member to join a cause to create a new country, but it was another to persuade them to kill an innocent person. Kelly had already made his value clear when an off-duty cop had overseen a transaction in Baltimore that should never have been going down in such a public place.

But Kelly also made Joe nervous. Joe knew that if Fred decided Joe was a problem and needed elimination, Kelly would handle that discreetly and quickly. It added an element of fear. It also made their early group feel as if they could not really quit the movement once they joined—at least not once Kelly had shown up. General Huerta had not liked him at all until the Baltimore incident. Kelly's actions that day had probably saved Huerta from jail time. From that day forward, Huerta had respected Kelly.

"Okay," Kelly answered. He never took notes either, something Joe had grown used to.

"Please be discreet and don't get detected. I think that within a week or so their role will be over, one way or another."

Kelly tilted his head sideways and looked quizzically at Joe. His unstated question was obvious.

"No, you will not need to kill them because everything will be public by then. But if they go sideways on us before they get close enough to something that we should take over, then yes, you might be doing something other than monitoring."

Joe had explained who Sean Johnson was and provided most of the other information Kelly would need to know.

Kelly nodded. "If there is nothing else, I'll head out."

"Check in with me at least once a day."

Kelly stood up from the desk. Even standing up was something Kelly did in a graceful but powerful way. But Joe had also seen how he could change his body language and behavior to match just about any situation.

"Be careful," Joe said. "we are now in a very critical and sensitive phase."

Kelly smiled. "Of course."

"I know you are probably the last person I need to say that to," Joe said.

Kelly smiled, nodded and left the little room. Joe watched him leave and then glanced at his watch. He grimaced when he saw how late it was. *It's going to be a long week*, he thought.

CHAPTER THIRTEEN

Washington D.C.

Agent Talie had been in the office since dawn. After processing a stack of administrative tasks that he had avoided the previous week, he turned his attention to Supernova. Alice and Dana had both completed some reports and he digested them.

Just as he was about to get up to take a walk out to the break room and grab some coffee, an email came in alerting him of a flagged report filed in the system. He clicked on the link and a report from Agent Lentz appeared on his screen. Even though Emmitt was very much a paper guy, he read this in its electronic form.

"Okay, Agent Lentz, great job," he said aloud when he finished reading it. He then punched some buttons on his desk phone and waited.

"Hi, Sir," Alice's voice said from the speaker.

"Agent Chapman, did you even go home last night?" Emmitt asked.

"No, Sir, I napped in my office some, though."

"Your dedication is noted," Emmitt replied. "Have you read Agent Lentz's report?"

"No, Sir. What report?"

"He just filed it. Read it and then come on down so we can talk."

"Will do." The phone clicked dead and Emmitt swiveled around to look out the window and think for a few minutes. He was still facing the window when Alice came in.

"Okay," she said, sitting down. Emmitt swiveled around and examined her for a moment.

"Your thoughts?" he asked.

"Very suspicious behavior. Meeting another man at a highway restaurant after dropping Ms. Poole off at the airport sixty miles away. Conversation along with the passing of an envelope across the table. Too much for me. Mr. Johnson is doing something out of the ordinary. Since he also matches our tip almost perfectly, I think he has to now be a focus for us."

"Agreed," Emmitt said. "We have a license plate for the person he met with as well. Seems to me that person is even more important. Lentz's description makes it seem like Johnson was getting instructions and perhaps being paid."

"Yes, Sir," Alice replied, kicking herself for not focusing on that fact. "Shall we dig into him as well?"

"Dig into? I want him identified, thoroughly investigated and monitored as well. And for Johnson, I want to get surveillance on him. No searches or wiretapping yet. I am not sure we have enough to get a court order for it anyway. But I'll start chasing that down."

"What about his team?" Alice asked. "Ms. Poole appears to have flown somewhere."

"Let's focus on Mr. Johnson and whatever he's doing in Gettysburg. No wait..." Emmitt interrupted himself and thought for a moment. "Let's bring him in for questioning, or at least see if he will come in. He has been cooperative. Hell, he was in our building last week. Us calling him will either cause him to panic or it won't. Get surveillance on him right away and then call him in. Let's see how he reacts."

Gettysburg

"Good morning, young man," James said into his phone, sounding as professorial as he could. James was sitting at his hotel desk looking out the window at Gettysburg Square.

"Good morning, Professor," Thomas mumbled back.

"Did I wake you?" James asked, not actually sounding sympathetic.

"No, no, not at all." Thomas sounded, though, like he was waking himself up to a higher level of alertness for the call.

"Very well," James replied. "I have a new assignment for you, if you will take it."

"Sure. Glad to. Let me get a notepad."

There was some rustling and then Thomas came back on the phone. "Okay, go ahead."

"I need you to find out everything you can on the Mecklenburg Declaration," James instructed.

"I'm sorry, Professor, the what?"

"The Mecklenburg Declaration," James replied. He spelled Mecklenburg out. "It's an alleged declaration of independence signed in what is now Charlotte, North Carolina. It was supposedly signed before the real Declaration was. By at least a year."

"Okay, yes, Sir." Thomas sounded confused. "Can I ask what this is for?"

"In a way, it's the same task you were on. It appears our painting hunt was a form of test for us and the real target was the Mecklenburg Declaration all along. We passed, thanks to you, and so now we have our real target."

"Okay," Thomas replied, still sounding confused.

"What we want is every document out there mentioning it, mentioning the Mecklenburg Resolves, which is another document. The Resolves exist also. Find out where they are physically located. The declaration is almost mythical and no copy is known to exist. We are supposed to find a copy of it. We have a clue, but I won't drag you into that yet. I want you focused on the Declaration first. Just put together all the information you can find on it."

"Yes, Sir, I'm on it right away."

"Great, and thanks, Thomas. Your work and support on this have been excellent."

"Thank you, Professor. I appreciate the work and the opportunity."

They hung up and James turned back to his computer and notes, humming happily.

*****

A beautiful day was getting started in Gettysburg. Sean was about two miles into a power walk through the Gettysburg battlefield park. He had taken an entrance to the park that originated only a few blocks from the square, behind a school. It started with a paved road going mostly straight across a set of fields before turning uphill. He had followed the road up the hill and was now standing at the foot of a large observation tower. An informational sign told him that he was on Culp's Hill. It was apparently actually two hills. It had been the "barbed" end of the J-shaped fishhook of Union lines that had run along the ridges south of town.

Shrugging, Sean decided to climb the tower. There were a couple of cars here already and he assumed the people that had parked them were already up in the tower. But just then, his phone vibrated and he pulled it out of his pocket. It was a number he did not recognize, but the area code told him it was Washington D.C.

"Great," he mumbled. "More FBI?" He answered the call. "Hello."

"Mr. Johnson?" It was a female voice that sounded very authoritative.

"Yes, this is he," Sean replied.

"Good morning, Mr. Johnson. I'm Agent Chapman with the Federal Bureau of Investigation."

"I've heard of that organization." Sean felt annoyed by how the agent sounded out all three words. "But I usually just hear it as FBI."

There was pause and Sean could tell he had thrown the agent off her planned script. She then went on, though, as if he had not said anything. "I am calling you regarding a very important investigation where you have emerged as a potential source of information."

"You mean the shooting of Agent Nazimi? I've been getting interviewed and investigated by some colleagues of yours already on that. And please don't take offense to this, but I don't think it's accurate to say I have 'emerged' as a 'source of information' in that. I caused Agent Nazimi's death." Sean started walking away from the observation tower, staring at the trees that surrounded the tower and the parking lot.

"None taken, Mr. Johnson. Yes, I am very aware of our ongoing investigation into your role and actions resulting in Agent Nazimi's death. However, I am calling about another matter that we believe you have information about."

Sean stopped walking. *Another matter?* "What would that be?" he asked.

"I would rather not discuss it on the phone. Let me just say it is a matter of both extreme importance and urgency."

"Okay, so if we can't talk about it, why are you calling me?" he asked. But Sean realized the answer to his question as soon as he finished asking it.

"I'm calling to ask you to come into our D.C. office as soon as possible. The same building you were at last week."

I knew it! Sean began walking along the parking lot, feeling frustrated.

"Agent Chapman, why would I want to do that when you won't even tell me what it's about?"

"Because you have been cooperative so far, Mr. Johnson. I think you know that it's a lot easier to do this cooperatively."

Sean thought things through for a few moments. Part of him wanted to tell the FBI where to go. But another part told him he should cooperate or it would just make things worse. He was also very curious about what they might want to ask him about, if not about Agent Nazimi. Perhaps there is something else entangled into the South Carolina find?

"Okay. You're right. I do wish to be cooperative," Sean agreed. "But I'm also a bit busy. How soon do you need to meet?"

"We would like to talk to you today if possible."

"No, that's not possible. I'm in Gettysburg. But you probably know that. I think I told your colleagues where I was headed last week."

"Correct, we know where you are. Tomorrow then."

"Why not up here?" Sean asked. "If it's so urgent, come up to me."

"We really prefer to have you come into our offices, Mr. Johnson."

"You mean you want to meet with me on your turf, to help make me feel less settled," Sean replied. "No, no, don't answer. It's okay. I'll meet with you. How about nine o'clock?"

"That's fine, Mr. Johnson. See you tomorrow."

"Yes, good day."

Sean hung up the call and shoved his phone back into his pocket. He was now over at the edge of the parking lot. The road led down the hill and towards other monuments in the park. Sean suddenly noticed a car that had come up the hill and parked. But no one had gotten out. Something about the way the car had pulled up the hill and parked raised his antennae.

It's got to be the FBI. They're monitoring me. Something is definitely going on that I am not privy to.

Sean stood there for a full minute, thinking. He finally decided he needed to do something, just to send them a message. Looking around, he realized there was no reason why he could not simply take off into the woods below Culp's Hill. They were thick, but not thick as to be impassable.

Let's see them follow me cross-country!

Sean grinned and suddenly took off in an easy jog off the parking lot and down the hill into the woods. He suspected he was following the path that some poor soldier had to follow back when the battle was raging.

Harrisburg

"Hello," Joe answered his cell. "I was not expecting to hear from you."

"It's important, but I will keep it short," Fred replied. "The FBI has identified you and is sending units to your home. My source is not sure whether they're setting up to start tailing you or if they're also seeking a warrant to search your home."

Joe jerked slightly at those words. He then settled his mind and replied, "We knew this would happen. My home is secure and clean."

"Yes," Fred replied. "But our effort is better off with you outside of their grasp."

"True," Joe admitted. "I guess that means it's time for me to get out of here."

"Yes, I think that would be wise."

Joe sighed. "I'll leave immediately. Any idea why I was identified so early?"

"No, none at all," Fred replied.

They hung up. Joe looked around his home. He realized that this might be the last time he ever looked at it. Mentally, he went through all of the precautions and procedures he had followed to ensure that he would not leave anything behind related to the FSA.

I take my computer and that's it, he thought. He then proceeded to shut his laptop down and begin packing it up.

Kansas City

"So that's it?" Kim asked her attorney.

"Yes," Katherine replied from across her desk. "We've done everything we can do to be ready for tomorrow's hearing. Go home and get a good night's sleep."

Kim reflected that she really did not like being in her lawyer's office. It was just too businesslike. She thought her lawyer was good and dedicated to her client's cause. But, Kim realized, she was not personally dedicated. It was just business. Her lawyer was a mercenary. But she seemed like a good mercenary.

"Easy for you to say," Kim replied. "But I will do my best."

"Good," Katherine said, standing up. She offered her hand to Kim, who took it. Kim then picked up her papers from her lawyer's desk and left the office. The receptionist waved to her as she exited into the hallway.

Kim mulled over the prospect of losing custody of her daughter. *I just need to think positive!*

As she worked her way out of the building and to her car, she called Sean from her cell. He answered on the first ring.

"Hello, how's it going?" Sean said.

"Okay, I guess," Kim replied. She proceeded to tell Sean about her meeting and the preparations for the custody hearing.

"Well, Abigail is doing fine. She's helping the professor with research for our new quest."

"New quest?" Kim asked. "What new quest?"

"After I dropped you off at the airport, I met with Joe," Sean began explaining. It took him a few minutes and Kim had managed to reach her car and was now driving.

"So now we have something that seems more historical to look for anyway," Sean finished. "And we're being well paid."

"Wow, okay. Well I'll head back out I guess, though my shop could use me for a few days. I'm headed there now."

"Well, take the time you need. Your daughter is in good hands and you might even be able to help from there," Sean replied. "I'm about to meet with that guy who came up to me yesterday. The one who said he had something we would like to explore. Maybe you can take the lead on that? Of course, we're not going to get paid for that one, I bet."

"Maybe," Kim mused as she pulled into her parking spot at the shop. "Listen, I've got to go to work. Thanks for talking to me." They said goodbye and Kim hung up. She sat in her car for a moment looking at the phone.

Do you want to be a shopowner or a historian? she asked herself.

Gettysburg

Sean hung up his phone and kept walking down the now-crowded sidewalk. *It's amazing how many people descend on this town. It is much more than just a battlefield!* Around him, families were bustling in and out of shops, crossing the street, even crowding tables. Sean spotted the coffee shop where the man had said they would meet and crossed the street.

The coffee shop was entirely indoors and Sean pushed the glass-paned door open and looked around. He quickly spotted Tom Kinneson sitting at a small round table. He seemed to be wearing the same slacks and shirt as the day before, though Sean suspected he simply had quite a few similar outfits. Sean walked over to the table.

"Mr. Kinneson?" Sean extended his hand.

"Hi, Sean," Tom replied as he shook his hand. "Have a seat. I can't tell you how happy I was to get your call this morning."

Sean slid into the empty chair at the table.

"Well, you had me intrigued," Sean explained. "When I told my team of my encounter with you, they were quite firm that I should meet with you."

Tom's eyes lit up. Sean noticed that when Tom smiled he looked twenty years younger.

"Oh?" Tom asked. "The same group that was with you in South Carolina?"

"Yes, but really, I'm as much with them as they are with me. We have become a team of sorts, I guess." Sean grinned sheepishly. "Really, the whole adventure just happened to us and now I think we're just trying to figure out whether we have stumbled onto a new career."

"My my," Tom said. "And how is your searching here in Gettysburg going? Better than yesterday?"

"No, not really. We actually got thrown a curve yesterday. In fact we changed sports." Sean smiled at his joke. He could see that Tom understood and enjoyed the joke.

"Well, let me tell you my story. Maybe you can find time for a side mystery."

Sean pulled a notebook from his back pocket and a pen from his shirt. "Go ahead," he said, poised to take notes.

"You are quite the reporter, I see," Tom observed. "Okay, here it is. Shortly after the Civil War was over, my grandfather was an innkeeper in western Maryland," Tom began. "He told a story to me that he also told to my father and my uncle. One night he had a very distinguished guest, the former general, Ulysses S. Grant. He was traveling with a small entourage, headed back to the capital.

"Former general?" Sean asked. "Wasn't he president then?"

"No, no," Tom replied. "This was about a year before the election to replace Johnson. I am not a historian, mind you, but I have looked at this story some. There was a lot of tension then about how Johnson was treating the former Confederate states and Grant was frequently quoted as being unhappy with the direction the country was going. My grandfather thinks Grant was headed to the capital to reach an agreement to allow his name to be thrown in the ring for president in the next election. Anyways, he stayed at the inn just that one night. My grandfather was honored and served quite a feast. He said the men all stayed up late drinking and smoking cigars. He said the air was foul with smoke, but he was fine with it, my grandfather."

Sean had quit taking notes and was simply listening, not sure where Tom was going.

"So anyways, at various times people from the area dropped in to pay their respects to the general. So their merriment was frequently interrupted. At one point in the night, my grandfather heard the door open and shortly thereafter the room was silent. He went to the front and saw a middle-aged man talking to the general. He had pulled out some sheets of paper."

Tom paused and looked carefully at Sean.

"My grandfather said that General Grant was pretty drunk, in fact most of his group was. I think that is the reputation the general had. I hate telling that, but it has some bearing on the story. The man told the general the papers were presidential papers from Abraham Lincoln.

Specifically, that they were, and this is a quote, "his real words at Gettysburg."

"Real words?" Sean asked, taking notes again. "What does that mean?"

"My father said he saw the document and later realized it was a speech written by Lincoln, and that it was probably the actual speech that Lincoln gave at Gettysburg."

"The actual speech? We know what he said at Gettysburg. Heck, every American has learned that speech."

"If you pursue this, you will quickly learn that we actually do not know exactly what he said that day. Accounts and copies of the speech differ."

"Okay," Sean said. "What happened to the documents?"

"Ah." Tom smiled. "That is the question. The man left the documents with General Grant and left the inn. My grandfather told my father he suspected the man was embarrassed to be around the general so drunk. He never told me that piece of information, though. Anyways, the night goes on and my grandfather goes to sleep, leaving the men to their merriment.

"The next morning, after breakfast, the men are packing up. General Grant is thanking my grandfather for his hospitality. My grandfather asks about the visitor the night before. He said that Grant got an amused look on his face and said that it was something fascinating. My grandfather asked what it was but the answer he got was nonsensical. The general laughed and said, 'It's in the memory of Lincoln.'"

"What?" Sean asked.

"It's in the memory of Lincoln," Tom repeated.

Sean wrote for about a minute and then looked up. "Okay, this is a good story, Tom," he said, trying to sound kindly. "But it's a little loose on facts."

Tom smiled. "I know, but there is one more part of the story. My grandfather said that several months later, while Grant was a candidate for president, a gentleman who was a champion of Grant's stayed at the inn. My grandfather told the story to him. That man's eyes lit up. The man said he knew exactly what it meant but that he couldn't tell. But he said to my grandfather, 'Grant hid it in the memory of Lincoln.'

"My grandfather never let this go. He researched it later and realized that the document was a speech and probably the Gettysburg Address. He said he had no idea what the Gettysburg Address was at the time, but when he was older he came to realize that Grant had held what was probably the actual manuscript Lincoln had read and that he had apparently hidden it somewhere in order to protect the image of President Lincoln."

"Well, that's making this pretty interesting," Sean replied. "So I assume the original speech has never been found."

"Right, and I think you are just the person to find it."

Sean laughed. "You're not the only one telling me these kind of things. I'm not sure I believe it, though. I'm just a reporter who stumbled onto something."

"No, Mr. Johnson," Tom replied, getting serious. "You are an accomplished historical miracle worker. If anyone can find that speech, you can."

"Maybe," Sean said. "Tell you what, let me get some more information from you and I'll present this to my 'team.' If they want to pursue it, then we will."

"Thank you, Sean!" Tom smiled. "That's what I was suspecting you would say."

Sean proceeded to ask Tom a long series of questions about his family history, the inn location, the dates, everything Sean could think of. They finally finished and Sean realized he needed to get back to the professor. He thanked Tom and left, promising to call him and let him know if they were taking it up.

On the way back to the hotel, he shook his head. *Is this what's going to keep coming my way? Every old man with a family secret?* Still, Sean had to admit that Tom's story was very intriguing. *We'll see what the professor thinks.*

*****

A few minutes later he was back at the hotel. He knocked on James's door and shortly thereafter, James answered. "Sean!" he said happily. "Come on in."

Sean followed the professor back to the table and chairs they had been at the day before. "My meeting with Mr. Kinneson was very interesting."

He proceeded to explain to James everything that had occurred, reading from his notes periodically.

"Fascinating," James replied. "Fascinating."

"So what do you think?" Sean asked.

"I think we should dig into this. We have a decent chance of un-earthing something about this, especially compared to our Mecklenburg quest."

"Is it true that we don't actually know what Lincoln said at Gettys-burg?"

"I think that, yes, it is true," James said. "But honestly, I haven't stud-ied the speech myself. It's always been too popular for me. The Grant tie-in is also very interesting and much more up my alley."

Sean waited while the professor thought. Finally he spoke. "Let's look at it," James said as he smiled. "You know, this is kind of fun! For me, it beats sitting around in a university office. Of course it helps we're getting paid for one of our tasks. And I think we have some time to spare."

"All right by me." Sean said. "I spoke to Kim earlier. We'll hear from her tomorrow about the hearing and if and when she is coming out. I told her that Abby was doing fine." Sean paused. "Oh, shoot. Listen, I agreed to another FBI interview tomorrow in D.C. I need to head down tonight. Are you fine taking care of Abby?"

"Fine? Of course I am," the professor replied. "But why does the FBI keep hassling you?"

Sean laughed. "Partly because I won't let them talk to you. Seriously, though, I'll be back tomorrow afternoon at the latest."

"Abigail and I will be working on all of our mysteries," James replied.

CHAPTER FOURTEEN

Knoxville

Thomas put his coffee cup down and picked up another page of the document he had printed. He scratched his head with his free hand and then rubbed his face. He realized he had not shaven for several days and the stubble was actually starting to feel smoother, like a beard. *Maybe that's when I look like the nutty historian I'm acting like? When I have a beard?* Shaking his head to wake up a bit, he focused his attention on the sheet of paper in front of him.

Thomas had been hard at work since mid-morning Monday. After sleeping long and hard Sunday night, his plan for Monday had been to relax and catch up on world events. And do his laundry. But professor Enloe's call Monday morning with a new quest had forced him to change his plans and dig into something new.

At first he found little other than the material cited on the Internet about the Mecklenburg Declaration. But like everything he had been doing for the professor, the more he dug the more he began to learn about what to actually look for.

He had found some microfiche records of personal diaries from the early days in North Carolina. He printed hundreds of pages and took them home. It was now Tuesday and his efforts had been slightly productive. He had found some references to the meeting in Mecklenburg, but most were references long after the fact. But he had also found some references to a town called Lenoir in north central North Carolina. So now he was trying to make a list of new search terms and trying to decide whether he should work from home or head back to the library.

Sighing, he sipped from his coffee cup and began reading the last of the pages he had printed. A few minutes later he came upon an entry in a diary by a woman named Elizabeth Stark. She had written: "Stoneman did not get anything from us, including the real declaration. Tom will be proud how well I protected his legacy."

The word "declaration" stood out to him. But so did the name "Stark." He thumbed through various piles of paper that covered the kitchen table in his apartment and then he remembered. There had been a Stark at Mecklenburg. Or he thought there had been. The clue seemed too good to ignore so he began scribbling on his notepad.

Washington D.C.

Sean leaned back in the pathetic version of a chair that was apparently all the FBI could afford in their "interview" rooms. He had been sitting for at least ten minutes all by himself. If there had been a mirror in the room he would have been certain that he was being watched through two-way glass. Instead the room was similar to the room he had been in last week: table, chairs, and a cheap print in a frame on the wall.

When he arrived, a polite young lady had led him to the room and told him someone would be right there. Sean was now ready to just get up and walk out. But something told him he needed to stick around and see what was going on.

After another ten minutes or so, the door to the room opened. A veteran-looking agent with graying hair and a young dark-haired woman came into the room. Both wore suits, Sean noted with a smile.

"Mr. Johnson?" the senior agent asked, reaching his hand out.

"That's me," Sean replied. He had decided to let them refer to him in the formal.

"I'm Agent Emmitt Talie," the gray-haired man said. "This is agent Chapman."

Sean Shook hands with each of them. He noted that the only items they had brought into the room were white lined pads of paper. They both put them down on the table in front of them and pulled out pens. Sean worked hard to avoid smiling at their stereotypical behavior. They both seemed very intelligent and very sharp, however, which helped Sean feel enough tension to maintain a serious look on his face. Agent Chapman spoke first.

"Mr. Johnson, thank you for speaking with me and coming in to talk with us," she said.

"You're welcome," Sean replied. "I have to tell you that while I strongly desire to help the FBI in any way I can, I also feel like you have little regard for me and my work and schedule."

Agent Talie cleared his throat. "That's actually a question we have for you, Mr. Johnson. Please explain what you are doing in Gettysburg. It seems odd to us that you went from a miraculous discovery in South Carolina to suddenly busy on something new in Pennsylvania."

So you're playing bad cop, Sean thought. *But this is not going to go well.*

"I don't see why I need to tell you anything about what I'm doing now, Agent Talie," Sean replied. "You asked me to come in here to speak to you about something. You would not tell me about it. Why don't you start by telling me what you have me here for."

"Mr. Johnson," Agent Talie replied, "perhaps you don't understand your circumstances. You killed an FBI agent. You are under investigation for that murder."

"Whoa, stop," Sean interrupted him. "It was no murder. If you want to talk like that then we are done."

Emmitt looked at Sean for a moment. "Accepted. I apologize. So here is why you're here. We are investigating the murder of an off-duty police officer in Maryland. We have reason to believe his death is associated with a historical researcher similar to you."

"Why would I have anything to do with this police officer's death, just because I'm doing historical research?" Sean asked, sounding confused. "And why is the FBI investigating a local crime?"

"I cannot reveal our source or the reason why you're a person of interest in that crime," Emmitt responded. "But I can tell you that the local crime, as you call it, has national security implications."

"Look, I'm not sure what's going on here, but all I'm doing is research.

I'm not considering any crime, let alone murdering a police officer."

"Who are you researching for? And what are you researching?"

Sean smiled. "I can't tell you. We are contracted to maintain the confidence of our employer until we complete the work."

Agent Talie seemed slightly startled and then irritated. He looked away and Alice jumped in. "We believe you're working for Samuel Franklin," Alice stated firmly. "Isn't that correct?"

"I can't tell you. I just told you that," Sean responded quickly and firmly, as he had been trained years ago, but his mind was racing. *That's our Joe! This just got really complicated. Joe must be associated with the murder. What does that mean about what we're doing and who or what he's really trying to accomplish?* Sean tried to think of a tactic to work information from the two agents but Alice jumped back quickly. Sean knew that her quick response was her training on interrogation. *Keep the opponent on the ropes, with no time to think.*

"Mr. Johnson, we are the FBI. We are investigating a serious crime and threat. You simply telling us you can't talk about what you're doing makes you look very suspicious, doesn't it?"

"Yes," Sean admitted, sighing. "I admit it does. But it is the truth. We're doing research for an organization, trying to find a historical document."

"An organization?" Agent Talie's head jerked forward, strongly reacting to Sean's use of that word.

"Yes," Sean said, trying to keep up with the pace of the interview. "And there is nothing criminal about what we're doing."

"Were you doing this research when you killed Agent Nazimi?" Agent Chapman jumped back in.

"No," Sean began and then he paused and looked quizzically at Alice. "What in the world does your rogue criminal agent have to do with my research? Or is it that he had something to do with the crime you're investigating?"

Agent Talie's face twitched some with Sean's last suggestion. *You guys aren't sure what you have,* Sean thought. *But I'm not either. What have we gotten tangled up in?*

"Mr. Johnson," Agent Talie said, regaining his composure, "you need to answer our questions, not the other way around. We are investigating a crime with national security implications. You could be in a lot of trouble."

"I am not in any trouble," Sean said, "because I and my team aren't doing anything wrong. We are conducting confidential research for a confidential client. Frankly, if I understand things correctly, our work will be done shortly."

The two agents glanced at each other. Talie spoke. "We need to know who you are working for. We also need to know your relationship with Samuel Franklin."

"I have not told you that I have a relationship with this Franklin," Sean replied, getting tired of the back and forth. "But even if I did, if he were our benefactor, I could not tell you. Do you understand that?"

The agents glanced at each other again. Talie nodded at Chapman. Alice then spoke. "What were you doing meeting with Mr. Franklin at a highway stop? And what did he give you?"

Sean reeled a little. *They were watching us? Who were they tailing? Joe or me?*

"What's your answer, Mr. Johnson?" Alice persisted.

It's time to end this. Something is out of hand, Sean thought.

"I think I'm done with this interview. Clearly you were watching our meeting. Which was in an open place and had nothing sinister or criminal associated with it." *Did it?* "I have no problem with you watching it, either. Because we were not doing anything wrong. But I'm done talking for now." *I've got to figure out what is going on. What is Joe really up to?*

"Mr. Johnson," Agent Talie said, "perhaps you do not understand. We think you might be a terrorist. Does that scare you?"

"It sure does," Sean replied. "But for two reasons. The first is the obvious one. I don't want the FBI thinking I'm a terrorist. But the second reason is more important. If you actually do think I'm a terrorist, then you are lost, because you are wrong. So if you have a real security threat, then I'm concerned you're not on top of it at all. Because I'm not a terrorist." Sean stood up.

"We are not done here," Agent Talie said. "Sit down."

"I'm leaving unless you can show a court order. I'll help you in any way I can, but I am done with this for the moment." Sean half-turned to the door. "Do you want to escort me out or can I leave on my own? I'm getting good at finding my way out of this place."

"Leave," Emmitt uttered. "But watch yourself, Mr. Johnson."

"I will," Sean replied. He then turned and left the room.

Kansas City

Kim was shocked. The judge had just announced the decision she had been dreading: custody awarded to her ex-husband. She was also fuming. After speaking briefly with her attorney in the hallway, she turned and walked the other way from her ex-husband, his girlfriend, and their lawyer. Tears were flowing down her cheeks as she reached the exit and passed back into the unsecured public world outside the court building.

She had also been ordered to cooperate in transferring Abby to her ex-husband as soon as possible. What she was now torn over was whether she was going to do so or not. She hadn't told anyone that Abby was not actually even in the state, not even her lawyer. So she now had to decide what she was going to do.

And I have no idea what to do!

Kim reached her car in the parking lot and fumbled with the keys at first, her hands trembling.

Once in the car and driving, she called Sean. After four rings it went to his voicemail.

"Sean, it's Kim. I lost. I'm supposed to turn Abby over to Jason. I don't know what to do. I'm so angry. Where are you? Please call."

She hung up and stared out the windshield at the red light. She did not even know where to go. *Home? To the shop? Should I book a flight for Abby and get her back here? Should I go back out there?*

The last thought resonated. She could go to Abby and take her dear sweet time getting Abby back. *But what do I tell Abby? I need to ask her what she wants.*

The light turned green and Kim made up her mind. She was going to drive out instead of flying. It would give her time to calm down and develop a strategy to drag out the custody transfer. She was so angry.

Washington D.C.

Sean was walking back to his hotel room with his mind going a mile a minute. He had failed to notice Kim's call because his phone was still on silent from the meeting. He was working his way through the facts he had learned at the meeting.

The FBI has a terrorist threat. Something they know connects it to historical research. They were either tailing me or tailing Joe. Joe is supposedly advancing a political cause. That does not make him a terrorist!

Sean continued to think through what was happening. Was this a real threat or was Joe's organization being confused as being terrorist?

Suddenly a horn beeped behind him. He turned and spotted a taxi driving slowly behind him, next to the curb. The driver waved at him. Sean waved him off. Or at least he tried to. The taxi pulled up even with Sean and the driver rolled the passenger-side window down.

"Mr. Johnson?"

Sean whirled around, confused, but also feeling his sense of alertness rising. "Yes," he replied, keeping his distance. The cab driver was moderately heavy and had a thick black beard on a Middle-Eastern looking face. "How do you know who I am?"

"Joe sent me," the cabbie explained. "I'm supposed to pick you up."

Sean stood for a moment and thought. A car had stopped behind the cab and was now honking.

This just got even more complicated.

He examined the cabbie some more and decided the driver was not a threat. Shrugging, he got in the cab.

"So, where are you taking me?" Sean asked, looking around the backseat of the cab and reading the cab driver's identification card hanging from the visor.

"No worries, Mr. Johnson," the driver replied with a toothy grin. "I'm taking you to a garage. I'm supposed to give you this."

The driver reached back and offered Sean a single car key through the space in the Plexiglas.

"What's this?" Sean asked, taking the key. But he recognized it as the key to his rental car. Except it had been clipped off the little wire cord that had attached it to another key and a tag.

"2 K, as in Kidding," the cabbie said laughing. "2 K. That's all I know. I pick you up, I give you that, I tell you '2 K' and I drop you off. Here."

The cab stopped next to an entrance to a parking garage. Sean looked at the cab driver for several moments. "Okay, thanks," Sean said.

He got out of the car and watched it drive off as he stood for a moment, thinking. Then he shrugged again and entered the stairwell leading up to the second floor of the parking garage. Once on the second, he hit the alarm button on the key and was awarded with a horn honking from the far side. *In row K,* Sean noted. He began walking towards the car, watching his surroundings. He saw no one, not even any suspicious cars. He approached the car and walked around it while also looking into the cars on each side. Everything empty. *My car looks like it did when I left it. It's just in a new location.*

Sean then hit the unlock button and the trunk button on the key. The doors unlocked and the trunk popped up partially. Hesitantly, he lifted the trunk up farther, not sure what he would see inside. What he saw surprised him. There, in the trunk, neatly arranged, were his bags and items from his hotel room. A note, hand-written on a small piece of paper, rested on top. He picked it up and read it.

You will best be able to help us in our mission if the FBI does not bother you anymore. There are people in the establishment that would like to see us fail. Please leave the city and continue to pursue your task.

It was not signed and Sean wasn't sure he knew what Joe's handwriting looked like.

"FSA, what are you really?" Sean asked aloud as he looked around the parking garage again. He stood there thinking for a few minutes, trying to come up with a plan. Finally, he developed some resolve. He got in the car and began his drive back to Gettysburg.

A few minutes later, as a truck hauling what looked like a load of landscaping pruning passed him by, he reached out with his left arm and nimbly flipped his cell phone up and into the truck bed.

Time to gain the tactical advantage, Sean thought, as he felt himself easing into his old life as a special operations agent. *Time to get ahead of everyone else.* He and his team had clearly been drawn into something dark. Sean's first and foremost thought was to protect his team, the people who were beginning to feel like family to him.

CHAPTER FIFTEEN

Gettysburg

James had rented the room adjacent to his own. It was accessible through a door from his room. He had also had the hotel bring two tables in and place them against each other. With Sean gone, they were car-less, so James had decided to set up a workroom in the hotel and start organizing their efforts. Abby and James were now sitting across from each other, both with laptops opened up and various documents scattered around. Behind James, a large map of the eastern United States was tacked to the wall.

"So, Professor," Abby said, "how does the Gettysburg Address relate to the Mecklenburg Declaration?" She was working her way through a long Wikipedia page on the Mecklenburg Declaration and trying to keep her concentration.

"It does not, my dear," James explained. "We are now taking on two mysteries that are not related. Perhaps I should have you focus on the Gettysburg Address?"

"That would be awesome," Abby immediately replied. "It's not that early history doesn't interest me, it does. But I can totally relate to the Gettysburg Address and President Lincoln. It also seems closer to the last job we were on."

James leaned back in his chair and stretched his arms. "Well, you can help on both, but let's focus you on the Gettysburg Address. We're not getting paid for that anyway, so Sean and I probably should focus on the Mecklenburg Declaration."

"So, what should I do?" Abby asked.

"Since we have Thomas focused on the Mecklenburg job, you can help a lot by compiling information on references to all copies of the Gettysburg Address that were in Lincoln's handwriting. Try and also build a list of references to scholarly work on the versions of the Gettysburg Address. And see if you can learn how the written version that he read from might have given General Grant a reason to hide it."

"Okay, okay," Abby groaned. "That's going to take me a few days."

"Just get started on the versions of the Gettysburg Address," James said, laughing. "But if you want to become a historian, you better get used to layers of research like that."

"Okay. Can you answer a question for me, though?"

"Sure," James replied.

"If we don't know what Lincoln said at Gettysburg, then why do we all learn his speech? Is it made up?"

James sighed. "Real history is much more complicated than the simplistic version we offer the public. I understand why we dumb it down, but sometimes we go too far. I'm not sure whether that is the case with the Gettysburg Address or not. I think what you're going to find is that the various versions of the Gettysburg Address differ only slightly.

"Understand," James went on, "that there were no recording devices back then. So mostly speakers provided a written version of their speech afterwards, if it turned out there was interest. Thus the speaker ended up putting out what they wanted to be remembered as saying. They could also say things that were more provocative or controversial but then put out a written version of their speech that lacked those elements afterwards. And speakers might meander off of their intended remarks as well.

"So, really, we don't know exactly what Lincoln said that day. He spoke briefly after a very long speech by a speaker who was famous for his speeches. Most reporters probably barely started taking notes when it was over. The published versions in the paper probably came from a version Lincoln's secretary handed out afterwards. I recall that there were several versions that emerged in the months after his speech and a couple after his death. Your job is to identify those versions and try and see how they differ."

"Okay, that helps," Abby replied. "Thanks."

"You're very welcome. I'm going to call Thomas now to see what he is accomplishing on his Mecklenburg research."

Abby nodded, so James pulled the hotel room phone closer to him and hit the speakerphone button. Shortly, Thomas came on the line.

"Hello?"

"Good afternoon, Thomas," James said. "I'm here with a young assistant in Gettysburg. Abby, say hi."

Abby looked horrified for a moment but then said a weak, "Hello."

"Nice to meet you, Abby," Thomas's voice projected from the speaker. "Is this the hotel phone line?"

"It sure is."

"Okay."

There was a pause and then James spoke. "So how goes the Mecklenburg Declaration?"

Thomas sighed. "As good as it can. I found plenty of material about the meeting and the Mecklenburg Resolves. It gets murkier when we dig into the Dec." Thomas has shortened declaration to "Dec" and had also begun referring to the "Mec Dec" as a faster way to talk to librarians about his topic.

"We expected that," James said. "Anything interesting?"

"Well, I've been digging through everything I can find that was written back in that era or not long after. The most interesting lead has been a reference in a diary that connects Stoneman and a town called Lenoir to some possible location of the Mec Dec during the Civil War."

"Hmm," James mused. "That's quite interesting. Since we're pursuing a theory that the Mecklenburg Declaration might have been in Gettysburg at the outbreak of that battle, a sighting or reference a couple of years later not too far to the south is a good lead."

"Right," Thomas agreed. " I thought the same thing. I've been studying more about the history of Lenoir, though I'm not done with that. There are so many different directions to go on this."

"I understand. Keep up the hard work, Thomas."

"Will do, Professor." Thomas replied.

"Nice to meet you," Abby called out.

"You too, Abby."

James hung up and looked at the phone for a moment. He then got up and turned around to look at the map on the wall. A few minutes later he found the town of Lenoir in North Carolina.

"There you are," he said, pushing a small red pin into the map and the wall where Lenoir was located. Abby got up and walked around the tables and looked at the map with the professor.

"Maybe the Mec Dec is in Lenoir," she offered.

Highway towards Gettysburg

Kim was clutching the steering wheel and trying to think calm thoughts. But criticism and fear kept rising up. *What are you doing, Kim?* She had been driving for eight hours now. The sun was setting and she was still eight hours out from Gettysburg. She wondered what her ex was thinking. He had called her cell phone several times. She was trying to decide what to do. Should she take his call or keep ignoring him? If she took the call, what should she say? She knew she had to turn Abby over at some point, but there was no specific deadline in place.

And where is Sean? She had called his cell probably ten times and he had not answered. On the last few calls, it had kicked over to voicemail instantly, suggesting his phone was off, dead or out of range. Overall, Kim felt panicky and unsettled. She didn't know what to do other than just keep driving as fast as she could.

But not so fast that I get pulled over, she thought, almost giggling to herself. *Maybe there is an all-points bulletin out on me? Be on the lookout for the kidnapping mother flying to hide her daughter.*

Kim actually laughed aloud at the thought. Then she settled back down into driving east. A few minutes later her phone rang. The number was one she did not recognize but she knew it was not from Texas or Kansas City. She decided to answer it.

"Hello?"

"Hi, Kim," Sean's voice replied.

"Sean, where the hell are you?" Kim almost yelled into the phone, feeling both angry and relieved at the same time.

"I'm calling from a pay phone on I-42 north of Baltimore," Sean replied, sounding tired and apologetic. "Abby is safe with the professor."

"Did you lose your phone?" Kim asked.

"No, I threw it away. Listen, a lot has happened and we need to talk."

"Tell me about it. I've been driving all day to get to Gettysburg. I'm still more than seven hours away. I'm going to stop somewhere soon."

"Huh?" Sean sounded confused.

"I know, I know. I'm probably nuts. Listen, Sean, I lost custody of Abby. The stupid judge awarded Jason one-hundred-percent custody."

"Uh-oh," Sean replied. "So what are you doing?"

"I'm driving to you, you idiot. I couldn't think straight and you haven't answered or returned any of my calls!" Kim was frantic now.

"I know, I know. A lot has happened here as well." Sean paused and thought for a moment.

"Okay, listen. Things will work out. But you need to meet me somewhere where we can talk. I will call you again tomorrow, from a different number. Okay?"

"Sean, what's going on?"

"Something larger than all of us, I think. But I don't want to say anything more on this line. Don't call anyone else. Don't take any calls until you get a call from a number you don't recognize. Okay?"

"'Okay," Kim replied, feeling anything but okay.

"Hang in there, Honey," Sean said, trying to sound reassuring. "Things will work out okay with Abby and everything."

"Okay," Kim repeated.

FSA Headquarters

The map on the table was covered with a sheet of rigid plastic. General Huerta was studying it, while Joe stood by the table on his cell phone. Finally, he made a short comment and ended the call.

"Sean took the invitation. That's a good sign," Joe reported.

"It's not clear to me at all why we're not simply terminating that situation," General Huerta replied.

"Because Fred, as well as our politicos in D.C., really want that declaration," Joe explained. "If we killed them now that option would be off the table. Plus, killing them might attract more attention than we want."

"Okay, but you and I both know this Mecklenburg Declaration thing is a long shot. I'm not certain we really need it anyway. We have the political argument and we have the physical force we need to preserve ourselves."

"We *will* have," Joe corrected. "*If* everything goes as planned."

Huerta snorted. "Many things can go wrong and we will still prevail. Don't worry. We have redundancy and conservative planning throughout this."

"It remains the case that only our political position and logical and moral argument are done. The tactical, physical situation is not yet achieved."

"Sure," General Huerta replied. "But our senator could mess up his speech. Someone could come up with a better or more influential argument. Nothing is certain that can be spoken. But strength and military capability is real. It can't be undone by some political circumstance."

"Admittedly," Joe replied, "you are correct. But just as you want every physical edge you can have, we want every political edge as well."

General Huerta looked up from the map on the table and grinned. "You are right, my friend. You are right."

"But there's something going on," Joe said, sounding concerned. "The FBI has gotten on to me, and also to Johnson, much faster than they should have. I sense that there's something going on that we're not aware of. My worst fear is that we have a leak."

"That has always been a possibility," General Huerta replied. "But we have prepared for that. We have limited knowledge of all of our plans among our members. We have parallel monitoring in place. Advance knowledge of our political plans is not a concern. Advance knowledge of our tactical plans could be."

"Tell me," Joe replied, "how soon will we be ready to deploy?"

"As early as this coming weekend. And this week we'll be recruiting, gradually. This means that we'll be achieving a size by this weekend or early next week that we won't be able to contain much longer. I think we'll have to deploy within two weeks."

"So our day is clearly close at hand," Joe said.

CHAPTER SIXTEEN

Gettysburg

"So that's where we are," Sean said. He and James were sitting in a booth in a diner-style restaurant across the street from the National Historical Park. Sean had gotten in to the hotel late and had spent the evening sitting in the bar downstairs nursing a beer and thinking about what to do. This morning, he and James had driven over to the edge of the battlefield to have breakfast at the diner. "Amazing," the professor said. "I'm not sure why you didn't just tell the FBI everything."

"Because I'm not sure who the good guys are and who the bad guys are," Sean explained. "I mean, I know the FBI are good guys, generally."

Sean could see James making a sarcastic expression. "Our previous experience notwithstanding," Sean said. "But what if Joe and the FSA are good guys and some other bad person out there is manipulating the FBI, using them?"

"Point taken," James admitted.

"But I still am very suspicious of Joe and the FSA. I'm not ignoring it. Something is odd about how they want this Mecklenburg Declaration." Sean paused. "No, that's not it. Something's odd about how secretive they're being about wanting it. That's what is off here."

"And we have our new mystery," James added. "I like this one a lot more. Partly because it's more modern, so there are more documents out there to find and examine. But also because it's something that we know existed. But the only clues we have now are oral history. We need to pin down some facts on that to confirm enough parts of the story to make the other part real."

"I think the strategy here is to ensure that I and most of you focus on the Mecklenburg Declaration," Sean said. "But I have a plan."

"Let's hear it then," James said.

Sean walked James through the elements of his plan. James agreed to it and they parted. Sean left James behind in the diner, since James was meeting with a bookstore historian around the corner in a half an hour.

James watched Sean go and then pulled his cell phone out of his pocket. He called Thomas and soon heard Thomas's voice on the line.

"Hello, Professor."

"Hello, Thomas. How is the research on the Mecklenburg Declaration going?"

"Okay," Thomas said. "As you know, that far back there are few records. I'm also searching in the following fifty or so years. But much of the material is not searchable by word."

"Okay, well, listen. Sean is going to head south, probably to Charlotte to give us some presence where it all happened. It would be great if you can give him some guidance on where to go and what to look at. Material not available online."

"Will do," Thomas promised.

*****

Back in the hotel room, Abby was lying on her bed, her laptop open. She was working her way through the story of the Gettysburg Address. For this first time she could remember, she was finding herself truly into something historical. She could remember hearing about the Gettysburg Address several years ago, but her recollection of actual details had been poor.

"My history teacher should see me now," Abby said out loud as she continued to read and take notes.

Washington D.C.

Alice Chapman and Dana Misler were sitting across from Emmitt, who did not appear to be in a good mood. "Updates, Chapman."

"Not very many, Sir. We lost Johnson after our interview yesterday."

"Lost him?"

"He hopped into a cab, and then got out just as quickly, about seven blocks later. We didn't have a vehicular team, but they sprinted to try to keep up. By the time they got to where he'd gotten out, they'd lost him. They returned to the hotel, but his vehicle was gone and the hotel reported he'd checked out."

"Humph," Emmitt snorted. "More suspicious behavior. Presumably he will resurface in Gettysburg. What are they doing in Gettysburg, of all places?"

"We'll find out, Sir," Alice promised.

"We better. I think we need to treat Mr. Johnson and his team as suspects. Let's see if we can get warrants. Same with this Mr. Franklin he met with. Let's put a tail on him as well." Emmitt paused and then looked at Dana.

"Find out everything you can about Franklin. Let's also dig into Johnson's accomplices. I'll get the budget approval today to step this up a notch."

"Yes, Sir," Dana replied.

"Chapman, what do you think?"

Alice looked up from her notepad. "I don't think Johnson fits the bill as a disgruntled ex-serviceman. I'll get his service record if I can to better examine him. But he is acting suspicious. At that meeting he took what looked like money from Franklin. And Franklin fits the tipster's profile perfectly."

"You don't think this is all nothing?"

"It can't be," Alice said, shaking her head. "At a minimum there's someone telling us confidential information about a cop killing and telling us it's connected to a serious plot. They told us to look for someone doing historical research and we find an FBI-agent killer, of all things, who was doing historical research, of all things, when he killed the FBI agent and is doing more historical research in a very suspicious manner."

"Okay, thanks," Emmitt said. "You just nearly perfectly described my feelings. Get to it. And get me an update on Johnson. He must have surfaced in Gettysburg again."

Alice and Dana jumped up and left Emmitt's office.

FSA Headquarters

Joe was standing at a window in the raised meeting room. Down below, Ken was addressing a unit of FSA soldiers who were standing in two crisp lines. For Joe, it seemed a bit surreal. No one was in uniform. Instead they were dressed in various nondescript sporty casual clothes. That was intentional. For their effort to succeed, they had to prepare undetected.

But it seemed off to refer to the eclectic mix of people as soldiers. It helped that they were standing in straight lines and at attention. Joe could not actually hear what Ken was saying but the men nodded and then began dispersing. Several were staying in the facility now. Joe was as well.

It's going to be crowded for a while. But not much longer, Joe knew.

Outside Gettysburg

Sean was getting tired of meeting people at highway restaurants. The food was usually not great. And the tension of the meetings often ruined his appetite. Even getting here had been hard for Sean. He had driven all sorts of different routes to satisfy himself that he had lost anyone who might be tailing him. In spite of a thorough search inside and under his rental car, he still worried it might have a GPS tracker in it. So now he was standing in a shadow of a tree watching the parking lot. A few minutes earlier he had called Kim from a payphone by a set of bathrooms at the gas station next door and told her to come on in off of I-15.

He spotted Kim pull in, park, and go into the restaurant. She had looked around a bit but Sean didn't think she had spotted him. Sean stood still for about five minutes until he was satisfied they could meet in privacy. Privacy in a public restaurant, anyway.

Sean walked across the parking lot and entered the establishment. As he knew, there were only three other people eating, a younger couple and a middle-aged man. He slid into the booth next to her.

"Hey there," he said simply.

"Sean, I'm so glad to see you," Kim breathed. "What's going on?"

"A lot," Sean replied. He then began walking her through his meeting with Joe, the D.C. events and his conversation with James. "So we have a plan."

"I'm not sure I like it that much," Kim replied. "If there's danger, why don't we tell the FBI what's going on?"

"James essentially asked the same question," Sean admitted. "We need to shake things up. And we're still being paid right now to find the Mecklenburg Declaration, or Mec Dec, as Thomas has started calling it."

"So the three of us sit around as targets while you run off to North Carolina?" Kim sounded miffed.

"No, the three of you research and work hard on both mysteries. I'll be focused on the Mec Dec, with support from Thomas and James. You and Abby can focus on this new mystery, the Gettysburg Address. You should see how Abby has suddenly found her inner historian."

"Is she okay?" Kim asked. "What does she know?"

"She doesn't know the outcome of the hearing. At least neither of us have told her. But she's sharp enough to know why she hasn't heard about it. She's just having fun with the professor being an amateur historian."

"She's tough," Kim said, a tear forming in her eye.

"Yes, she is," Sean replied. "Look, can you buy some time from your ex-husband?"

Kim smiled. "I kind of have already. I called him today and told him I was picking her up from out of state and would get her home, get her done with her make-up school work and then get her packed. He wanted to talk to her, though. So I need to make sure Abby is okay doing this."

"A week may be enough. Abby can handle it. I can tell you that there's no way she wants to go down to Texas. Get your lawyer working on an appeal or whatever she can do. Let's let Abby talk to the judge directly. I think she'll convince the judge to keep her with you. We will win."

Kim was smiling. "You used 'we.'"

Sean clutched her hand. "I meant the word we. I feel the word we. We're in this together. Now listen, the plan is for me to disappear. In part, this is to throw everyone off. It will also allow me to work outside of whoever it is that's watching us. I threw my cell away and am now using this." He pulled a cell phone out of his pocket. "It's a prepaid cell. And you can call me on this one."

Sean pulled another phone out and set it in front of her. "Just use this to call mine. The phone number is in there. Don't use it for anything else. If you call, I'll answer or call back right away."

"Okay," Kim said, sounding unconvinced. "How are you going to disappear? You recall how it seemed like everyone was tracking us by our credit cards."

Sean smiled. "I have a plan for that also." He stood up. "Let's eat, I'm hungry." He offered his hand to Kim and squeezed it.

CHAPTER SEVENTEEN

Washington D.C.

The team was back in the inner meeting room with the pathetic tables that depressed Emmitt. Today it seemed to make Emmitt even grouchier.

"Let's begin. We are mostly all here and Agent Lentz is on the speakerphone. Let's start with Lentz. Give us a report on Gettysburg and on Mr. Franklin."

"Uh, well, we regained Johnson yesterday morning but then lost him again in Gettysburg." Lentz sounded like he was cringing.

"Again? How is this guy escaping our surveillance so easy?"

"He's a pro, Sir. He went into a café and sat down at a table that was visible from the street. The person following him saw him order food. He then stood up and went to the back, presumably to use the restroom. He never came back. We believe he went out the back through the kitchen."

"And I assume he never surfaced at the hotel?" Emmitt sounded more irritated.

"No, and his car is gone from the parking garage. We observed the professor and the young girl several times later in the day and believe they are both still in Gettysburg. But they have not emerged yet. I had agents cover the entire hotel last night. The mother, Ms. Poole, also returned last night, very late. We believe that is their only car at this point."

"Okay, well today you're getting more support up there. I want you to set up a command center somewhere north of Baltimore on a major highway. We'll up the level of monitoring on our quarry. Assuming we can find him. Chapman, where are we on search warrants?"

"Still in progress, Sir. Hopefully we get them today. Though counsel tells us it's iffy. Mostly circumstantial evidence and an unknown source to tie them to a cop murder."

"I assume still no Franklin?"

"Correct, Sir," Lentz responded from the speakerphone. "No one has come or gone from his house and there is no sign of activity."

"Misler, who is this Samuel Franklin?"

"Businessman. Mostly imports and art. Still pulling all the public files on him and his businesses, but nothing suspicious yet. No record either."

"Well, he acted suspicious the other night, so there is something in there. Dig into his past. Find out where his money comes from and where it goes."

"Yes, Sir." Dana scribbled on her notepad.

"Everyone, we are now in an all-out effort to determine what this group is doing and what they mean to do. Since we've been told action is imminent, we need to treat this as urgent.

"And I want Mr. Johnson found. When we get warrants, get a trace on his cell phone and cell phone records as well. See if we can find Franklin that way." Emmitt looked around the room. "Anything else?"

Everyone shook their heads. "Okay, then this meeting is over. Get to work."

Baltimore Outskirts

The house looked very ordinary. It had a neat lawn, trimmed shrubs. Just like the houses next to it. *A nice house in a nice neighborhood,* Sean thought. *That's all we wanted.* He walked up the path to the door and pressed the button. A few moments later the door opened and Sean immediately recognized his friend Ronald Marsh.

"Sean," Ronald said from behind the screen door. He pushed it open and embraced Sean. Sean could sense that Ron had kept himself in shape.

"Ron, you look great."

"You too, my man." Ron gestured into the house. "Come on in."

Sean walked past Ron and into a living room. There were pictures on the wall. Some were of kids that had to be Ron's. He looked around the room and turned to face him.

"Your family?" he asked, gesturing toward a photo of Ron, an attractive brunette and two smiling kids.

"Yeah, that's mine. At school and work but if you're around, you can meet 'em tonight."

Sean shook his head. "In a pretty big hurry. I actually came by to ask a pretty big favor."

Ron tilted his head a bit and smiled. "Sit. At least have a drink of water. I'd offer a beer but it's too early for that."

Sean grinned. "Water it is."

Ron left the room to get the drinks and Sean studied the surroundings a bit more.

*****

A half-an-hour later Sean was back in his rental car, heading south. But now he had a driver's license and credit card that identified him as Ronald Marsh. Height and build were pretty close. So was the hair. Eye color did not match but Sean had little concern that anyone would look very closely at the license. He now had a busy day ahead.

Gettysburg Hotel

"Okay, so where are we?" Kim asked. She, Abby and James were around the set of tables in their war room.

"Sean is headed to Charlotte, I think," James replied. "Thomas will or should be getting him some guidance on what to do there. We are presumably being watched while we work on both mysteries. You and Abby are going to focus on the Gettysburg Address."

"And you?" Kim asked.

"I will support both mysteries."

"I've got a lot on the Gettysburg Address," Abby reported. "We're not actually sure if any of the current copies of the speech are the real one or not. Some people think one version is real because it's on two sheets of dissimilar paper, which matches the version of events told by one of Lincoln's secretaries. But there are inconsistencies." Abby looked up from her computer and smiled.

"Wow," Kim said. "My daughter has become an historian. Sean said I would be impressed."

"She is," James said. "And quite a remarkable one. What we need to start doing is homing in on Grant. Why would he hide a copy of it? We need to get everything we can about where he was and who was with him at the time of this story."

James turned around in a swivel chair and looked at a map on a wall. "It appears that Grant was crossing back to D.C. at the time of this story so we have a first confirmation of a fact in Tom Kinneson's story. That's promising." He swung back around. "I've got to go through some more material on the Mecklenburg Declaration though." James looked at Kim.

"Have you heard what young Thomas calls it? The Mec Dec." The professor smiled, clearly amused.

"Yes, I have," Kim said. "Sean used that term last night."

"Speaking of Sean, why don't you call him with your special cell then," James said.

"My super-agent phone?" She pulled it out of her purse. "It's pretty plain vanilla," she said, holding it up. She then called up Sean's number. As promised, he answered on the first ring.

"Good afternoon," he said.

"Hi there. I'm here with Abby and the professor. How are you doing?"

"Still in Maryland at the moment taking care of a few more things," Sean replied. "Then I'm headed south. Does the professor still think Charlotte is the place for me to go?"

"Yes. Thomas should have materials soon to direct you once there. Heard from anyone?" Kim knew that Sean knew who she meant.

"No, but until I call them, they can't reach me. But I can check voice-mail on my old cell. I'm going to let them all stew for a day or more and just focus on research."

"Be careful," Kim admonished.

"You too," Sean replied. "Stay in public areas. If the FBI is up there, at least it's likely they won't let anyone hurt you."

"Do you think physical violence is a possibility?" Kim asked, sounding alarmed. Abby and James looked over at her.

"No, but after our last experience I just think all precautions should be taken. And the FBI is worried about a national threat, a terrorist threat. So you should be careful."

"We will," Kim promised. "We will."

"I'm hoping we can figure out what Joe and the FSA really want with the Mecklenburg Declaration," Sean said. "That's at the heart of our involvement, so hopefully finding it will answer some questions. But even if I don't find it, we may still get some insight into what's going on. And the temptation of it might flush Joe and the FSA out some so we can see what they're doing."

"Just be careful," Kim repeated.

"I will," Sean promised.

CHAPTER EIGHTEEN

Washington D.C.

Emmitt and Alice were back in his office.

"We have warrants?" Emmitt asked.

"We do," Alice replied, sounding cheerfully surprised. "We drew a judge who is anti-terrorist. Pretty liberal allocation of warrants."

"Good," Emmitt replied. "Let's get Johnson's cell pinned down. And get access to his voicemail. That communications unit in Kansas City handles our interaction with the cell phone companies. They should co-operate. I want to know where Johnson is and what he's doing."

Alice nodded.

"Get young Misler digging hard into Franklin. Bank records, how he bought his home. His businesses as well. My instinct tells me Sean is a pawn but this Franklin guy is the bad guy. Misler is pretty good too, by the way." Emmitt smiled. "But don't you tell her I said that."

"Mum's the word," Alice promised. "What about the rest of Johnson's team? Our warrants don't include them, so the most we can do is keep looking for Johnson. Apparently they have four rooms at the hotel, all next to each other."

"Four rooms," Emmitt repeated. "Pretty good for a reporter, a history professor and a single mom. Franklin must be bankrolling their effort.

Well, let's ratchet up the surveillance."

"Already done," Alice interjected. "Twenty-four hours, multiple agent units."

"The burn rate on that is going to be high," Emmitt said. "We better produce something soon. What about the command center?"

"Being set up today and tomorrow. Should be ready by Sunday."

"Okay, what else?" Emmitt asked.

"There is Franklin's house. We can search it now."

"Let's hold off on that for a few days. I don't want to spook him. He might just come back. Then we'll be able to tail him again."

"Yes, Sir."

"Anything else?"

"That's it on my end."

"Oh, one more thing," Emmitt said. "Don't forget we're looking for an organization. So there are more people out there. Phone call records will be helpful. See if we can find a cell registered to Franklin. And let's get the landline records for Franklin's house."

"Will do," Alice promised, standing to leave.

Gettysburg

James stood and looked out the window. Outside it was a nice warm-looking afternoon. The square was busy with foot and vehicle traffic. He turned back around and faced Kim and Abby. Both were hunched in front of computers.

"So, why do we think Grant might have hidden a copy of the Gettysburg Address?" he asked.

Abby looked up. "To protect Lincoln, right?"

"Maybe," James admitted. "But General Grant had more than that on his mind after the war. President Johnson was taking the country down a path that Grant disagreed with. And he felt that Lincoln would never have wanted. Johnson felt a desire to punish the South. Grant felt it had been punished enough. That the war was enough."

James paused and looked at them. Kim glanced at Abby and they smiled. They knew a lecture was coming.

"Grant and Lincoln both needed each other but also created the legend of each other. They are both forever entwined in the Civil War. Lincoln had gone through just about every other general he could trying to find one that would wage war. He promoted the new upstart Grant who did just that for Lincoln and delivered a Union victory.

"Grant was struggling to find a life for himself after the Army and just trying to provide for his family. He was a West Point graduate and served in the war with Mexico. He was an officer in the force that occupied Mexico City. But he later found himself out of the Army and unable to succeed in his business ventures. His drinking was part of that too.

"The Civil War erupted and really saved Grant. Lincoln's faith and trust in him gave Grant a chance to redeem himself. And he did. Today he is a hero because of two things: his own actions and decisions, and Lincoln. He restored the Union by force, but then wanted peace to resume over the land. He became president to do that.

"But he was never a politician, either. He was a soldier. His administration was full of corruption scandals primarily because he trusted too many people around him to be as clean and honest as he was. But he still stands as a great leader and a great president. It was under his leadership that the South was truly rejoined to the country. That was his legacy. It was also Lincoln's legacy. They were very different people but they shared the same legacy, the same desire to keep the United States whole."

James sat down. "Sorry, I was getting into that for a little bit."

Kim smiled. "You're good, though. I wish I could take one of your classes."

"Well, you both make a good audience," James said, getting a hint of red in his face.

"I'm still not sure what reason Grant would have had to hide the Gettysburg Address other than to protect Lincoln's reputation," Abby said.

"He would have also hid it to protect their legacy, or at least what they wanted their legacy to be," James explained. "What if the script included a sentence or phrase wherein Lincoln spoke of punishing the South?"

James paused and stood up. "But we're getting distracted. We do want to know the 'why' of it. But it's the 'where' that we need to solve. Let's go back to our two quotes from Kinneson's story."

"Yes," Kim spoke up. "I haven't even seen them or heard them yet."

"Hold on, I've got Sean's notes here," Abby said. She shoved some documents around by her computer. "Here it is." She picked up a notebook and began thumbing through it. "Okay, the man said 'real words at Gettysburg.'"

James walked over to an easel at one end of the room. He picked up a black marker and began writing the phrase out on the pad of paper resting on the easel.

"Real words at Gettysburg?" Kim repeated out loud, only as a question.

James finished writing the quote on the page and turned back to Abby. "And the other one?" he asked.

"Oh, right," Abby said. "Here it is. 'It's in the memory of Lincoln.' That was from Grant himself."

James turned and wrote the second quote down on the sheet under the first one. He then came back to his chair and sat down. Kim was staring at the chart.

"So, the first one tells us it was the Gettysburg Address," she said.

"That and also the observation of Kinneson's grandfather," Abby added. "The second one tells us more about why Grant hid it."

They all stared at the easel for a minute.

Finally, James spoke up. "So, this version of the Gettysburg Address never surfaces. We need to know everything about who was with Grant, where he was going, et cetera. I guess we can presume one of his traveling partners had the speech?"

"Perhaps," Kim said. She seemed deep in thought. "But I agree, we need to know more about his party."

"Okay," James said. "We will."

*****

Down in the square, Kelly was standing in front of a store, looking like one of the hundred tourists wandering the area. In front of him, through the plate glass, was an assortment of Civil War artifacts for sale. In reality, however, he was not interested in those artifacts.

Instead, he was interested in the FBI agent sitting at a café table pretending to read a newspaper. It was pretty pathetic, in Kelly's judgment. The man was in the shade, yet had dark sunglasses on. Kelly knew that he would struggle to read the print on the paper in such lighting. Instead the sunglasses allowed him to observe the sunny reflecting face of the

Gettysburg hotel. Which is what the man was doing.

His dress was also pathetic. Kelly had on jeans, a sport shirt, and a ball cap and carried a small knapsack. He looked like a tourist that had briefly escaped his kids. This man wore an open-collar, long-sleeved dress shirt over slacks. To Kelly, he had 'FBI' written all over him. The man also had a clear plastic cup of iced tea. Except the ice had long melted and the waitress was not bothering him at all. *Table renting.*

Kelly decided he needed to move on or attract attention so he turned his back on the man and began walking around the square. He had spotted a woman in the lobby who was trying to look like a businesswoman working on her computer. He had spotted a van with dark windows parking in the alley behind the hotel: perfect to observe both the rear door of the hotel as well as the parking garage behind it.

So the FBI is all over these three. And there is no Johnson anywhere. Kelly realized that Sean had to have seen the pitiful attempt at surveillance. Kelly also realized that the FBI was expending a serious amount of resources on the surveillance. Clearly the FBI was after something important. Kelly knew what it was, but he felt surprised that the FBI was aware enough to devote the resources that they had. *I'm going to have to tread very carefully.* It would not do for him to get caught spying on the FBI spying on the research team.

FSA Headquarters

They were gathered around the large table with the map under plastic. Joe was on one side, General Huerta on the other. Ken and Alex were sitting next to each other at one narrow end.

"So, we are ready," Huerta summarized. "Our units are at full strength, we have reconnoitered the targets and basic plans have been briefed."

Joe nodded. He noticed that Huerta, Alex and Ken liked to look at the map when speaking. *Must be a military thing.* "What does the countdown look like?" he asked.

"Six days from order to go to action," Huerta replied.

"Okay, then I think it's next Friday," Joe said. There was a silence for a few moments. Ken and Alex looked harder at the map. Huerta smiled.

Finally, Huerta replied, "Friday will work. That also matches our general preference to initiate this on a weekend. We expect the resistance and vigilance to be lower then."

Joe and Huerta looked at Ken and Alex, who simply nodded.

Ken muttered a short, "Yep."

Joe stood up. "Okay, I'm going to call the senator then."

He walked into his little office, but left the door open, knowing it was better if there were no secrets. He sat down in the chair and pulled up the senator's cell phone number on his own cell and called it. A full minute later Senator Hines answered.

"Good evening," he said. That signaled to Joe that the senator was in a public setting, meaning that he would be limited in what he could say.

"Good evening, Senator," Joe replied. "We're ready to begin on our end."

There was a pause before the senator replied. Joe suspected he could sense a slight change in the tone of the senator's voice, a hint of tension.

"Very well. We are as well."

"Does next Friday work?" Joe asked. It was an amazingly simple phrase, as if Joe were setting a dinner date.

"Yes, I think it will," the senator replied. Joe knew the senator wanted to say more, wanted to express some excitement or perhaps dread. But he could not.

"Where are we on the document?" Senator Hines asked.

"Nothing yet, but the team is doing remarkably well," Joe replied. "I will amplify the pressure on them."

"Okay, we can wait until near the end for that. We're prepared either way."

"I'll keep you informed of any news regarding it," Joe promised.

"Good," the senator replied. "Talk to you soon."

They hung up and Joe went back into the main room. He knew that they had heard all of Joe's side of the conversation.

"The senator agrees. Next Friday it is."

Huerta grinned, but Alex and Ken looked at each other briefly and seriously.

They're nervous, Joe thought. *So is the senator. So am I.* But those thoughts comforted Joe. He felt one should be nervous. It was Huerta who looked fearless and eager. That was unsettling. But Joe realized that you wanted your military leader to be fearless. *His job is not to question what we plan to do, but to accept it and complete it.*

"I will pretty much be right here for the next week and more," Joe said. "Let me know of any needs, any problems."

They all nodded.

CHAPTER NINETEEN

Washington D.C.

Steven was sitting at his dining room table enjoying some coffee while reading the latest news from his computer. He missed the days of newspapers, but they were no longer nearly as current as online news. They also lacked as much depth and original content as they used to have. But it was certainly more tiring staring at his computer instead of relaxing with a newspaper.

His cell phone began vibrating on the table next to his coffee and he glanced at it. *The senator!* He picked it up and answered. "Good morning, Senator."

"Good morning, Steven."

"I can assume you're calling me with news," Steven said.

"Yes. Joe called me last night. We set the date for this coming Friday."

So that's it. We are a go.

"I see," Steven replied, suddenly feeling some nerves work their way through him. "What about the Mecklenburg Declaration?"

"No word yet. Joe sounded less pessimistic than he did last time."

"Well, we're ready to go forward with or without," Steven admitted. "But I sure would like to have it. Showing a separate Declaration of Independence off would add a nice distraction as well as help our case."

"I agree. Joe promised to keep me informed."

"Good."

"I'll be arranging for my press conference Friday evening. Your job is to ensure the media carries it live."

"I know that," Steven responded, sounding irritated. "I made this plan, you know."

"I know that, Steven," the senator said kindly. "I'm repeating it for my own benefit."

"Sorry, Senator," Steven apologized. "Now that the moment is here, it feels a bit overwhelming."

"Yes, I know the feeling," the senator admitted. "I barely slept last night. And we're a week away."

"Soon enough we'll be in the thick of it."

"I won't call you anymore. I am also going to toss this cell phone," the senator said.

"Understood."

"You need to proceed very carefully with your job."

"I'll begin sensing who our supporters might be but do so very discreetly," Steven promised.

"Good. We need you to be our man on the inside when all of this goes down."

"I will be."

"Well then, good-bye. See you soon." The senator's words sounded ominous.

"Yes, see you soon." Steven hung up. He looked at his phone a moment and then stared outside. *The time is arriving.* Steven knew he had lots to do this weekend to be ready for all of his tasks in the coming week. After glancing at his cup, he decided to make some more coffee.

Charlotte

"A good Saturday morning to you, Paul," Sean was saying into his cell phone. "I'm just calling to get you an update. I should have my second story to you this coming week. I'm also now in the middle of not just one, but two mysteries. I think both will be worthy of stories. I'll probably be able to deliver one per week over the next three weeks." Sean paused and looked at his watch. "I'll call again early next week. I'm not able to answer my cell right now, but I am getting messages. So just leave me a message if you need anything."

Sean hung up the call and put his phone down. He began drinking his coffee a little faster. He was sitting in a small breakfast café across the street from the main Charlotte library. He had gotten in late the night before and gone to sleep early. On the way down he found a self-service computer-printer set up at a copy store and had managed to print the various documents Thomas had sent him. They were stacked up on the table in front of him. He had not read them as much as he wanted to, but it was enough to get him started.

Sean took a last gulp of his coffee and packed up his files, shoving them into a black leather shoulder bag, next to his computer. He then left the café and trotted across the street. The library was in an old stone building that had some modern parts connected to it. Still it looked elegant. He strode up several steps and approached the entrance. The library had opened just a few minutes earlier.

The first set of double doors swung inward and Sean walked in. The second set gave way and Sean found himself standing in the entranceway of a large, high-ceilinged room. In front of him, metal detectors guarded a path around a large book checkout counter. Sean walked through the detector and also through a turnstile. On his left he could see a middle-aged man with a bald head behind the counter. He was staring at a computer screen. As the turnstile squeaked the man looked up. He looked at Sean for a moment and then swiveled on his high stool to face him.

"Good morning," he said. Sean thought immediately that the man had to be a real librarian, not just a counter clerk. He had a kind scholarly air about him.

"Good morning," Sean returned the greeting. He began walking towards him.

"How can I help you?" the man asked.

"I'm here from out of town to do some research today," Sean explained.

"Oh." The man looked at Sean for a moment. "Where have you come to us from?"

"Mostly Seattle," Sean said, smiling. "But lately I've been everywhere." He reached his hand out. "Sean Johnson."

The librarian shook Sean's hand as he replied, "Henry Myers."

Suddenly Henry turned his head sideways a little and examined Sean more closely.

"Are you the Sean Johnson of that caper down in South Carolina?" he asked, his eyes lighting up a little.

"One and the same," Sean replied.

"Oh, well it's very good to meet you, Mr. Johnson. It's an honor." He extended his hand back out to Sean and this time shook his hand firmly and repeatedly.

"Please, it's just Sean."

"Certainly, Sean. Wow." Henry paused and sat up straight. "So how can I help you?"

Sean looked around. As near as he could tell he was the first and only patron of the library. "Well, first I would like to ask a favor of you."

"Anything, anything at all," Henry replied.

"You see, I'm on an important research project that is supposed to remain quiet until I'm done. But I tend to draw a lot of attention. So it would be great if the fact that I'm here and what I'm looking at can remain, well, a secret for a little while."

Sean tried to give Henry a full and attentive smile.

Henry paused for a moment and then replied. "Certainly, Sean."

"Great, I really appreciate it. So I'm interested in early Charlotte history. In particular, the files on the Mecklenburg Resolves and the meeting that took place here in 1775. But also references to the meeting afterwards."

Henry smiled. "Well, you came to the right place. We have a significant repository on that. You know it's not very common for a public library to hold such ancient files. Usually they're at the state library or at some university."

Sean smiled. "I know. That's what brings me here."

"Oh, of course." Henry suddenly twitched and a frown came over his face.

"Oh, but I have some bad news. It's Saturday and those materials are locked up in an archive that only our head librarian can access. She's gone to Norfolk for the weekend. Normally, she would come in for a guest of your stature."

Sean frowned slightly but then smiled. "I see," he said. "Well, I can wait until Monday. In the meanwhile, I could use the time to go through general Charlotte history and perhaps some materials I brought."

Henry's face lit back up. "Certainly. We have some files in a back room I can provide today, too. In fact, this afternoon, I can set you up in a small research room." Henry looked around. "It's pretty calm right now, but soon our homeless will start coming in. Mostly they're harmless, but they can be a bit loud and awkward sometimes."

Sean laughed, but politely. "It's that way all over America. I understand."

"I actually thought you were a homeless man," Henry admitted and then seemed shocked by his own words. "I mean, not that you look homeless or anything, just that you were the first person to come in."

Sean laughed again, a bit louder this time. "No worries, I know exactly what you mean." Sean looked at his watch. "I better get busy."

"Oh yes, sorry." Henry pointed to the right. "I suggest you head to the tables around that corner. That will put you right in the middle of the history area and also close to the room I'll set you up in this afternoon. Sorry, but I can't leave this post until our afternoon folks get here."

"I'm fine. Thank you, Henry." Sean turned and headed around the corner to the history section.

Knoxville

"Good morning," Thomas said groggily. "Why do I think my weekend just got ruined?"

James laughed. "That's a fine way to greet your employer. I also know you better. Giving you more research isn't going to ruin your weekend. It's going to make your weekend glorious."

"At this very moment it doesn't feel that way."

"Now now, Thomas," James chided. "Did you get all those files to Sean yesterday?"

"I did. And last night I went to sleep early. I must have slept twelve hours." James could hear some rustling and he sensed that Thomas was waking up.

"Great. That means you're well-rested for your next assignment."

"Sure," Thomas replied. "Give me a second."

There were more rustling sounds and then Thomas spoke, sounding clearer and sharper. "Okay, I'm ready. Fire away."

"I need you to find everything you can about Grant's movements in the year before his election."

"1867?" Thomas asked.

"Very impressive."

"I memorized all the 19th century presidents for a U.S. History class. I recited their statistics in front of the class for extra credit," Thomas explained. "It's been stuck in my head ever since."

"Well, yes, 1867, at least the middle part and then going back one full year to mid-1866. The period around the inn encounter. We need a list of all the sources of information about who he traveled with, who he met, what he did and the like."

"Understood. I'll get right on it."

"Great. Thanks, Thomas."

"Glad to help."

*****

Thomas hung up the phone and glanced at the clock on his table. He was glad he had gone straight to sleep the night before, even if it was a Friday night. He had been exhausted. He now felt rested and ready to go at it again.

He got up and headed for the shower, knowing the Saturday librarians at the University Library were going to notice his presence all weekend again.

Gettysburg

James hung up the phone and walked back from the window to sit down. Kim was sitting at the table. Abby had not yet shown herself.

"Okay, Thomas is on it. We should have something from him tomorrow or tomorrow night," James said. "Any word from Sean?"

"No, nothing. I assume he's in Charlotte?"

"Thomas said that he got the files, so yes."

"Well, here we seem to be stuck a little bit," Kim said. "How do we know this story is true?"

James smiled. "This is coming from the woman whose family harbored an even more unbelievable secret?"

"I know, I know. I'm being the skeptic. But someone has to be."

"Your question is a good one," James said. "Don't get me wrong. In fact, good historians don't presume anything. But it's also worth noting that your family secret was a good example of how oral histories are often rooted in truths and sometimes fly in the face of accepted, established history."

"Okay. Are you avoiding my question?" Kim looked at James quizzically.

"No. Not at all. Just setting the background. In fact, one way to decide the credibility of a story is to confirm pieces of it. We have done some of that. We've identified in genealogy records that Tom Kinneson's grandfather lived when he was alleged to have lived. We've found records of the inn and also a deed in the grandfather's name that was probably where the inn was. It was an intersection of roads that crossed over the Appalachians and also along the foot of them. We can also place Grant traveling through there at that time."

"That does not prove the story, though," Kim pointed out.

"No, but it tells us the first part, that the oral history is rooted in truth. We also know that it is not certain whether the actual script of the Gettysburg Address has been found. We also know the versions vary somewhat." James paused and looked at the quotes on the easel. "So all in all, the story seems plausible and reasonable. We'll never know for sure what was said. But if those clues take us somewhere, then we'll have good reason to believe that even the quotes are correct."

"Okay, I give," Kim said. "That takes us back to those quotes."

They both stared at the easel in silence.

CHAPTER TWENTY

Charlotte

Sean was sitting at his hotel desk sipping coffee he made from the in-room coffee maker. After a long day at the library, he had headed out in his car and driven around until sunset. Charlotte was a pleasant city, perched on rolling hills that gave lots of great views. The soil in the area seemed rich, even still after hundreds of years of extractive agriculture. He understood how it would have been an attractive land to settlers and immigrants.

His hotel was also nice. It was an older hotel remodeled and part of a modern chain. The lobby areas were nice, even if the rooms were a bit cramped. He had been so tired Saturday night, that all he had done was eat in the bar while half-watching a baseball game on the television. He then stumbled up to his room and went to sleep.

Now, Sunday morning, he felt much more rested. He also felt like he had a bit of a free day. He was determined to use the time to think through what had been happening. He was also determined to finish his second article and get it to his editor early.

Looking at his watch, he decided to call Kim. He picked up his cell and called her special cell phone.

"Hello," he heard her mumble.

"Good morning," Sean replied. "I'm sorry, I've woken you."

"No. I mean yes, but it's okay," Kim explained. "Hold on a minute."

He heard rustling, then the click of a door and the sound of running water. Then after a minute she came back on. "I'm so glad you called. I was getting worried about you."

Sean chuckled. "I can tell. You had to brush your teeth before you talked to me."

"Listen, Sean," Kim began and then realized Sean was teasing her. "Fine. You're lucky I took your call at all."

"I do miss you," Sean said, suddenly feeling sad. "It's lonely down here in Charlotte."

"Are you done?"

"No." Sean proceeded to tell Kim about his day at the library. "So I've got a good day tomorrow. And it looks like Lenoir may be next, which is at least northward from here."

"Lenoir?"

"Thomas found a few references up there that are promising."

"Well, up here we're making decent progress on things. But I think we might be at a wall. How much longer are we being paid for the Mecklenburg work?"

"Really, we're half-paid already. But we're supposed to pursue it until we're told it's too late. We're burning through the advanced expenses as well. I think we'll be done this week, one way or another. I kind of plan to force it that way with Joe."

"Do be careful, Sean. Something tells me this could get ugly. Abby and I both spotted the people watching us yesterday. They look like government."

"Yes, I'm pretty sure that is the FBI. Like I said, they're really your protection, though they don't know that. Even if the FBI is being played, I trust them to be good honest people."

"I'd have said that about all FBI agents before what happened," Kim pointed out.

"That was one man, not the organization," Sean replied. "And they treated me fairly in investigating my killing of their own agent. That's what makes America America. We respect freedom and human rights."

Sean decided to change the topic. "How's Abby?"

"Sleeping hard right now. That's the reason why I came in here to the bathroom, you oaf."

Sean laughed and Kim went on. "You're right, she's totally into what we're doing. We also had a great mother-daughter talk last night. She's fully on for going to the judge and telling him there is no way she will go to Texas cooperatively. She's also more than willing to lead her father on, though I feel guilty about that. I've always tried to show her that I respect her father, even if I don't."

"She really doesn't think that much of him," Sean said. "But she may later."

Sean paused as an idea came over him. "Hey, I just had a great idea. I'm going to do stories on both of our new mysteries. How about if I co-author the Gettysburg Address piece with her?"

"Oh, she will love it."

"Okay, then the next time I see or talk to her I'll ask if she'll join me on it."

"Thanks, Sean."

"You're welcome, but I really want to do it for her and for me."

"I don't mean that," Kim said. "You know what I mean."

Sean sighed. "I do. But it's me that wants to thank you. When this work is over, we need to sit down and talk about how to craft our lives together."

"Agreed," Kim said.

"But in the meanwhile," Sean replied, sounding serious, "let's carefully finish this off."

Eastern Pennsylvania

The highway restaurant was a chain known for its country theme. But Ken and Alex really just wanted a chance to talk. They both had lunches and coffee in front of them.

"So, when you joined this, is this what you expected?" Ken asked.

"Pretty much," Alex said. "But, I'll admit it's pretty overwhelming."

"Yeah, but I would follow Huerta anywhere. I served with him in Iraq when we were called up."

Alex picked at his food. "Most of our recruits are like us. Pretty ticked off at the lack of appreciation the government has. And disgusted with our government. I'm not sure this is the way to fix it, though."

"Are you kidding?" Ken asked. "It's the only way. We're getting bloated and fat as a country and as a government. Nothing is going to fix itself. It needs us to shake things up."

"But we're now essentially terrorists."

"No, we're not, Alex. We're patriots. That's yet another example of how stupid things have become. We're not trying to hurt Americans, just help them. But we will be a threat to our government, to the bureaucrats in control in D.C. You watch how fast Pennsylvanians join us."

"If they get a chance," Alex replied. "But that's our job. To make sure they get a chance to choose."

"Exactly," Ken agreed. "We're only using the amount of force necessary to preserve our cause. That is one of our core principals."

"Well, it's going to get hot. My team will do its job, though."

"Mine also," Ken replied.

FSA Headquarters

"Good evening," Joe answered Kelly's call, trying to take the same stiff professional tone that Kelly preferred.

"Good evening," Kelly replied.

"Where are you?" Joe asked.

"In Gettysburg. But there is no Johnson here. The rest of his team, yes. But Johnson must be somewhere else."

"Hmm, that's probably good news," Joe said. "What is the team doing?"

"They're mostly holed up in a hotel room, in a war room they've set up. Sometimes they come out for a walk, like to a restaurant. The professor has gone to a few shops and talked earnestly with people there."

"About what?"

"I don't know and that brings up another dynamic. This place is crawling with FBI agents. They're maintaining a smothering twenty-four-hour surveillance on Johnson's team."

"That's interesting."

"But they're so incompetent it's pathetic," Kelly replied, showing a rare hint of emotion. "They stand out like sore thumbs. They have to know they're being watched."

"Or protected?" Joe asked.

"No, it's surveillance. The FBI is acting pretty incompetently, but they don't seem to know it. They're truly trying to secretly watch Johnson's team. And that's why," Kelly went on, "I don't know what they're talking about. I can't get that close to them without risking detection by the FBI."

"Understood," Joe said grimly. "We need you for more important things in the coming weeks, as you know. These people are not worth taking risks over. Maybe we should pull you out?"

"I'm being careful," Kelly replied. "Fred told me about their mission. It seemed important to him."

"Okay. It would be good to know now if they're close to finding it."

"Well," Kelly said, "I think I could sneak into their war room while they're out during the day. The FBI seems to significantly drop their attention toward the hotel when all three of them are out."

"That's risky," Joe pointed out. "The FBI could have video surveillance of the hotel."

"No, I don't think they do. So far there are few signs of electronics being used here. I kind of sense they threw this together at the last minute."

"Your decision then," Joe said. "I'll contact Sean and find out where he is. Anything else?"

"No, that's it," Kelly replied.

They hung up. Joe put his phone down on the desk and walked out to the mapped table. He stared at the map under the plastic for a minute while thinking about the implications of intense FBI surveillance on the research team. He couldn't understand how the FBI could have determined that Johnson's group was doing anything that could be connected to something dangerous. The level of effort also surprised him. That told him they were after something that they perceived to be a big threat. *That's us. But how did they know that?* As Joe thought, he reached the inevitable conclusion. *We have a leak!*

Washington D.C.

Chapman came into Emmitt's office. He looked up and waved at her to sit down. She plopped herself down heavily.

"We still have no idea where Mr. Johnson is," she said simply. "There's been no communication from his cell phone since the afternoon we interviewed him."

Emmitt turned his head. "Really. So he dumped it right after our interview."

"Most likely," Alice replied.

"Hmm. He's a professional."

"Yes he is. We don't have his service record yet, but I got someone to walk me through its contents. First, it has classified portions. They must be pretty classified because the level of classification is classified. That means he was a spook," Alice surmised.

"Yes, it does," Emmitt agreed. "Okay, we need to treat him with much more respect." Emmitt paused for a moment. "Christ, our effort at interrogating him must have been buffoonery to him." Emmitt put his head in his hands. "His voicemail?"

"Not yet, the phone company is being a bit slow on the weekend. All the recent stories of spying on citizens has them more methodical. They provided information, the phone's whereabouts, but their lawyers have to examine the warrant. So probably not until Monday."

Emmitt thought for a moment. "Misler's research?"

"She and a few others are working hard right now. Probably all night. She's getting access to material now. So far Franklin looks clean."

"And Franklin himself?"

"We haven't been able to find a cell phone registered to him. No sign of him either."

"Well then, it's time to search his house. Hit it tomorrow morning. I think it's time for you to move up to the command center anyway. Have a good IT team ready to evaluate his computers on site right after you get in."

"Yes, Sir." Alice looked at him questioningly.

"Because otherwise it will take three days, Agent Chapman. But if we bring them on the raid, sit them down in front of the stuff we find and tell them they get to go home when they produce something, well, then things will happen very quickly."

"Understood." Alice smiled. "If I'm heading out into the field, I'll put Dana Misler as contact point for all the various leads out there. Yes, she can handle it."

Emmitt smiled. "Thanks."

"Where do we contact you?" Alice asked.

"Right here, or at least in the building. I will be using the bunkroom for the time being."

"Okay," Alice replied. "I better get moving if I'm going to hit Franklin's house by tomorrow morning."

Emmitt watched Chapman leave, and suddenly felt tired. He turned and looked out the window of his office, trying to make sense of all the pieces in his hands. *There is always a solution to a puzzle*, he remembered being taught. *The trick was solving it before the solution was made obvious by more pieces.*

CHAPTER TWENTY-ONE

Harrisville

Agent Chapman pounded on the door.

"FBI," she yelled loudly. "Open up, we're here with a search warrant."

After waiting an obligatory time, she stepped back and aside and nodded at a young man wearing the same style blue-colored jacket as she with the word "FBI" in large yellow letters on the back.

The man pulled a kit out from under his jacket and examined the locks on the door. Then he flipped open the kit, selected several slender metal picks and deftly inserted them into the two locks. He began wiggling and twisting the tools and in about twenty seconds the front door opened, causing a deafening siren to hit their ears. He immediately jumped back next to Chapman and a small team of agents covered in battle dress advanced inward with pistols and riot guns brandished.

The agents entering also called out "FBI" as they stormed in but the siren mostly drowned out the sound. Alice waited for about one minute before she decided to head in. She gestured to the others behind her to follow. She stepped into a large living room nicely furnished with plush chairs, a sofa, and art adorning the walls and most surfaces. There was no one in the room. Doors led in several directions.

She looked behind her and saw the IT personnel she was looking for. "Karl, Beth!" she yelled to make herself heard over the siren. "Find the computers, make sure they're safe and start cracking!" Two young looking people jumped forward with large briefcases in their hands. They stood in the living room for a moment and then split up, each taking a different door. Just then one of the battle-dressed agents came back.

"All clear, Agent Chapman!" he yelled. "We'll keep two armed guards present in the building and start through the grounds!"

Alice nodded and then set off on her own to find the siren and disable it. She found it right around the corner of the first hallway she went into. It was up against the ceiling just beyond her reach. Frustrated, she retreated back to the living room.

She spotted her lock picker. "You, go disable that alarm. I don't care how you do it, just shut the damn siren off."

The young man nodded and headed down the corridor. Very shortly after that Alice heard the sound of shattering plastic and the siren ended. Silence finally descended on the team.

"Okay, let's go. Everyone has an assignment," Alice directed.

FSA Headquarters

Joe looked at the email that had just popped up on his computer. *It took you long enough*, he thought. Still, his thoughts went back to the revealed fact that the FBI was closely monitoring the team in Gettysburg. They had clearly held off on his home, hoping he would return. At least Fred's warning had been solid. That meant that his source in the FBI was credible. But for the FBI to be this close with so many people, they had to be getting information from within his team. He could not, however, for the life of him, think of who it might be. He had set up essentially everyone to be equally exposed should things fail. Except for one. They had mostly sheltered their lobbyist partner, Steven Ableman. *Is it you, Steven?*

It had to be either him or they had a true spy or mole. In either case, Joe decided, what did not make sense was why the FBI wasn't already beating down the door of the warehouse.

Sighing, Joe began deleting the forwarding trail of the alarm email that had reached his computer. He knew they would still trace it, but it would take longer and still not actually reveal where he was.

North of Gettysburg

James, Abby and Kim settled into the living room of the house they had driven up to. Across from them an elderly man lowered himself into his chair. He looked to be in his eighties. His hair was thinned and his frame seemed a bit shaky, but his eyes were sharp.

John Manning spoke up. "Welcome to my home, Professor. It's an honor to have you visit. I heard you were down in Gettysburg." John's voice had a certain sing-song quality that James Enloe knew came from northern Alabama.

"It's my and our honor, John," James said. "You're an esteemed expert on Grant. I'm just a history teacher."

"No, you're all quite amazing historical sleuths," John said, smiling. "Your find in South Carolina sounds fascinating."

"All in a day's work," James said humbly but clearly pleased with the praise. "We do really appreciate your time today."

"So, you want to know about Grant and Gettysburg?" John asked.

"Yes," James said. He then briefly summarized the mystery they were working on.

"Fascinating," John said when James was done. "But I don't believe a word of it. Even if it happened, and Grant was handed this missing copy of the Gettysburg Address, why would he hide it? Grant was too honest of a man. Now, he might have handed it to someone else who might have done something with it."

James started to speak, but Abby beat him to it. "How can you say that?" Abby asked. "Aren't you supposed to have an open mind?"

Kim reached her hand across Abby's lap. "Abigail, you need to be much more polite. We are guests in this man's house."

"It's okay, Ms. Poole," the old man said. He looked at Abby. "You're right, Miss. I am just an old historian quite stuck in my ways. I'm also used to expressing my opinion. And what you just heard is my opinion. I might be wrong. But I don't think I am."

"Mr. Manning," Kim said, "let's pretend that the encounter happened like it was described. Do you have any insight into what Grant might have meant?"

John Manning thought for a moment. "He admired Lincoln. So the phrase sounds like something he might say. I will give you that. But you need to understand something. The Gettysburg Address was not a big deal at that time. Really, Lincoln's speech becomes a minor event for a decade or two or three. But it gradually re-emerges and takes on a legendary status. But at the time it was not major news. It was not a rallying cry for Union soldiers heading into battle. It's possible that Grant never even knew about the speech until much later, perhaps after the war or even while he was president."

John paused and thought. "So, if he did react to this version and put it somewhere out of sight, it had to have been about what it said and what it meant for the legacy of Lincoln and perhaps the war. Perhaps even for his own legacy. That all suggests that speech contained something related to post-Civil-War reconstruction. But I really doubt it did. It was a short speech to dedicate a cemetery. That was all."

Gettysburg

Kelly had walked the corridor twice and decided it was time. He stopped at room 408, put on a pair of latex gloves he'd stashed in his pocket, and slid a master key he had lifted from a maid's cart in through the slot. The door clicked open and Kelly moved quickly into the room. He turned around and shut the door behind him. He knew he was now trapped if it turned out the FBI was watching the door. Fortunately he had nothing incriminating on him and could later claim he got lost. He had also brought nothing with him at all, not even his wallet.

He glanced around the room, seeing piles of papers, computers and the like. His eyes were drawn to a particular set of papers taped to one wall. One had a timeline on it with dates in the 1860's. Another had dates in the 1700's. The third one had two phrases written on it that made no sense at all. He quickly repeated the two phrases until he thought he could repeat them from memory. He then examined the two timelines. It became apparent that one was about the Mecklenburg Convention and the other was about Grant's movements and activities during and after the war. He then walked around the table looking for any other clues. He read some of the notes, moved a few papers around.

A few minutes later he emerged in the hallway, shut the door behind him and began walking down the hallway to the stairs that connected all the floors. As he passed a trashcan built into the wall, he tossed the room key into it. He also pulled off the latex gloves and stuffed them into his pocket. He then began trotting down the stairs like a tourist eager to see the sites.

Baltimore Command Center

Alice was sitting at a desk in a cubicle next to a large meeting room table. They had found a recently vacated company office in a commercial building and quickly moved into it. The office had plenty of desks, cubicles and chairs. It also had a massive meeting room table that they had pulled from the meeting room and shoved right in the middle of the cubicles. Techies were still walking around connecting things, but they already had usable landlines and a connection to the Internet. Their own mini-network was supposedly a few minutes away.

She had stayed at Franklin's house for about a half an hour and then made the drive back down to the command center, where she knew she would be more effective.

After skimming her email she settled in to study the report Misler had completed on Franklin. *Still not very much.* Franklin clearly brought money in from overseas, but it was all declared and spent or invested in an open manner. Then an email reminder popped up on her screen. She clicked on it and saw it was an email from one of the techies at the house. She opened it and read for a few minutes. It was an email in an account they had found had been used by the alarm system to email another account when an alarm went off.

He had a trip wire waiting for us, Alice thought.

But that email had revealed the next email address and they had been able to access that one for a little while using information from another computer. Then, suddenly, the account access ended. *Did he see us hacking in?* The technician had captured one email and sent it to her. It read:

"*Thanks for the information. As you know, secrecy remains our most important weapon. If found out, there will be some who accuse us of wrongdoing. Of course, in reality, what we are doing is nothing less than what our founding fathers did when they declared independence.*"

The excerpt was unsigned and both email addresses, the to and from, revealed nothing in their names.

Alice hit "reply" to the technician, telling her to keep digging and to forward the email account information to the technology center in Kansas City so they could go after the account records. It had been a free Internet email account from one of the big mega-hosters. They would likely cooperate with the FBI.

Alice then picked up the phone to call Agent Talie.

CHAPTER TWENTY-TWO

Charlotte

The room was really more of a cage within a room. He could see that the room had its own ventilation system, which was probably to better preserve the documents. Still, he couldn't help but think that the whole collection would be better off in a state or university archive where specialists could oversee its care.

But right now, Sean was not complaining. This was because it seemed like the entire library was bending over backwards for him. Clearly, Henry had not managed to keep it a secret that he was here. The head librarian had come in early Monday morning and pulled some files she thought Sean would be interested in. And she had been right.

He was sitting at a table with a notepad next to him and using only a pencil. He also had latex gloves on so as to not rub his oils on the documents. He had adopted this as his special document handling process, but it didn't appear that the library would have required special precautions from him.

Open in front of him was the fourth file from the stack of documents. It was a correspondence file from the early 1800's. The particular letter he was examining was from someone who was then a state senator, writing to a university president. Most of the correspondence involved this senator, who had clearly been an advocate for the fact that the Mecklenburg Declaration had existed. This particular letter intrigued Sean because it made reference to a Mason named Frederick Rellman. The senator was explaining that Rellman claimed to know where the Mecklenburg Declaration was. That was pretty significant to Sean so he began jotting down all sorts of information on the file, the senator, the dates, the names, et cetera.

Gettysburg

"Hello?" James answered hesitantly.

"Hi, James. Sean here."

"Oh, hello, Sean. I didn't recognize the number."

"It's the head librarian's office phone at the Charlotte Main Library," Sean chuckled. "So it's no wonder you did not recognize it."

"Ah, so I suspect you will now tell me you found the Mecklenburg Declaration."

At James's words, Abby looked up sharply. Kim was not in the war room at the moment. James smiled at Abby as if to tell her he was joking. She scowled at him.

"No, I wish it were so," Sean replied. "But I examined some correspondence around a state senator that truly believed in it. Back in or around 1810."

"Interesting."

"So there were clearly a bunch of Masons in this group. There's reference to one Mason named Frederick Rellman who told people he knew where it was."

"Go on," James prompted.

"That's about it. I mean I now have a handle on most everything contemporaneous with the Mecklenburg Convention. But it isn't much. But I do have to admit that I'm a bit lost when it comes to Masons. I mean, I've seen a few movies that mention them. And I see the old Mason halls in every town. They must have been a pretty big group at the time."

"Ah, now I understand your inquiry," James said. "Correct, the Masons were a centuries-old men's club that spread like wildfire in the first century and a half of American history. Most respectable men of means wanted to join a club that was selective in who it allowed to join. The

Masonic Society is still a decently strong organization. Back in the day, though, they were very selective, very secretive. They used code and ciphers to write each other. In fact, the Freemasons, which is the full correct name of the Masons, provided coded communication for American spies operating under the noses of the British in the Revolutionary War."

"So, you're saying there were lots of them?" Sean asked.

"Yes, and they liked to dramatize and sensationalize some as well."

"Okay, well that's it from me. I better get off this phone soon," Sean said. "How goes the hunt for the Gettysburg Address?"

"Not well," James admitted. "I expect to get some details from Thomas in a bit on Grant and his activities at the time. With that, we're going to read and brainstorm and see if we can think of anything else to solve the riddle of Grant and what he might have done with the Gettysburg Address. We just had a historian essentially tell us we were wasting our time."

"Okay," Sean said. "Understood. Gotta go."

James took the hint and said goodbye.

Washington D.C.

Ted Hines swept his arm towards the chair.

"Hi, Rick," he said to his chief of staff.

Rick Seals was Ted Hines's long-serving supporter and political leader. But Ted knew he was about to set him back on his heels.

"What did you need, Senator?" Rick was always formal and deferential to Ted. He always had been. When Ted ascended to the Senate, Rick had become even more devoted and deferential.

"I need a press conference set up and announced for Friday at five o'clock."

Rick tilted his head. "What? What for, Senator?"

"You know very little about this other than you know my political views about states' rights versus our obscene federal government."

Rick smiled. "We share those views. I almost feel like I talked you down that path."

"Well, for a number of years I've been working with a select group of folks to start a movement back towards states' rights."

Rick smiled some more. "This is funny, Senator."

"Don't laugh. I even did this under your nose. Not because I didn't want to share it with you, but to protect you."

Rick looked confused. Senator Hines knew the moment of truth was at hand. If he could not sway Rick to his cause then he knew they were all wasting their time.

"What we are going to do is demand the right for our state, Pennsylvania, to decide whether or not to stay within the United States."

He let that sit for a moment. Rick's confused look gave way to astonishment.

"Our organization is the Free States of America, or FSA. We are very, very well funded. I'm going to give a speech Friday night to announce ourselves and our intentions to the country. When I do this, there will be some who will brand me a traitor. Probably even a terrorist. I expect to be at least placed under house arrest. But my words will resonate with many, including some other senators and representatives."

Rick started to say something, but Ted held his hands up.

"Wait, let me finish. We have established a special state militia and will be simultaneously taking some actions over the course of the night to protect Pennsylvanians' right to vote whether or not to exit the United States. We will propose a constitutional convention to be attended by other states that wish to reshape things. I will be protected very effectively. And I'm not afraid of what fate may bring me. I will consider it an honor to serve my country in this manner. Okay, Rick, you can breathe."

Rick sat silently for a long moment. He started to speak twice and then closed his mouth. Finally, he took on a grin that looked almost evil to the senator.

"Count me in, Senator. I've believed in you this far, I'll follow you to the end."

It was the senator's opportunity to be stunned. *Hallelujah!* he thought. *We have a chance.*

Gettysburg

"Joe," he said simply into the phone.

"Kelly, here," Kelly replied. He was sitting in his car by the highway that ran along one side of Gettysburg.

"How was your day, Kelly?" Joe asked.

"Good, I made it into the war room when the trio took off in the car somewhere. They're definitely hard at work on the document. It also looks like they have somehow connected it to Grant and the postwar years."

"Really?" Joe sounded very interested now. Kelly briefly explained what he had seen in the room. When he finished, he waited for Joe to digest the information.

Finally, after some scribbling, Joe spoke up. "Grant and the Gettysburg Address? I would never have thought that. It makes sense that Sean is in North Carolina. I left him a voicemail yesterday but haven't heard back at all." Joe was rambling, which was a fault as far as Kelly was concerned.

"Do you need anything else from me?" he asked.

"Just stay handy and safe down there. Something may come of this yet."

"Roger," Kelly said and hung up the phone. He looked around his surroundings for a moment and then decided to drive back into downtown Gettysburg and enjoy a better meal than anything he would find out on the highway.

CHAPTER TWENTY-THREE

Washington D.C.

"Talie," Emmitt said as he snatched his phone up.

"Good morning, Sir," Alice replied.

"Ah, Agent Chapman. I didn't recognize the number."

"It's the landline at the command center."

"Okay, fire away."

"You saw my report on the raid on Franklin's house?"

"Yes," Emmitt replied.

"And the email we captured?"

"Yes. Pretty amazing that they, or he, compared the effort to the American Revolution."

"Yes, Sir. I think we now know they're planning something serious."

"I'm scheduled to brief the high brass in two hours," Emmitt explained, looking at his desk clock. "What else?"

"I understand that we have been given access to Mr. Johnson's cell phone voicemail. If that produces anything, I will let you know right away."

"Good. What else?"

"Only that we still have no sighting of Johnson and Dana hasn't gotten any farther on records."

"Very well, don't let me slow you down. Besides, I need to polish up my report."

Emmitt hung up his phone and went back to the presentation on his computer.

Charlotte

"Good morning," Thomas said, answering his phone. "Based on the area code this is either Sean, Professor Enloe or Kim."

"Right on the first one." Sean said, smiling.

"Oh, hi, Sean, what's up," Thomas said. "I was really expecting it to be Professor Enloe. He seems to love dumping research on me in the morning."

"Now it's my turn. I came across a Rellman, a Mason." Sean continued to explain what he had found and what he wanted.

"Okay, this sounds like a quick search. I'll tackle it right away," Thomas promised.

"Okay, thanks." Sean hung up his phone. He was sitting at his desk sipping room-made coffee again. He decided he was going to leave Charlotte in the morning and head north. Either to Lenoir, or back up to Gettysburg. While he was trying to think of what to do next, he realized he had not checked voicemail on his old phone. Sean considered whether calling it from either his phone or hotel room mattered. He decided going straight into voicemail wouldn't register anything traceable.

So he picked his cell back up and called his voicemail. The first message was from his editor, Paul, asking for the promised story. The second one was also from his editor thanking him for his story. He deleted both, smiling. *Two stories done.*

The next message was from Joe. It was a short, simple message asking Sean to contact Joe right away. He listened to the time stamp and found it was Sunday. The next message was from FBI agent Talie, asking Sean to contact him. The final message was from Joe again, this time, Sean determined, last night. He said the fuse was burning out and he needed the document as soon as possible or it would be a scratch. *I guess I need to call him. I've stalled him long enough.* He hung up the phone, not actually having deleted the last message.

He sat there at his desk for a few more minutes and then decided to call Kim. It rang but the person who answered it was James. "Hi, is this Sean?" James asked.

"Yes," Sean replied, the hair on the back of his neck rising. "I thought so. Kim and Abby are out taking a walk, but she forgot her special bat phone."

"Oh." *Whew!*

"How are things in Charlotte?"

"Fine, I guess," Sean replied. "I am leaving in a little while, trying to decide where else to go, if anywhere. Also, I think it's time to call Joe." He elaborated on both calls from Joe.

"I agree," James said. "Are you going to string him along?"

"Yes, that was the plan but I think it's time we spoke. I can't keep him dangling forever."

"Well, good luck."

"Thanks." Sean ended the call. He then looked up Joe's number from a short list he had and decided to call Joe from the hotel phone. He dialed the number and Joe answered on the third ring.

"Hello."

"Hi, Joe, this is Sean."

"Sean, I've been wondering why you've been avoiding me."

"Not avoiding. After you arranged for me to disappear, I took it to heart and really disappeared. I'm down in Charlotte and just cleared my voicemail. I hadn't wanted to call you unless I had some good news."

"Ah, so no good news then?" Joe asked, slightly disappointed.

"Well, actually, I have moderately good news. We've been unraveling a very complex set of clues and I think we're close to finding it, if it still exists."

"So you think the Mecklenburg Declaration actually exists?" Joe asked.

"Yes, I do. I've found references to it by enough people that I think it had to have existed, that it had to have been real. But we also have some later references to individuals who say they had it. So I think it survived into the 1800's."

"Well, that is good news. But I have to temper it some. I need it in my hands by Friday."

Sean paused for a good five seconds. "That hardly seems reasonable, Joe. I may not have it by then."

"You remember our conversation where I told you we were preparing to go public?" Joe asked.

"I do."

"Well, we are doing that Friday night with a major speech and a major splash. We either have it by then or we don't."

"Okay." Sean tried to sound frustrated.

"But I do have some good news. Our benefactors will double again the finder's fee for it. Just get it to me by Friday night." To Sean's ear, Joe was partly lying. *He wants it by then for sure. But he just made up the part about paying more.*

"Okay, I will do my best. But if I reach Friday, you want me to stop?"

"Let's just say everything changes on Friday. But let's not talk about what happens if you don't have it. I believe in your ability to find it in time."

Knoxville

Thomas found something very quickly. He quickly called the number that Sean had called from. It barely rang before Sean answered.

"Hi, Thomas."

"I think I have something for you. And it's related to Lenoir, that town north of you."

"Go ahead," Sean said.

"I found some other references regarding Mecklenburg up in Lenoir. It was not clear if it was the Mecklenburg Resolves or the Mecklenburg Declaration. Some of the references related to raids by a Union General named Stonemason, who came through Lenoir in 1865. Anyway, I now think there's a chance that there is a coded diary of a Mason at the museum in Lenoir. I think that Mason might be the Rellman you're looking for, because I think Rellman itself was a simple code for the name Robert Fellman."

"Okay," Sean said, slowly digesting the information. "Am I going to be able to read the code?"

"Oh, sorry," Thomas said, "It looks like the diaries, they're actually something like eight of them spanning 40-plus years, were decoded by a Duke history grad student. They were returned to Lenoir along with the translation."

"Hmm," Sean said. "It's safe to say then that the diaries do not say 'This way to the Mecklenburg Declaration.'"

"Well, they kind of might. Some Masons used code upon code. So the grad student could have deciphered the simple code but still not understood a reference to one thing was a reference to another."

"I'm headed to Lenoir then," Sean said. "Can you email a summary of where I'm going?"

"I sure will," Thomas promised.

"Great work, Thomas!"

*****

Sean hung up the phone. Suddenly he felt in a hurry and downright excited. But he forced himself to sit and think through the implications of all of his calls.

"Things are getting interesting!" he said out loud as he got up to pack up his room.

CHAPTER TWENTY-FOUR

Washington D.C.

Emmitt scanned the report that had just arrived and decided to print it. He sent it to the printer out in the hallway and then headed out there to pick it up. Several minutes later, he picked up his phone and called Misler.

"Hello?" Dana's pleasant voice answered.

"Misler, Talie. Have you seen the report Chapman just filed?" Emmitt asked with little preamble.

"Yes, Sir," she replied. "I just finished reading it."

"Well, I want you to get me everything on this lobbyist, Steven Ableman. All of his required reports, anything else you can find. You've got thirty minutes."

He hung up and called Chapman next.

"Chapman," Alice answered smartly.

"Chapman, great report. So, we have a message from our Samuel Franklin, going as 'Joe' to Johnson. He's putting the pressure on Johnson to deliver. Something is going to happen. I'm putting two agents down here to work trying to find this lobbyist that we connected to Franklin. Misler is digging up everything we can find." Emmitt paused and Alice quietly waited for him. He finally realized he hadn't asked her a question or told her to do anything.

"Sorry, Chapman, I'm feeling the fatigue around the edges. I want you to go all out on finding Johnson. Have Lentz pay a visit to the team in Gettysburg. Have some people start tracking down every one of his contacts. I want Johnson."

He hung up the phone and leaned back in his chair. "Something is going to happen on my watch," he said aloud to the ceiling. "And I don't know what or exactly when. But it's soon."

Lenoir

Sean pulled his car into the Caldwell County Heritage Museum parking lot. In front of him was what looked like an old schoolhouse. He grabbed a set of files and pulled a notebook out of his pocket, hopped out of the car and headed up the steps and into the museum. As the door closed behind him, he found himself looking at display cases in front and to the right and a registration area on the left. There was an older lady sitting in a chair reading a book. She looked up at Sean and smiled.

"Good morning, Sir," she said in very clear voice. "Welcome to the Caldwell County Heritage Museum. Won't you sign in?"

Sean smiled. "Certainly."

He put his materials on the counter and signed the book. He saw a note about admission costing three dollars. So he pulled a five-dollar bill out of his pocket and placed it on the counter.

"Admission?" he asked, still smiling.

The lady stood up and walked the few steps to the counter.

"Oh, yes. Thank you." As she was processing his admission, Sean asked, "Is Mr. O'Malley here?"

The lady hesitated. "Oh, I'm sorry, he's out doing an interview today. Did you have a meeting with him?"

Sean noticed that she had stopped processing his admission.

"No, it's spur of the moment, but important." He gestured at the money on the counter. "Please, I do want admission. And please have the museum keep the change."

"Certainly, Mr. ah…"

"Johnson, ma'am, Sean Johnson. And who might you be?"

"I'm Alice Divans, Mr. Johnson."

Sean decided she would truly prefer to refer to him as "mister" so he stopped himself from correcting her.

"Well, Mrs. Divans, I am glad to meet you. I would love to look around some and then probably come back tomorrow. You don't have a number for Mr. O'Malley, do you?"

Alice Divans handed Sean a receipt she had filled out. "Yes I think I do. He carries a cell phone. Let me find that number." Alice walked off to the desk behind where she was sitting and began rummaging around.

"Is this an old school?" he asked.

"Yes, in fact this was a girls college at the time of the war." She came over to him with a business card and handed it to him. "This building was built in 1926 and was part of the Davenport College of Lenoir for women, which opened its doors in 1858. It survived the war but not the Depression." Alice shook her head sadly.

"You certainly know your history," Sean said smiling.

Alice blushed slightly. "Oh, I'm just a volunteer here, but I do care much about our museum."

Sean thanked her and began wandering through the exhibits. Finally he came back to her.

"So, I suppose you wouldn't be able to point me to some records you have on microfiche."

Alice shook her head. "I'd try Mr. O'Malley."

"I think I'll head over to the library and give him a call on my way. Thank you so much for your hospitality."

Alice beamed. "You are very welcome, Mr. Johnson."

Sean walked out of the museum and headed to his car. He looked at the card and punched in the cell phone for the director, Jeffery O'Malley. A few moments later it rang through to his voicemail.

"Hi, Mr. O'Malley, I was just at the museum where the pleasant Alice Divans helped me look around a little. I'm in town briefly for some urgent and important research that I think your museum can help me with. I understand you're out of town today, but if you get this message in time, I'm willing to come by anytime this afternoon or evening. Otherwise, I will plan on coming by first thing tomorrow. Thanks." Sean said his name and left his number twice.

He then sighed and got in his car and began following the directions he had for the library. He decided to contact the team back in Gettysburg and put in the call. A moment later, Kim answered.

"Hello, there you are," she said. "Hold on, I'm going to put you on speaker phone." There was a click and then she said, "Are you there?"

"I sure am," he replied.

He got back "Hi, Sean" in unison from James and Abby.

"Hello yourselves. How goes the hunt?"

"We're pounding through a ton of material Thomas sent us," James reported, sounding tired. "I think this is our last stab at it."

"Well, hang in there. I'm hot on the trail of a good lead but am stuck for the day. I think." Sean elaborated on where he was, what had brought him there. He finished by repeating Joe's latest comments about it all happening Friday.

"I'm afraid I led him on some, which seemed to work to get him to open up. I'll keep playing him along. I sense we'll be done getting paid Friday one way or another, but if my leads pan out, we'll still have something to do."

"Hopefully, we'll find our answers today," Abby called out. She had clearly regained her optimism and energy.

"What about you, Kim? Are you still hopeful?"

"I'm determined," she said. "You know me. I never like to give up. And I think there's still something we haven't thought of."

"Well, keep at it. I'm headed to the county library to bone up on Lenoir, the Stoneman raids and everything Mason."

They said goodbye and Sean hung up just as he was reaching what looked to be a very large library.

Gettysburg

Kim pushed the button to end the call and then looked around at her team.

"Okay, let's dig into this material. I think we should all read it through and then discuss it."

James and Abby agreed and she began parsing it out.

Washington D.C.

Emmitt finished reviewing the latest report. Misler had given him a full rundown on the lobbyist Ableman. It turned out that they had an old file on him that went back twenty years. They were still trying to find it. In the meanwhile, he now had a tail on the lobbyist, who appeared to be doing exactly what lobbyists do: talking to other lobbyists and meeting with elected officials or their staff.

He sighed and stood up to look out the window. He noticed how nice it seemed outside and realized he hadn't actually been outside for at least three days. As he thought about all that was going on, he decided that the Baltimore Command Center seemed like a better place for him to be. Or at least visit.

Having made up his mind, he turned around and began packing up some materials. He also unlocked his cabinet and removed his service pistol and holster and strapped it to his body. Finally ready, he shut down his computer and headed out the door with a briefcase in his hand.

Eastern Pennsylvania

"We're ready to deploy," General Huerta said. "Ken's group will go out first thing in the morning. Alex's team will leave at two in the afternoon."

Huerta and Joe were standing, staring at the map on the table. Outside the meeting room, down on the floor they could hear the sound of all the preparatory activity. Joe walked over to the window and looked down. He knew there were about forty men below, but it seemed like a very small group to take on a country. He sighed. "I will confirm with the senator and also see what the latest is on our historical document. The senator got excited when I told him we might have it in hand shortly."

"I always thought it to be a pipe dream," Huerta replied.

Joe turned away from the window and went into his mini office. He pulled up the number Sean had called him from and called it back. Sean answered promptly.

"Sean, Joe here. How goes it?"

There was a pause and then Sean replied, "I think I'm going to find it!"

Joe sounded less than impressed. "Today or tonight?"

"I'm going to look at a painting tomorrow morning," Sean replied.

"Based on a coded diary by a Mason that I just worked my way through, it was hidden behind a painting when Stoneman's raiders came through here."

"Who? What?" Joe sounded confused.

Sean laughed. "I'm in Lenoir, North Carolina. It's a long story, but I'm close to it. I can feel it."

Joe thought for a minute. Something told him that Sean was not being entirely truthful with him. But he could not find a reason for Sean to lie to him. *Except maybe greed.*

"Okay, Sean. This is great news. Keep me informed and tell me as soon as you have it. If you get it in your hands, please make plans to get it up here to Pennsylvania as fast as you can. Do you understand?"

Sean's voice came back without hesitation. "Completely."

Joe hung up and stared straight ahead. Finally he got up and walked out to the room to update the general.

CHAPTER TWENTY-FIVE

Lenoir

It was eight o'clock a.m. on the dot when a large sedan rolled into the parking lot. Sean got out of his car as a large man emerged from the sedan.

"Mr. Johnson?" the man asked.

"That's me. You must be Mr. O'Malley."

"Guilty as charged." The man smiled sheepishly and extended a huge hand to Sean.

Sean took it and they shook firmly.

"You can call me Jeff," he said.

"Great. And I'm Sean."

"You're the famous Sean Johnson," Jeff laughed. "That was some humdinger down in South Carolina. I read your own story on it just the other day."

Sean shook his head. "I've been so busy, I didn't even know the first one ran. I delivered the second story the other day."

"I'm certainly honored to have you stop by our little part of the country," Jeff said. "Come on inside and let me get a pot of coffee going."

"Now you're speaking my language," Sean replied, as he followed the large man inside.

A few minutes later, with cups of coffee in hand, they were standing in a back room of the museum building.

"So, you're after a peek at the Fellman diaries, I understand?"

"Yes, exactly."

"What exactly are you looking for?" Jeff asked.

"I'd rather not say just as yet. To be candid, there are a whole bunch of moving parts going on that are above my pay grade. It's all about something important." Sean paused and continued, "Really two important things."

"Fine by me. Your credentials are impeccable. Do you know what you're getting yourself into with these diaries?"

Sean shook his head and Jeff smiled.

"Okay, here's the inside scoop, Sean. Apparently Mr. Robert Fellman was a very dirty old man who was also very smart and also a Mason. He started his life down in Charlotte and ended up living it out here until just after the Civil War."

Jeff took a sip of his coffee and continued. "He kept a diary for a large portion of his life. When he filled up one book, he moved onto the next. About twenty years ago a young man stumbled upon the books when he was cleaning out his grandparents' house down near Hickory. They looked like a bunch of mumbo jumbo, but on impulse he brought them to us. We sent them to Duke, where the department of history realized we had provided a series of diaries written by a Mason, in code, covering roughly 1815 to 1858. A Duke University history master's student made it his thesis to decode them."

Jeff paused again, and this time, after a sip, he seemed to hesitate further.

"The books are amazing, Sean. The guy wrote down what he did, what he thought. But he also wrote extensively about other women, and it's very vulgar and blunt. I won't repeat it out loud. I just want you to be prepared for what you will find."

Sean nodded. "I can handle it," he said.

Jeff patted a small box. "The microfiche translation is in here as well as the un-translated version. We actually sent the originals back to Duke, where we felt they could be better cared for. You know how to use this reader?" Jeff patted the reader next to the box.

"Yep," Sean replied. "Too well."

"Okay then, I will leave you to it. Come on out for coffee when you need some. Let me know if you need anything else."

Sean moved up to the machine, took another gulp of coffee and then began his task.

Gettysburg

Kim was tired and finally ready to give up. Thomas had sent them an amazing amount of information about Grant's travels after the war. Yesterday, into the night and again this morning, they were sharing, discussing and even arguing about the importance of some fact. But it had gotten them nowhere. The simple truth was they had no idea what Grant might have done with the speech. *And that's even assuming he had it.*

Kim shook her head and looked over at Abby. Her daughter was scrolling through words on her computer screen. Across the table, even James looked like he had had enough. Kim stood up and stretched her arms. She too was ready to give in. But she still had a nagging feeling they had left a stone unturned. She walked to the window and then turned around to look at the papers strewn around the table. On the wall were sheets torn off of the easel pad. Her eyes came back to the two quotes they had gotten from Tom Kinneson. For the tenth time she read her way through them. *Real words at Gettysburg? That seems plain enough. In the memory of Lincoln? That was obvious enough as well.* But then she noticed one discrepancy. Grant had not just said "In the memory of Lincoln." He had said "It was in the memory of Lincoln." *That's weird.* She walked closer to the sheet of paper, staring at the words. Then it hit her.

"Oh my God!" She put her hand to her mouth.

Abby jumped up. "What? Mom, are you okay?"

James twisted around, looking confused. Kim stepped back.

"We've been misinterpreting this second phrase. Remember that Grant was drunk the night before? And he was half-joking in the morning?"

Kim backed farther away. "It's in the memory of Lincoln!" she shrieked.

Abby looked at James and they both looked concerned.

"Mom, maybe you should sit down," Abby pleaded.

But Kim was now unstoppable. She quickly walked back around the table, passing her daughter by. She stopped at a stack of paper and started roughly sorting them.

"It was in a letter…" she mumbled, searching. Then she found what she was looking for. It was a scan of a letter. She held it out for them to see.

"It's in the memory of Lincoln was a joke by a tired, perhaps hung-over general," Kim exclaimed, excited. "It was literally in the memory of Lincoln. It was in his head!" She thrust the page at Abby, who took it gingerly. Kim went on. "The joke was that they had stuffed the letter up into a bust of Lincoln that one of Grant's traveling companions was carrying to D.C. as a gift to a friend."

Kim looked at Abby and James. The fear and concern on their faces began to shift to shock and then wonder. Abby started reading the letter.

"We would pass old Abe around each night and make a toast," Abby read out loud. "Oh my God!"

James sat there looking stunned. "Could it be?"

"It has to be," Kim said, crossing her arms.

Abby passed the letter to James. He read the letter, and then looked at the words on the wall. There was a long silence. Then he said, "I guess we need to find this bust."

Lenoir

Sean rubbed his eyes and stood up. He was mostly through the diaries but could not keep going without a break. He was also beginning to suspect he wouldn't find the answer he was hoping to find. He began slowly at the beginning. Jeff had been right. Robert Fellman made comments about just about every woman he met. It had to have been because he felt no one would ever understand his diaries.

But then Sean had jumped ahead and worked his way through the era he thought would be most likely to produce an answer. He looked for obvious words. He looked for suspicious abbreviations. He looked for suspiciously used words. Nothing stood out.

It's time to make a plan, he thought. *You're not going to find the Mecklenburg Declaration.* But the key question was whether or not to come clean to Joe. He stood up and walked out onto the museum floor. Jeff saw him and waved. "Hi, Sean. How's it going in there?"

Sean yawned. "I'm not finding what I'm looking for, but I am being entertained." Sean smiled at Jeff.

"I warned you," Jeff said.

"Yes. It's funny. Some of it is more vulgar than anything we say today. Yet we look at ourselves today and assume we are more vulgar and blunt than all previous generations."

"Those were his thoughts, not his words," Jeff commented. "I like to think that if he talked like that, then he would have been locked up."

"I agree." Sean headed towards the door. "I'm going to stretch out a little and also make a call."

"Okay," Jeff said.

Sean headed outside, where it was a mildly warm day. Nothing too oppressive. He looked at his phone and made up his mind. *Time to come in from the cold.*

Sean pulled a business card out of his pocket and dialed the number on it. A few seconds later the phone was ringing. Then it was answered.

"Hello?"

"Hi, is this Agent Talie?"

"Yes. Who is this?"

"Sean Johnson."

There was a long pause of pure silence. *I've surprised him.*

"Mr. Johnson," Emmitt began, "you know we've been looking for you."

"I know. But I needed to work, shall we say, more quietly."

"I'm not sure I know what that means." Sean could tell that Emmitt was being guarded. He suspected he was also scribbling something down on a piece of paper. *Probably something like 'Trace this call!'* Sean thought.

"Look, I won't beat around the bush. I have information for you. I think my employer is planning something that might or might not be legal. I'm not sure."

"Hmm, you're singing a different tune now, Mr. Johnson, than you were a week ago."

"I haven't totally changed my tune yet, Agent Talie. I think it's possible you're being manipulated. Do you believe in freedom of speech?"

"Of course," Agent Talie replied. "Because it's in our Constitution. I gave my oath to defend that Constitution."

"So did I," Sean replied. "It's possible the Free States of America are simply planning a speech event."

"The who? Wait a minute." Agent Talie sounded confused, but also excited.

"Tell me this, Agent Talie," Sean spoke strongly, "why are you looking for me? Why are you watching my team in Gettysburg? Tell me the truth. I swear to you, I am not the enemy."

There was another pause. Then Talie took a breath. He had clearly made a decision. "An off-duty Baltimore state trooper was killed more than a month ago. Several months ago, in fact. We got a tip that included details of the murder not publically known. The tip came from a Washington D.C. pay phone. It said that the murder was connected to a dangerous plot against the federal government. We got more tips. One of them said we were looking for a historical researcher. You fit that bill. We saw you meeting with Samuel Franklin north of Baltimore and taking what looked like money from him. Then you disappeared. So has Franklin. We have connected Franklin to some strong statements about revolution in an email earlier this year."

Emmitt paused for a moment. Then he went on. "I just told you most of what I know and most of which I am technically not supposed to be telling you. But to be honest, I am a bit desperate."

Sean stood there under a large tree, the phone at his ear. He felt pieces fitting into place.

"You did the right thing, Agent Talie. Listen. The organization is the Free States of America. They are planning something tomorrow, I think. I need to go get some things done. I promise you that you will hear back from me as soon as I can."

Sean hung up, knowing that Talie was probably cursing him at this very moment. He stood under the tree for a few more minutes before heading back into the museum.

CHAPTER TWENTY-SIX

Gettysburg

"Is that it?" Kim asked. All three of them were staring at a computer screen. On it was a small picture of a bust of Lincoln.

"It's the best chance," Abby said. "There weren't many originals and it's clear that Grant's party was carrying an original. We traced all the other originals. This one is a mystery bust."

The picture was accompanied by a description that declared the bust to be original. It was for sale at a history shop in Madison, Wisconsin. Abby had not been able to find any information online about the shop, though. All they knew was that it was right on the square that surrounded the state capitol building.

"Okay, let's go," Kim said eagerly.

"What?" Abby asked. "Right now?"

"Yes, right now," Kim said. "We've been cooped up here for days, and we're almost dead certain that the hiding place of the missing Gettysburg Address is sitting in a shop in Wisconsin."

Kim seemed a little hyper to James and Abby, but she had been since she solved the puzzle they had been wrestling with.

"I'm staying here," James said. "We still have our main mission, the Mecklenburg Declaration, and Sean needs support on that. But you should go."

Abby nodded, feeling the excitement. "All right. Let's go. But how do we get there?"

"Philadelphia Airport, I think. It's probably the closest," James said. "Head to the airport now and I will work on booking a flight. Just call me when you get there and I'll tell you where to go."

Kim nodded. "Come on, kid, let's grab a few things and head out. Bring your computer."

Lenoir

Sean had finished going through the diary entries. He had forced himself to do that, feeling he would never get another chance and also because he was hoping for some inspiration. As he had gone through the entries, though, his mind kept drifting off to Agent Talie's words. Had murder just been added to the picture? And why kill a cop? Had the cop seen something?

Finally, with the diaries exhausted, Sean admitted to himself he had not found the Mecklenburg Declaration, or even a clue about its existence. It was disappointing. All the coincidences had seemed to align for something to be in the diaries. On a hunch he called up Thomas, who answered on the first ring.

"Hi, Sean," he said. "What now?"

"I just finished going through the Fellman diaries. I didn't find anything. Not even a suspicious word."

"Hmm." Thomas, too, seemed disappointed. "It could still be in there in multiple layer code. He might have used a word on one page to provide the key for a code on the next page."

"I guess you could spend a career looking for ghosts in this thing," Sean said.

"Exactly."

"Okay, thanks, Thomas."

Sean hung up and then dialed the Gettysburg hotel and asked to be patched through to room 408. It rang a couple of times and then James answered.

"James, it's Sean."

"Oh, hi. This is the first time you called this number."

"Yeah. I have surfaced. But I'm trying to figure what to do now. I thought I would brainstorm with you."

"Well, it's just me here. Kim and Abby are headed to Madison, Wisconsin."

"What?"

James explained what they had deciphered.

"Wow, that's awesome," Sean said. "That just leaves our original mystery that I think is at a dead end. Of course Joe doesn't know that. I had a talk with the head FBI agent examining us. He told me more about what's going on. But they are still lost, I think."

Sean explained what he had learned talking with Agent Talie. "So what do you think?" Sean asked.

"I'm trying to think about what they might be trying to do," James said. "Their version they got from the tipster is pretty close to our view of things. Don't you think that is interesting?"

"Yes, but more I wonder who the tipster is," Sean replied. "Listen, I need to think things through as well. Let's talk again tonight and come up with a plan."

"Sounds good, Sean."

"I'm going to give Joe a call and tell him that I'm still one day out from getting the declaration. I'm just not sure what to do when I run out of days."

"I think that happens tomorrow," James replied.

Sean hung up the phone and began putting the fiche back in place. There was a lot because there was one for every page, and it was doubled because there was fiche for the un-translated, original pages as well. Sean had not even bothered to try to decipher those.

Then it hit him. *You didn't look at the actual diaries!* If there was a Mecklenburg clue it would not have come through in a straight translation. He needed to look at the actual documents. As exciting as this realization was, he knew it meant another few hours on the machine. He got up and went out to the main floor.

"Hi, Jeff," he called.

"Hi, Sean," Jeff said back happily.

"Hey, I just realized I need to do one more search. I don't suppose you can put a pot of coffee on?"

Jeff smiled. "Certainly!"

Sean thanked him and went back into the room and sat down in front of the machine. *Back to the grindstone.*

*****

Two hours later, Sean had found it. There, in the first letter of each of the eleven pages covering 1855, were the eleven letters that spelled M-E-C-K-L-E-N-B-U-R-G. He knew that was no accident. The next question was what Fellman had to say in those eleven pages. Sean called up the pages in the translated form and printed those out. He printed the un-translated pages as well. His brain was too tired to do anything more, so he began packing up a second time.

He made his final walk out of the room and up to the counter. Jeffrey O'Malley looked him up and down. "You look really tired," he said. "Staring at microfiche can be hard."

"Yes, it's that and the mystery, which is not yet solved. But I have a more pressing deadline to deal with."

"Well, this will be waiting for you anytime you want to dig in again," Jeff assured him. "You're always welcome here."

"Thanks," Sean said.

The director stood to shake his hand and Sean was again reminded how small he felt next to the man. He had to be the largest museum director on earth.

*****

An hour later, Sean was sitting in his little hotel room along the highway that ran north-south through Lenoir. He had brought a beer up to the room from the little bar downstairs and was nursing it. *Time to call Joe.*

He selected Joe's number and dialed it. Joe answered shortly.

"Tell me you have it," Joe ordered.

"Almost," Sean said. "We made a mistake in the decoding and went to the wrong picture. I just finished figuring it out. I should have it tomorrow morning."

There was a long silence.

"Sean, are you being truthful with me?"

He knows! Sean thought.

"Look Joe, I have no reason not to be."

"Then tell me why two other members of your team just left to Madison, Wisconsin."

Sean was stunned that Joe knew that. And angry.

"You mean you have your own men watching my team?" Sean asked.

"Of course."

"They're on another project. But I've got some news for you. I talked to the FBI. I know why they are after you."

It was Joe's turn to be stunned.

"Please tell me, Sean," Joe said.

"They say you killed a cop north of Baltimore. Not you precisely. Someone is ratting on you from within your organization."

"That is not true, Sean We are not a violent organization."

There was another long pause. Sean was trying to drag it out as long as he could.

"Okay," he said finally. "I will accept that. If I get this document tomorrow morning, do you still want it?"

"Of course," Joe said.

"I'm going to need more money than you're offering. I'm figuring this thing is worth millions. I just gave up one treasure because I failed to realize how much it would be worth to me. I'm not doing it again." Sean tried to play his most greedy self, but it was a struggle.

Joe paused for a moment and then asked, "How much?"

"One million in cash."

"You've read too many books, Sean. No one has that much cash anymore. Look, I can offer $250,000. $50,000 when you produce it and $200,000 after we verify it. The $50,000 can be in cash. The rest will be wired to an account of your choice."

"$350, 000 and you have a deal," Sean replied.

Joe paused again and then conceded. "Very well. But I need to know the minute you have your hands on it."

"Understood," Sean said.

CHAPTER TWENTY-SEVEN

Road to Gettysburg

Sean placed the call and waited. He had tried to sleep the night before, but the tension of the coming day made him toss and turn hopelessly. Now that fatigue was eating away at his confidence. But he knew he had a plan. He just had to stick with it.

"Joe here."

"I have it," Sean said, trying to sound excited. "It's on the back of a painting, very yellowed and very old. I did not dare remove it. So I'm bringing the whole painting."

"That's great, Sean," Joe said. "Where are you?"

"I'm just on the highway headed north out of Lenoir."

"Tell me exactly how you found it," Joe instructed. Sean realized that Joe was interrogating him. Sean played along and built a story connected to the truth of the code he found in the diary. When he was done, Joe seemed satisfied.

"Okay, Mr. Johnson. I may just believe you. Of course I will need to see it before payment."

"I'm on my way, Joe," Sean said. "I prefer to meet somewhere neutral but also relatively discreet. I suggest Gettysburg. Maybe the elementary school parking lot that is just a few blocks south and east of the square?"

"That may work," Joe admitted. "Call me again in a few hours."

Eastern Pennsylvania

As soon as Joe hung up, he called Kelly's cell, but it rang through to voicemail and Joe hung up without leaving a message. He leaned back in the chair in his little office and thought, *Are you playing me, Sean? Did you really find it?* He realized he had no choice but to go see for himself if it had been found. But he also knew he needed to update the senator. The senator, in turn, would want to know what Joe thought. A "maybe" answer would be of no use. It had to be "yes" or "no." Finally ready, Joe called the senator, who answered promptly.

"News?" Senator Hines asked. Joe knew again that the senator was in a public setting.

"Yes, we have the Mecklenburg Declaration. Or we will tonight. I've verified the find." There was a long pause.

"Remarkable," the senator replied. "The stars are aligned. Great job."

The senator hung up and Joe did as well. *If only he knew that the degree of alignment of his stars was still very much subject to debate.* But it was better to have the senator confident than anything else.

Joe was left, however, trying to decide what to do about Sean. And about Kelly, who was now many miles away.

Madison

Kim and Abby stepped out of the cab that had transported them to downtown Madison.

"Wow, Mom, look at that mansion." Abby pointed at the State Capitol building. It was tall, round and shiny. It benefited by being on top of a hill, and by being at the center of everything. Four streets surrounded it, making a large square. The outer sides of the streets were filled with shops and stores.

"It's beautiful, Abby." Kim had not actually really looked at it. Instead she scrutinized a sheet of paper in her hand and then looked for a street sign.

"I think we need to go down there." Kim pointed across the rear slope of the mansion towards the other side of the square.

Together, Kim and Abby began walking through the capitol park. Spring was in full bloom in Madison and the park was alive with color and bird life. They each had a stuffed knapsack hanging on one shoulder. Between the beautiful foliage and their focus on finding the shop, both failed to notice the cab that had stopped a ways back behind them. They also failed to notice Kelly, who began following them from a very discreet distance.

*****

A few minutes later, they arrived at their stop. It was a narrow shop space with a setback center door. On each side of the door, glass-covered sections of the building protruded out to the sidewalk. The result was that by the time someone walked to the door, it almost felt like you were inside the shop. A look inside the shop revealed something often called controlled chaos. Shelves and aisles were jammed with almost everything that had ever been made. There were globes, mannequins, revolvers, games, toys, books, and on and on. Kim and Abby had both stopped and were staring through the glass into the store.

Finally Kim walked up and tried to push and then pull the door. It was locked. There were no signs on the door with any posted hours, or the word "Closed." Kim tried the door again and then looked at her watch.

"It's eleven o'clock. Maybe he opens in the afternoon," Kim said.

"I couldn't find any hours for this store anywhere online," Abby replied. "But this is the place." She pointed at a crude sign above the door that read "Kevin's Olde Time Curiosity Shoppe."

"Yep, this is it," Kim agreed. She tried knocking hard on the door and then stood waiting to see if someone emerged from behind a pile of stuff somewhere. "He could really use some space design or shelf organization."

Abby giggled. "It's certainly not neat like your shop."

After a few minutes and one more round of rapping on the door, they gave up. Kim led Abby up the street.

"I think there's a lake around here and I bet we can find a lunch table overlooking it," Kim said.

Just then her phone rang. She pulled it out of the front pocket of her knapsack and saw that it was Sean.

"Hey there," she said.

"How's sunny Madison?" Sean asked.

"Beautiful."

"Did you find the bust yet?"

"No, the shop is closed. We're going to come back in the afternoon."

"Okay," Sean replied. "Let me update you on what's going on down here." Sean quickly gave an overview of the events, omitting the fact he was setting up a face to face meeting with Joe to hand over a non-existent painting. He still earned a "be careful."

"You too," he said. "Things are weird enough that you should stay on your toes, even up there."

"Do you think they might have followed us here?"

"Maybe. They told me you were headed up there. So someone has either bugged your war room or followed you to the airport."

Kim looked around. "That's a scary thought," she said.

CHAPTER TWENTY-EIGHT

Baltimore Command Center

"Agent Talie."

"Hi, Agent Talie. Sean Johnson."

Emmitt waved to Alice and Ryan, who came walking over to Emmitt.

"Mr. Johnson, I've been patiently awaiting your call. Can I put you on speaker phone?"

"Yes, by all means," Sean replied.

Emmitt put the phone down on the table in front of him and pressed the speakerphone button.

"Sean, you are in our main conference room. With me are agents Lentz and Chapman."

"Hi, all," Sean replied. "Okay here's what's going on. First, I have the FSA, or at least I have Joe thinking that I have the Mecklenburg Declaration. We're planning a meeting to deliver it this evening. Second, and I think more important, it seems clear to me that something is going to happen tonight, and whether or not they have this document plays a role in their plans."

"I'm sorry, Sean, the what declaration?"

"The Mecklenburg Declaration. It's a legendary document from 1775 whereby the colony of North Carolina declared its own independence from Great Britain, a year before the Declaration of Independence. The FSA, or at least Joe, your Samuel Franklin, hired us to find it."

"Okay," Emmitt replied, sounding confused. He looked at Chapman and Lentz but they shrugged their shoulders.

"So, why is such a document so important to them?"

"Joe told me once that it acts as an extra piece of foundation for their platform, their cause."

"Okay, I get it," Emmitt said. "But what are their plans?"

"I don't know," Sean admitted. "My plan is to get close enough to them to find out. Listen, I have a cell phone number for you. It's Joe's."

"Great!" Emmitt exclaimed. "Ready when you are."

Sean read off the number. "I've been calling him on that number since day one. I'm betting you haven't had it."

"You would win that bet," Emmitt admitted.

"So, watch for my call this evening. It might be a good idea to have a unit stationed somewhere in Gettysburg. But my sense is that they are all over the region, if not the country. So who knows what they are going to do."

"Got it. Anything else?'

"Yes," Sean replied. "Kim and her daughter Abigail are up in Madison, Wisconsin. Did you know that?"

Emmitt looked at Lentz, who looked surprised. "Apparently not, Mr. Johnson. Have you been teaching them how to lose a tail?"

"No, I have no idea how they escaped your surveillance. But listen, Joe knew that they had gone up there. He sprang that fact on me, partly to surprise me and partly to show me that he didn't yet trust me. I'm worried they might be in danger. Can you get someone to them to help them?"

"We're on it. Do you have a contact number for them?"

"Yes, use this number." Sean read off Kim's main cell phone.

"That's it for now, I guess," Sean said.

"Okay, we'll be ready and waiting." Emmitt hung up the phone. "Reactions?" he asked.

"I trust him," Lentz said.

"Me too," added Chapman. "But he's being awfully commando. Of course he was one once. Still…."

Emmitt nodded. "I agree. But he hit the nail on the head. We need more information. Simply arresting Franklin might not do anything to stop them."

"He's basically trying to use himself or this declaration as bait, hoping to get them to tell him more," Chapman said.

"Exactly. Let's get to work."

Washington D.C.

"Yes, Senator," Rick answered his cell.

"It's a go, Rick," Senator Hines informed him.

"Very well, the space is reserved. I'll issue the press release and begin personally inviting major networks to urge live coverage."

"You're the best, Rick." The senator hung up.

Eastern Pennsylvania

Huerta tapped the map with his stick. "We are in position at all these points. The unit for the arms center is still moving into position."

"Good," Joe said. "It's a go."

Huerta looked up at Joe and grinned. Again it made Joe feel that the general was a little too happy.

"Understood, mission is a go," Huerta repeated. He picked up his cell phone and proceeded to make two phone calls.

Just then, Joe's cell phone vibrated. He looked at it. "Ah, Mr. Johnson," he said. "Perfect timing."

Pulling his phone to his ear he answered the call, "Mr. Johnson, are you near?"

"I'm one hour out from Gettysburg," Sean replied. Can we meet at the elementary school?"

"That will work fine," Joe said, glancing at the clock on the wall. "I can just get there on time."

"Okay, one hour then. See you there. And bring the cash."

Joe hung up on the call. Joe cursed himself for having let Kelly chase the two women to Madison. *That was a dead end. I guess I have to do this one on my own.*

"General," he said, "I'm going to need a pistol."

Highway South of Gettysburg

Sean hung up on his call to Joe and placed a call to Kim. It went over to voicemail and he hung up without leaving a message. *The FBI will take care of her,* he thought. He then placed a call to James, who answered on the first ring.

"Hello, are you in town?" James asked.

"No, I'm running pretty tight. Let's adjust our plan a little bit," Sean said and then began explaining what he had in mind.

Madison

Kim never sensed her cell phone vibrating. She had placed her purse on the cabinet right after they walked into the shop. Kevin Bollman had greeted them happily and proceeded to entertain them with the objects in his store. He was probably in his sixties, Kim judged, and not of great health. His clothes were untucked and a bit disheveled, but he seemed clean. His hair, what was left of it, was a graying messy bundle. He tended to run his hand over his scalp and hair occasionally and then rub it all about. In short, Kim realized, Kevin was a bona fide eccentric.

Abby was enthralled and loving every minute of it. Kim, however, was determined to get things on track.

"Mr. Bollman, if you can, we actually came here for a specific item."

Kevin's head popped up from behind a bookshelf.

"Oh, well yes, of course." Kevin walked out and around towards Kim. Abby reluctantly followed. In her open palm she was balancing, as if it were real, a giant metal tarantula.

"What is that?" Kim asked pointing at the spider.

"It's actually a poison holder, Mom," Abby said, flipping it over. "See, each of the legs unscrew."

"Abigail!" Kim shuddered. "Put that down right now."

Abby giggled but did as she was told.

Kim turned to look at Kevin. "We're here to look at your Lincoln bust," she declared. "But I don't see it anywhere in here."

Kevin smiled. "It's in a back room."

"There are more rooms?" Abby asked. "Cool."

"But before I show it to you, can I ask why you want to see it?"

"Well, uh," Kim replied, "you can probably tell we're not collectors or anything. We're actually trying to solve a mystery."

"Yes, I can tell, you're not even close to being like almost every other customer I get in here. Take for example this mini-Beretta." Kevin started to open a glass case that looked stuffed with little antique revolvers.

"Mr. Bollman, we're really just interested in the bust," Kim said, using her hand to politely interrupt him in his quest to open the glass case.

"Oh yes, right," Kevin said, looking more closely at Kim. "So, you're not collectors, but you're kind of like historians," he said.

"Right," Kim said. "And we're not really here to buy it. In fact we might be here to help you discover something great in it."

"Hmm," Kevin said, looking at the floor. "Twenty dollars."

"Excuse me," Kim replied, "did you just say 'twenty dollars'?"

"I did," Kevin grinned. "Is it a deal?"

"You want twenty dollars for us to see the bust?" Kim was beginning to think there was no bust.

"No, no to buy it."

Kim looked at him for a moment. "Mr. Bollman, you advertised this as an original work."

"Of course I did, because it is," Kevin smiled.

"Then why are you offering it for sale for only twenty dollars?"

"Because I like you and your daughter."

"I don't think I could live with myself if I bought that from you for so little an amount," Kim replied, starting to feel very confused.

"Well, you're going to have to buy it from me if you want to see it." Kevin crossed his arms.

"Come on, Mom, let's just buy it," Abby urged.

Kim thought for a moment. "Okay, Mr. Bollman, you have a deal."

"Great, let's go then." Kevin turned to walk away towards the back, but then stopped and turned around. "Gotta lock the front door."

He went up to the front door just as a man was entering the breezeway framed by the windows.

Kevin turned the lock closed. "Sorry, closed for a half an hour," he called through the glass door.

Abby and Kim turned around to see whom he was talking to. To Kim the man looked out of place. To Abby he was a shock.

"Mom, that man was sitting next to us when we were eating ice cream in Gettysburg."

"What?" Kevin asked. "Gettysburg."

Kim looked and suddenly felt vulnerable. "Everyone back right now! This man is dangerous!" she ordered.

Even as she spoke the man grinned and pulled a small metal object out of his pocket.

"That is a very nice, but old lock pick tool," Kevin said. "I have several of them myself. Yes, time to head to the back."

Kevin began herding them back to a door that led into a dark corridor. Behind them they could hear the door being rattled.

CHAPTER TWENTY-NINE

Washington D.C., Capitol Building

Senator Hines stepped up to the podium and looked about at the gathering of the press. His own office staff was also gathered in the audience at his request and they looked inquisitive and confused. The senator smiled at them. He then looked over at a reporter standing next to a CNN camera. The reporter nodded to Senator Hines, letting the senator know that CNN was live at his press conference.

The press conference was set up in a hallway of Congress. Ted could see several of his fellow senators at the back. *Boy, are you guys in for a shock*, he thought. Then he cleared his throat and began speaking.

"Citizens of the United States, and my fellow citizens of Pennsylvania." The senator paused and took the time to look directly and confidently into each of the several video cameras facing him. He then continued to speak as he shifted his attention from camera to camera.

"We have a great nation here in North America, but we can be greater. Recent times have shown that the United States has become bloated and ineffective in many of its efforts. We have also grown divided; our political divisions have never been as large as they are now since perhaps the Civil War."

He paused again, assuming that the reference to any war, especially the Civil War, in the context of current political divisiveness, would have raised the attention and concern of most viewers. If his speech was going to have the explosive effect it was intended to have, then his citation regarding the Civil War would be the beginning moment. He saw several reporters look sharply at him or at each other. *Yes, that's it, I said Civil War.*

"One issue that divides us is the role of our federal government in telling us what we, as citizens of our respective states, can and cannot do. This was never supposed to have been an issue; states were to have many, even most, powers. The United States Constitution defined very limited, precise powers for the central government and left everything else to the states. But we do not follow the Constitution any longer. We have allowed creeping judicial expansion of the role of the Federal Government through fabricated words that are read into the Constitution even though they are not there. I speak to you tonight on behalf of a group of citizens who say it is time for that to end.

"I do not speak of insurrection, or even revolution. I speak simply of the right of a state to secede from the union of many states. I believe that Pennsylvania, my state, wants to do just that, secede. I believe other states wish to as well. I speak tonight to declare that we, as Pennsylvanians, are demanding our right, taking our right, to vote on whether to remain in the United States as it is currently formed. A century and a half ago this basic legal right was crushed by force. There were other political necessities of the time, slavery being key among them, that were partly to blame for this most illegal taking of the people's rights. But it remains the case that the Civil War represents the use of military force to suppress a fundamental democratic right of a people to choose how and by whom they will be governed.

"I speak openly and honestly to you tonight. In doing so, I am now the face of a movement that has many supporters, The Free States of America. I ask you to join us."

Senator Hines paused again and looked around the room. Reporters stared back at him, most with open mouths and in shock. He could only imagine how the rest of the United States was reacting.

"Beginning with this speech tonight, the Free States of America is making itself known and asserting its right as a group of North Americans to self-determine their government. It will begin in my home, Pennsylvania. I believe it will grow beyond that because I believe that many of you feel the same concerns over the path the United States is on.

"There are many precedents for this. And there are many reasons why you should join us. The Declaration of Independence speaks of the right of a people to determine their future as a fundamental right. Our forefathers told us that a government obtains its powers only by the consent of the governed, and that life, liberty and the pursuit of happiness are fundamental human rights that allow separation or secession of a people from a union, that allow undoing the political bands that had united them.

"You should also know that one of our first thirteen states, North Carolina, declared independence on its own, long before the Continental Congress finally gained the courage to do so. That declaration is known as the Mecklenburg Declaration from the old name of the Charlotte, North Carolina area where North Carolina's leaders met to declare their independence. We will shortly publish online a long-talked-about but never-seen copy of the Mecklenburg Declaration. The Mecklenburg Declaration was really a vote to secede. So, too, was the Declaration of Independence. But the Mecklenburg Declaration stands for the basic precedent that all states have retained the right to exit the Union because it was the first step taken towards the creation of the new free states.

"The secession that led to the Civil War was, of course, also a series of votes to secede. But it was tainted by the hideous stain of slavery and quickly embroiled in physical violence against those who sought to exercise their rights. We hope to avoid that. But the decay and rot of the leadership of our country today cannot be tolerated any longer."

The senator paused again and looked calmly but sternly at the cameras. "Violence and war are not necessary and should not occur. But whether or not there is violence will depend on how your current leaders react to the efforts of the Free States of America. Our great leader in the Civil War, Abraham Lincoln, was a lawyer who resorted to violence to answer the question of whether a group of states could exit the Union. His army general and future president, Ulysses S. Grant, fought the war to complete the answer to that question. But war was not and should not have been a necessity. And it does not need to be today.

"In his Gettysburg Address, Abraham Lincoln told us we needed a 'new birth of freedom' for a government 'of the people and by the people.' Most recently, Great Britain and its leadership allowed one of its states, Scotland, to freely vote on whether or not to secede. It would be ironic if the government that we once fought for our freedom should turn out to be, today, more able to embrace fundamental human rights than the American government born from its own great struggle for freedom against that country. Tonight I am exercising another cherished human right that is clearly declared in the Constitution: freedom of speech. For exercising freedom of speech, none of us should be deprived of any of our other rights. Thus I, and those of you who join with us, should not suffer any mistreatment by our current government in seeking to exercise a right to declare independence.

"There are many reasons why you should join the Free States of America. Imagine the people of North America reborn with a new focus and conviction. If you think your community, your state, is getting the short end of the stick, or if you think the government of the United States has become lazy, bloated and ineffective, then you should want the Free States of America to succeed. The end result will be a stronger voice and power for the American people, both to defend our borders and interests, as well as to create wealth and success for ourselves.

"Make no mistake, the entrenched power elite of the United States will seek to oppose us. They may even attempt to illegally and immorally use force to suppress us. But I am confident that the Free States of America will persist. An idea, once expressed, cannot be extinguished so easily. I am confident that we will vote in Pennsylvania and that that vote will be to secede and form a new Constitution with those other states that have both the desire and courage to act. I believe that in my heart.

"This is where you, citizens of the great states that currently make up the United States, should become involved. Call, write, email or text your friends, neighbors, colleagues and leaders to tell them where you stand on the right for a free people to exercise its right to choose its government. Tell the press where you stand. Blog and comment online. Exercise your constitutionally-guaranteed right to freedom of speech. Demand one simple right: the right to vote on whether to continue or part ways with the government of the United States.

"The Free States of America has taken actions to defend you, should the federal government or your state government attempt to act oppressively, immorally and illegally to stop us and you from exercising your rights. They are likely to shut our websites down. Or, at least, they are likely to attempt to stop you from accessing them. But we have prepared for many of these expected actions and can and will defend your efforts and rights. I will not list those actions tonight, but I will warn the governments that they should not take such illegal actions. Instead, the only just and right action of the governments should be the same as that which I now take: speak. Attempt to dissuade us through logical argument, not through suppression of life or liberty.

"There will be a lot happening in the coming days and weeks. You will and should hear arguments for and against secession. I encourage you to think carefully. I firmly believe that, together, we can form a newer union of states in North America, one stripped of the burdens the current union has accumulated. This new union shall be the Free States of America!"

Senator Hines completed his speech and looked again around the room. Now, with his words done, he was able to see the room in its completeness. For the first time in his memory, the press was so shocked, so surprised, that they were not moving at all. The space in the Capitol building was silent. Cameras remained fixed on him. He assumed that commentators back in the studios were equally stunned into momentary silence.

It has begun, he thought. *Time for darkness followed by great light.*

As if on cue with his thoughts, the lights around the press conference area went out, came on momentarily and then flickered. Then, about half the lighting went dark and the remaining lights significantly darkened.

It has begun. The senator gestured to his Chief of Staff, who quickly began herding his staff back toward the back end of the hall.

Time for me to win over my own team.

CHAPTER THIRTY

Western Pennsylvania

In six locations around a power transmission corridor known as the PJM, short for Pennsylvania, New Jersey, and Maryland, units of two or three men executed their tasks. One involved teams launching metal cable slings into the air, sending them cascading down onto four major transmission lines that were critical to supporting the east coast power grid. Each heavy cable had even heavier weights at each end, allowing it to be thrown by a specially-made launcher that used a coiled spring to throw the two weights. One weight was more aerodynamic. Thus, it gradually got ahead of its mate, stretching the cable out so that it became a graceful metal arc flying through the sky until it landed on its target transmission line. Then the air above them lit up in a massive show of sparks and explosions of melting metal. Each group simultaneously fired at four locations. The men then quickly retreated to their vehicles and drove away while the transmission lines quickly severed themselves in the surge of power from the grid.

The other task was simpler, but more violent. Two men launched hand-held tank-busting missiles at transformers at two massive power plants. One was on the east coast of Pennsylvania. The other was near Pittsburg. Both power plants went down instantly. Between the four major downed transmission lines and the two power plants taken out, a massive blackout hit the east coast of the United States and parts of Canada. It reached as far as Chicago, Toronto, and Boston. To the south it reached down to Norfolk and Knoxville. This had been the flickering lights in the Capitol building.

Darkness settled on the land as the sun set on the east coast. But so too did chaos. Many people went from listening to Senator Hines's stunning words to feeling and hearing the power go dead.

Madison

Kevin locked the second door behind them. Kim felt just a little bit of relief that there were now two doors between them and the man Abby had identified.

"Who was that?" Kevin asked, as he began looking through a pile of odd objects on the floor.

"I think it's someone that thinks we're about to get something. I think he wants it, and…" Kim paused, realizing how hard it was to describe the situation to a stranger. "Nevermind. I think he means to rob us."

Abby and Kim looked around at the room they were in. There were even more rows of stuff jamming the room. In front of them was a path that led to a third door.

"Ah, here it is!" Kevin exclaimed. He pulled out what looked like a bar with a shoe on one end and a fork on the other.

"What is that?" Abby asked.

Kevin grinned "The stopper. It was sold on late-night television in the seventies. Watch!"

The eccentric man then shoved the forked end of the bar up under the doorknob and jammed the shoe end down against the floor.

"Voila!" Kevin exclaimed. "Let's see him get through this. Come on." Kevin gestured and started walking towards the doorway at the back of the room.

"Come on, Abby," Kim said, nudging her daughter forward. She was determined to keep Abby in front of her.

They walked behind Kevin into a dark room. Kevin was making stumbling noises as he walked forward. Abby and Kim stopped at the doorway. Kim looked back at the now-jammed door, expecting it to burst open at any time. Then suddenly the room was flooded with light. Kim looked around at the room, which seemed remarkably empty. Then she noticed two things. There were piles of large pieces of paper stacked everywhere. She quickly realized they were maps. But the second thing caught all their attention. There, resting on a table in the corner of the room, was a white bust of Abraham Lincoln.

"This is the map room," Kevin explained as if he were giving a tour of a mansion. "You better grab your purchase."

Kim was too shocked to move immediately, but Abby wasn't. She quickly walked over and looked at it for a long moment. She then reached out and tried pulling it towards her. Kim could see that it was heavy.

"It weighs about 35 pounds, I think," Kevin commented.

"Let me get it, Abby," Kim said, as she trotted across the room, avoiding the piles of maps.

"Okay," Abby replied, realizing it was a bit much for her.

Kim reached her side and pulled the statue over to her. With one hand resting against Lincoln's forehead, she leaned it forward and then slid her other arm under his torso. She then lifted it cleanly off the table. It was heavy, she realized, but manageable. She was not going to be moving fast, though.

"Okay," she grunted. "Where now?"

"Follow me!" Kevin exclaimed again.

"Abby, stay close to him but keep me in sight," Kim ordered as she began walking after them, clutching Abraham Lincoln against her chest.

Kevin had run out yet another door. The space lit up and she could see it was a stairwell going down. She worked her way gingerly down the steps, being careful not to trip or even lean too far forward. Finally she reached the bottom, where she found Kevin and Abby waiting at the door. *Blessedly*, Kim thought, *it's labeled exit.*

"Thank God," she said between breaths. "I thought this building went on forever."

"It is a bit of a mystery place," Kevin said. He looked out a peep hole and then said, "All clear."

"Okay, let's go!" Kim almost yelled. "This thing is heavy."

They pushed open the door and exited the back of the building. The heavy door closed behind them. Kim could see an alley below the sloped edge along the back of the building. They descended the few concrete steps and began walking down the alley. Kevin was leading, followed by Abby, who looked back at her mom frequently. Kim brought up the rear carrying the bust. *We must be quite the sight,* she thought. They reached the end of the alley and Kevin looked around the corner. He turned around and pointed back the other way. "Wrong way," he said, and began urging them to turn around.

"No!" Kim exclaimed. "I'm not going to get much farther with this as it is."

Just as she was finished lecturing Kevin, the very man they were evading came trotting around the corner. He was tall, athletic, and powerful-looking, but she did not see a weapon. The light was growing dim, especially in the alley, but Kim could see a grin on his face.

"That's enough," he said. "Everyone freeze."

Kim thought that was the stupidest order she had ever heard, since she didn't think she had it in her to run anywhere. But Abby was too close to him for her comfort.

"Abby, get behind me," she ordered.

Abby backed up until she was even with her mom. Kevin turned to face the man.

"So, what do you have there, Ms. Poole?" the man said in a leering voice as he crept closer. "You've dragged me halfway across America for this. Is the declaration inside?"

He thinks we've been after the Mecklenburg Declaration, Kim realized. But that gave her the perfect inspiration.

"Yes," she said forcefully. "And it's very old. If I drop this, it will likely be ruined. If you come any closer I'll drop it."

The man stopped. "Put it down," he said.

"No!" Kim yelled. "Not until you let my daughter and this man leave."

The man had gotten closer and Kim could see a look of exasperation come over him. But he stood there for a moment and then said, "Okay."

"No, Mom!" Abby exclaimed. She took a half-step forward and put her arms on her hips. "I'm not going anywhere without my mom!"

"Christ!" the man cursed. "You guys are nuts. Look, I didn't come all the way here for nothing. Put Mr. Lincoln down on the ground and you all back away and then leave."

Suddenly the eccentric Kevin Bollman spoke up. "You know, I don't think you understand the situation. You obviously don't have a weapon or you would've pulled it out by now. Further, there are three of us and one of you. Finally, we have something that you want that we can destroy in a moment. I think you need to back off. Or we will destroy it."

The man looked incredulous with rage, but he continued to just stand there. Kim's arms, however, were reaching the breaking point. She couldn't hold the bust up much longer. As she struggled to think of a way out of the situation, lights suddenly lit up behind the man, silhouetting him.

A loud voice called out, "Freeze! FBI."

The man half-turned, trying to shield himself from the headlights flooding his face Then he simply put his hands in the air. Kim felt a surge of relief wash through her body as two men in suits approached the man from each side.

"Abby?" she said.

"Yes, Mom?" Abby replied,

"Please help me lower this thing to the ground before I collapse," Kim gasped.

Abby turned and put her hands underneath the bust, relieving her of some of the weight. Kevin reached in as well and helped her lower it to the ground. She then sat down appreciatively. She looked over to see the man up against a wall. One of the FBI agents was looking at the three of them.

"Now here's a sight you don't see very often," he said, chuckling.

Baltimore Command Center

The lights in the command center went dark. So too did the television they had been glued to. It was not quite yet nightfall, so some evening light came in through the windows on the perimeter. It was just enough to allow them to see each other and the major objects.

"Great," Emmitt groaned. "Just what we need. Chapman!"

"Yes, Sir."

"Get me some power in here now!"

"Working on it!" she yelled back from the other side of the room. He could see her exiting the room. He looked around and could see most everyone simply standing with their mouths open. *It's the shock of what they just saw. I can give them a moment to sort out their thoughts. We can't do much without power anyway.*

Emmitt pulled out his cell phone and punched up the number for his team in Gettysburg. He pulled the phone to his ear and waited for the ring. But it never came.

"What the....?" he said as he looked at his phone. The signal strength showed that he did not have a network. He turned and started walking to the perimeter of the room. When he reached the windows he looked out at the commercial area around him. The sun was setting and it was growing dark. But it was too dark. Emmitt saw that there were no lights on anywhere. The streetlights were dark. The buildings were dark. A realization struck him. *We were just attacked! By the FSA!*

Emmitt whirled back around. "Chapman!" he yelled.

She called from quite a distance. "Yes!"

"Everyone, listen up!" Emmitt yelled as he started walking back into the center of the building. "The FSA has just attacked the United States! There is a widespread blackout around us! I want everyone to look at their cell phones. Tell me if you have a signal. I do not. Chapman, get the emergency radio out and link up to the emergency network!"

He paused to let people start moving but most of them were standing still.

"Now!" he screamed. Everyone suddenly exploded into motion.

"Understand, everyone, if the FSA has done this, then it has to be a distraction from something else!"

CHAPTER THIRTY-ONE

Gettysburg

"Hi, Joe," Sean said as he stepped out of his car.

Sean had just driven into the parking lot and found Joe waiting for him as planned. He stopped his car in the direct path of Joe's headlights, which were creating a lit-up area that pierced the otherwise dark city. Joe had his right hand inside the waistband of the black windbreaker he was wearing. *He's armed.*

"Hi, Sean," Joe said nervously, looking around. "Where is it?"

Sean held his hands down and out in the open in a calming gesture. He looked down to avoid the glare of the headlights.

"You'll get it in a moment," he said. "But I want to know what's going on."

Joe pulled his hand out and pointed the pistol at Sean. Sean couldn't tell whether the safety was off or if a round was chambered, but he assumed that it was ready to fire. *But he's not used to using guns.*

"Bullshit," Joe said. "You're going to give it to me right now."

"Joe, take it easy," Sean replied, continuing to keep his hands still and in the open. "You're not used to handling pistols and if you kill me you'll never get the declaration."

"I am so tired of your games, Sean. I don't think you even have it," Joe said angrily.

Sean turned his head slowly to look to his left, into the dark beyond

Joe's headlights. There, about one hundred yards away, was James. He was standing by a defunct streetlight, shining a flashlight on himself and a painting that he was holding in his hand. Joe turned briefly and looked.

"What's that?" he asked.

"That's your declaration on the back of a painting, just where a Mason named Robert Fellman wrote that it would be," Sean said. "I've been driving all day to get it to you."

Joe looked carefully one more time and then back at Sean.

"You want money?" he asked.

"No, Joe," Sean replied. "I want to know what's going on. I heard most of the senator's speech on the radio. Is that what you based your plans on? An old declaration by a colony? Don't you know what the government is going to do to you?"

Joe looked at Sean carefully.

"Tell your professor to come here. I will tell you what you want to know if you give me the damn document."

"Give something to start, Joe," Sean responded. "I am not against you. If you're going to change things around here, then I can support you."

"You shouldn't have to," Joe replied. He seemed defiant, but Sean could already see him relaxing his focus on the gun in his hand.

"You mean how we have forgotten our roots? We were about people and people's rights. Now we're some bloated federal bureaucracy."

Joe tilted his head and looked at Sean as if seeing him in a new light.

"Yes," Joe said. "Okay, you're right. We're not just depending on the senator's appeal to moral righteousness."

"You mean because force and power matter," Sean said, looking Joe squarely in the eye.

"No revolution was ever successful without power and force," Joe replied.

"And that makes it legitimate," Sean said. "Joe, I agree, but I want to know that you have a plan that will work."

Sean hooked his thumb back towards James and the painting. "That document back there, it's just words. Show me that you have a plan to win by force."

Joe stared at Sean for a moment and then spoke. "Bring him in. I need this declaration for our internal politics. Then I'll tell you what you want to know."

Sean immediately gestured to James, waving for him to start walking in. The lighted area around the professor began to advance towards Joe and Sean.

"I admire you, Joe," Sean continued. "I spent a year fighting secret wars in South America that I think just helped make the establishment rich."

"That's just the start of it, Sean," Joe replied. "My father died fighting a war the CIA later denied. Our federal system is out of control."

Sean moved a little closer to Joe, opening his arms even wider. "I can be with you, Joe. I want to be with you. But I need to know that you're not some nut-job organization doomed to be destroyed by the American establishment."

James had finally reached the scope of Joe's headlights. As he walked into the lighted area, he stopped a few feet away from Sean.

"Okay, Joe," Sean continued, "we're here. Your declaration is here. Give me proof that you're not a nutcase."

Joe burst out in a laugh. He then wiped his mouth and forehead with the windbreaker sleeve covering his free arm.

He's losing it, Sean thought. *He's right on the edge.*

"I'm not a nutcase. We are a real organization. You're right, the declaration is not really significant. But the senator really wanted it. So I'm getting it for him."

Joe was waving the pistol back and forth. Sean was very aware that his finger was on the trigger.

"Maybe you are, maybe you aren't," Sean said. "But how does the Free States of America hope to stand up against the full force and power of the U.S. military complex?" Sean had let emotions seep into key words in his statement so that he conveyed disgust at the mention of the U.S. military. Joe finally bit on Sean's bait.

"Simple, Sean. Nukes!" Joe shouted. "As we speak, our forces are securing several tactical nuclear weapons right here in Pennsylvania. Northeast corner of the state, the middle of nowhere. With those nukes, nobody can touch us. We are guaranteed our own entry into true statehood. Not this miserable existence under the oppressive federal regime."

Now armed with the information he needed, Sean knew he had to get it to the forces capable of stopping the FSA. But he really wanted to protect and save his friend, the professor, from any harm. All sorts of old training tactics entered his thoughts, but he parsed it down to one truth: *He who acts decisively and immediately is much more likely to carry the day.*

Sean jumped towards James and snatched the painting from the professor with one hand while pushing the professor into the darkness, beyond Joe's headlights with the other. "Run!" Sean shouted as he shoved James out of sight.

Sean then turned and started running south towards the battlefield park, painting in hand. He remained in the direct path of Joe's headlights and knew the next few seconds were the most dangerous ones that he had to survive. He zigged as erratically as he could, trusting Joe's aim with a pistol to be inadequate. As it turned out, Joe failed to even get a shot off.

He kept on running across the parking lot toward the entrance road that led to Culp's Hill. Painting in hand, Sean still managed to pull his cell phone out and glance at it. *Signal! I've got a signal!*

He came to a stop just as the headlights of Joe's car started to move. Fumbling, Sean pulled up Emmitt's cell number and dialed it. He then clamped the phone against his ear as he continued sprinting. Joe's headlights swung onto the road, illuminating Sean. He knew now that it would be iffy for him to make it to the woods at the foot of Culp's Hill. So he jumped a fence that ran along the road to the right and started bolting across a field.

Emmitt's voice suddenly materialized in his ear. "Sean, is that you?"

"Yes!" Sean yelled as he pulled the phone away from his ear so he could keep running. Behind him headlights silhouetted him. Sean began mentally counting ten seconds. *It will take him ten seconds to get out, aim and fire.*

"Emmitt, listen!" he yelled at the phone in his hand, barely able to hold and expel the breath he needed. "Tactical nukes….base in northeastern Pennsylvania…..tactical nukes…..it's their insurance policy!"

He pulled the phone back up to his ear and slowed some. His breathing was screaming in and out of his lungs. He heard Emmitt say "tactical nukes, got it."

"Great, gotta go," he panted as he lowered his hand and kept slogging across the field. He heard Joe's car brake hard, its headlights illuminating his path. Suddenly the blast of a single gunshot exploded behind him. Sean tensed, but nothing happened. *Terrible shot, Joe!* Sean had reached the other side of the field and faced a fence. On the other side was another road, this one leading up a hill. He could no longer handle leaping the fence—he was too winded. He stopped and bent over, breathing hard. He dropped the painting, which fell to the grass. *What do I do now?* Sean asked himself.

Baltimore Command Center

Emmitt never hung up the phone. He walked over to the table with the map, shining his flashlight on it.

"Everyone listen up!" he yelled, feeling his voice start to go hoarse. "We need to identify a storage facility in northeastern Pennsylvania that could have tactical nuclear weapons. That's their target."

"That's easy, the Clipper Special Weapons Storage Facility," a voice called out.

Emmitt swung his light around to the source.

"Cooper. Show me where it is," Talie commanded.

Cooper ran up to the map. Emmitt turned to the far corner of the room. "Chapman, tell me you have linked up to the emergency command network," he yelled.

"Yes, Sir," she yelled back. "We have it."

"It's right here by Plymouth," Cooper called out. "My younger brother was stationed there a few years ago."

For the first time in at least half an hour, Emmitt felt hope. He rushed to the corner where Chapman and the radioman were sitting. "Clear the channel, emergency message," he said. The radioman repeated his words into the microphone. He waited and then nodded at Emmitt.

"Attack is imminent on Clipper Special Weapons Storage Facility near Plymouth, Pennsylvania," Emmitt said. "Say that twice." The radioman complied.

"FSA seeks to gain tactical nuclear weapons. Need to deploy force to defend immediately." Emmitt lowered himself to the floor and listened to the radioman repeat his words. He leaned his head back against the wall and took a long deep breath.

Gettysburg National Park

Sean had left the painting behind. As far as he knew, James had snatched it from a wall in the Gettysburg Hotel. All Sean wanted to do was escape the situation alive and unhurt. He rested for a couple of minutes and then leapt the fence to start running down the road in front of him at a moderate, sustainable pace. After about two minutes, headlights swung onto the road about 200 yards behind him.

Sean decided to jump off the road again. He was still clutching his cell phone in his hand as he hurdled the low fence. He landed among some large boulders. He quickly decided he was on Little Round Top, the location of perhaps the most famous defensive stand in American history. He recalled that the side he was on was mostly woods, and that it was steep. That had been part of the Confederacy's undoing.

Sean lay down on the dirt to rest again and calm his breathing so he could listen. After a minute he saw and heard a car driving up the hill to the main parking lot. It stopped and Sean heard a car door open and close.

He's on his feet again.

Sean quietly lifted himself up and stood upright to look around. He could see the beam of a flashlight swing around. It was moving up the paved trails away from Sean. He thought for a moment and decided to creep through the woods and towards the lighted car that Joe had left running.

Just as Sean reached the road, he saw several cars' headlights down below the hill coming towards his location. He prayed they were reinforcements, but he realized they might also be park rangers coming to investigate why a vehicle was up in Little Round Top. Sean raced across the road, carefully watching Joe's swinging flashlight. *A light in the dark is a beacon to your enemy.* Sean remembered learning that adage but not when or from whom. Right now, though, it made total sense. The flashlight swung back toward Sean and the car. Sean ducked down behind a large boulder and waited as the flashlight grew closer. Eventually he could actually hear Joe's steps approaching.

As Joe came closer, though, so too were headlights from two cars that were coming up the hill. Sean realized he was going to be caught in their light in a few seconds. He shrunk down low, hoping that Joe would reach and pass him before the additional cars illuminated him behind the boulder.

The timing worked. Joe passed by his position, obviously rushing to get to his car. The other cars pulled into the parking area and doors opened.

Several voices yelled "FBI! Freeze!"

Joe froze, silhouetted in the headlights, and raised his hands in the air. One was holding the pistol.

"Put the weapon on the ground and step back," a voice boomed at him from behind headlights. Joe did as ordered and was quickly overrun by several men.

Sean stood up, hands in the air. "This is Sean Johnson. I'm coming out."

A flashlight swung toward his face.

"Mr. Johnson. Good to see you. I'm agent Lentz. Agent Talie sends his greetings."

Madison

Kim had reconnected with her purse that had been left behind in the shop. She and Abby were sitting on stools in Kevin's store. FBI agents and police seemed to be everywhere, but they were leaving Kim and Abby alone. Kim pulled her cell phone out of her purse and looked at it. She had several missed calls. One was from Sean and she clicked to call the number back. Sean answered quickly.

"Hi, how are things in Madison?" Sean said as a way of greeting. To Kim he sounded exhausted.

"Pretty wild," Kim replied. "How about down your way?"

"Well, the lights are still out, but I just got told that the primary effort of the FSA has been defeated."

"Lights?" Kim asked.

Sean then walked Kim through his experience. Kim had no idea that half the country had gone dark. She also hadn't heard about the senator's speech. It was then her turn to explain that Kelly had been arrested while claiming he hadn't done anything wrong.

"So, you have the Lincoln bust?" Sean asked.

"I do," Kim replied. "In fact, it's sitting in front of me. I bought it."

"You bought it?" Sean sounded surprised. "That must have cost something steep."

"No, actually it was only twenty bucks," Kim replied. She glanced at Kevin, who smiled back.

"Wow! So was the speech there?"

Kim paused, trying to think of something witty to say, but she realized she was just too worn out. "No. It's empty."

"Oh, I'm so sorry."

"That's okay," Kim said smiling. "I'm just glad we survived the ordeal."

CHAPTER THIRTY-TWO

Gettysburg National Historical Park

Kim and Sean were walking hand in hand. Abby walked slowly on one side of them looking about at the monuments erected here and there. James walked next to Abby with his hands behind his back, thinking. On the other side of Kim and Sean was Emmitt Talie, also looking pensive. They were walking down an access road that led from Gettysburg into the historical park.

"So, we have rounded up most of the units scattered around the countryside," Emmitt said. "Thanks to your actions, most of the crisis is avoided. Power is back on. I think, though, that there will be effects from this reverberating in the capital for years to come."

"They were terrorists," Abby stated simply.

"Yes," Emmitt responded. "But they didn't have to be. They could have been peaceful advocates for secession and change. This is the land of free speech."

"They were bad people," Sean said. "They were trying to grab power and they tapped into other people's frustration with our government."

"They were cowards," Kim said. "That's why they wanted to use force. The senator in particular. He was not willing to risk his career without assurances they would succeed."

"To be fair," James responded, "our nation does not have a good history about peaceful efforts at secession. In the Civil War we decided the question of secession by force and by violence. I'm not defending this group, far from it, but I can understand how an American might think that the road to secession is force."

"Well, that was a reason they wanted the Mecklenburg Declaration," Sean said. "They wanted moral justification. I'm not sure why the Declaration of Independence itself was not enough."

"Because," Emmitt replied, "as you said, they harbored other motives. There is one person referred to as 'Fred' that we have not yet identified, let alone rounded up. We should be able to trace him however, because he was the source of the FSA's money."

"And we still don't know who the snitch was, your tipster?" Sean asked.

"No," Emmitt admitted. "Not that either. I'm leaning towards the lobbyist, that Ableman fellow."

"So that just leaves our missing Gettysburg Address," Sean said.

"If one is missing," James replied. "We may never know. We will also never know exactly what Lincoln said at Gettysburg, even if we identify the script he held in his hand. At this point, anyway, there is a firmly established belief in the minds of nearly every American, beginning in childhood, that the speech he gave is the one found in every history book, on every monument."

"I really wanted to find it," Kim said. "But I think I got a greater gift. My daughter is now an historian."

"Mom!" Abby groaned.

"Seriously, Dear. You could write a book about the Gettysburg Address or even about Grant."

"That's saying something," James said. "My college students seem to only know that Grant is the person on the fifty dollar bill."

"Well, the whole country should know what Grant did for us," Abby said sincerely. "He's right up there with Washington. He led us in battle and then led us in peace."

"Well said, my dear," James replied. "Well said."

"There is one more thing," Kim said, looking at Emmitt.

Emmitt smiled. "I have an agent contacting the judge in your custody case right now. I suspect it will not be hard to convince the judge that you had something very important to do."

Kim smiled. "Thanks."

"Glad to be of assistance. It seems like the least we can do to recongize your support in stopping the FSA."

"I guess we need to head back to Kansas City," Sean said.

Kim and Abby both turned to look at Sean.

Sean smiled. "Yes. I'm saying I would like to come back with you to your home. Is that okay?"

"Okay?" Abby replied enthusiasticly. "It's awesome!"